BREAK THE GLASS

OTHER TITLES BY
OLIVIA SWINDLER

Cynthia Starts a Band

BREAK THE GLASS

OLIVIA SWINDLER

LAKE UNION

PUBLISHING

Published by Lake Union Publishing, Seattle

www.apub.com

Amazon, the Amazon logo, and Lake Union Publishing are trademarks of Amazon.com, Inc., or its affiliates.

ISBN-13: 9781662516290 (paperback)
ISBN-13: 9781662516283 (digital)

Cover design by Eileen Carey
Cover image: © Angie Corbett Kuiper / Shutterstock; © George Munday / Alamy; © Evelina Kremsdorf / ArcAngel

Printed in the United States of America

To my dad, who has always been my biggest cheerleader.
And to my beloved Washington State University.
Go, Cougs!

Prologue

The world is watching. It is impossible to not feel it. The snap of a ball. The roar of the crowd. Two sides. For every winner, there's always a loser. Every time someone makes a game-winning catch, there's someone who missed their block. It's the way of the world.

It's the way the game is played.

It's the way the game is won.

It's the way the game is lost.

Someone will be celebrated.

And someone will be torn apart.

No one wins the game on their own, nor does one lose alone.

But there are always two sides. That's important for this story. That's important for every story. Somewhere there's always someone who has to break the glass. Someone who removes the extinguisher from its case. Who puts out the fire. Who makes the final play.

Meanwhile, the world is watching.

1.

NORA

December 10, Today

"Mrs. Bennet, can you tell me more about your mental state going into this football season?"

"It's Ms." His tired face didn't register that I had spoken. Or perhaps he simply pretended not to hear me. It would be an easy excuse; the noise of the crowd was overwhelming as players and fans rushed onto the football field. "It's *Ms.* Bennet," I repeated. I knew he heard me this time. Tension filled the air. Neither of us spoke. I wasn't going to be the first to crack. I didn't want to do this interview any more than he did; that much was clear.

On the surface, the difference between Mrs. and Ms. doesn't seem like a big deal. It's just the difference of one letter. But that one letter carries a lot of meaning. Especially in the world of sports. Especially as a woman. Especially after everything I've gone through to get to this position, all to be standing on this field.

I used the reporter's long pause as an opportunity to take inventory. I knew how I got here. The whole world knew how I got here. Half of the world thought I deserved it, while the other half still believed that I was simply a Title IX hire.

The world would never know how hard I had worked. I had wanted this my whole life. But there is a massive difference between wanting something and working to get it. Anyone can have a dream. It takes a different type of person to make it a reality.

I was used to this type of reporter. His questions were underwhelmingly predictable. I would have expected a little more fanfare to celebrate such a groundbreaking day. Not only for me and the team, but for all women. In the last few months, I had realized that my victories, my losses, were no longer simply mine. I had become the face of all women in athletics.

This reporter looked as bland as his questions. But unlike a woman reporter, he didn't have to be attractive or interesting to look at. Being proficient at his job was enough. Being smart was a bonus. He wore a generic navy suit. White dress shirt with an understated red-and-navy tie with an argyle pattern. Half the men standing in front of a camera on this field probably wore the same suit without anyone noticing. But if two women wear the same thing, it somehow becomes a competition of "who wore it better?" If a woman wears the same outfit twice, it's front-page news.

"I'm sorry, Mrs. Bennet, are you planning on answering the question? How did you feel going into the season?" the reporter prodded.

I stiffened. No matter how ridiculous this question was, it was my job to answer it.

I cleared my throat authoritatively, raising my voice above the noise of the crowd. "You can call me Nora." I figured that was easier than explaining the Mrs./Ms. concept again. "Yes, there was anticipation along with some healthy apprehension. We all knew that a win was possible, we've been working toward it all year, but no one wanted to say it out loud, especially given how the season started. For me, this win has different implications than for the players. This was my chance to prove myself. It feels like the whole world is watching."

"It's interesting that you identify with the team as if you're a part of it."

I paused. "I'm sorry, I don't think I understand the purpose of that statement."

"You weren't on the field. You sit in the box, and I assume that you do watch the game, but I mean, are you really going to credit yourself with the win in the same way we can credit Coach Ross or, I guess, now Coach Kennedy?"

I forced myself to exhale. He wasn't worth it. "Mr., I'm sorry, I can't seem to remember your name?"

"Dan Creek." He blushed. With his air of self-importance, my petty dig felt very satisfying.

"Right, Mr. Creek, have you ever heard the theory of fan identification?"

"I'm sorry?" I could tell I'd shaken him.

"Fan identification. I'm sure someone of your status knows what I'm talking about, but just in case you need a refresher, it's the theory that a fan can feel a psychological connection to their team, therefore using pronouns like *we* when referring to the team they support. They identify as part of the team. This is a very accepted and acknowledged fan behavior. I'm sure that at some point in your life, you've uttered the words *we won* when the team you support wins?"

He nodded.

"But you in no way contributed to the win, is that correct?"

He nodded again.

"Great, so as a fan, you're allowed to say *we* when referring to the triumphs and failures of your team. Given that logic, it is more than acceptable for me to say *we* when referring to the team of which I am the athletic director."

He regarded me silently. His expression made it clear that I had destroyed any rapport I had worked to build with him.

"Do you have any more questions for me, Mr. Creek? I'm sure that your boss wanted a little bit more content?"

He scanned his notes.

"Yeah, um, could you tell me how you think *your* victory impacts the future of women?"

"Wow, you're throwing softballs tonight." If I had a dollar for every time I was asked this question, I could fund our entire athletic program.

2.

NORA

August 10, 5:13 a.m.

Panic. That was my first thought. There are few worse things than waking up to the blaring ring of a cell phone. It's right up there with the late-night cries of a child. I didn't have to answer the call to know that something was wrong. There was no such thing as a good early-morning call from him.

He never called this early. Or this late. Who knew if he considered 5:13 a.m. night or morning. I suspected he hadn't slept at all.

I flipped on the light next to my bed. If I didn't answer, he'd just keep calling. Or worse, he might stop by.

It was too early for that.

"Yes, Higgins?"

"Is everything all right?" Nathan whispered from the pillow next to me. I nodded and watched as he pushed himself out of bed. He was an early riser, his alarm normally sounding at five thirty.

"Nora, what took you so long to pick up? I don't have time for this today."

I could tell he was already drinking. Or maybe he never stopped drinking. Both were equally possible.

"Because it's 5:13 a.m., and I was hoping to get a normal amount of sleep."

My daughter, Margo, had been going through a phase. It was just a phase, I kept reassuring myself. This was normal for six-year-olds. But it meant that she woke me up multiple times a night. Last night was a rare exception. She hadn't woken me up. My body was cherishing these needed moments of extra rest.

"Nora, this is important. Can I come over?"

"Sal, no, I'll see you at the office in like two hours. Can't this wait?"

"Nora, I'm not coming back to the office. The university and I mutually agreed to part ways. Well, technically, I'm being fired, but the wording of it is a formality. You know how these things work."

I was fully awake now. There was no way they'd fire Sal this close to the opening of the season. This could not be happening.

"Sal . . ." I didn't know how to finish the rest of the sentence. I didn't know what I was supposed to say. I heard Nathan downstairs making coffee, his world utterly unchanged.

"I wanted to call you before someone else did. I wanted you to hear it from me. I owe you at least that."

"What happened?" The rest of my sentence finally found its way to my mouth.

"A shady reporter let some things leak. He'd apparently been gathering intel for months, waiting until now, right before the preseason rankings are announced, to release his findings." He paused. I could hear him take a long sip of something. Searching for the liquid courage to keep talking. "Please don't ask me if it's true."

"Sal, I'm sure this is just some misunderstanding?" The sentence came out as a question, but as soon as I spoke the words, I knew the answer. This was no misunderstanding. He wasn't much different from other self-assured men I had worked for throughout my career in athletic departments. He was charismatic and knew how to be charming when he needed to be. How else did you raise money to fund an athletic department? How else does one convince coaches and players that your university is the right choice for them? I had always chalked it up to part of the job. A necessary evil. Sal was a man who used his personality to get what he wanted.

I was loyal to him. He had given me a chance four years ago when no one else would even read my résumé. He had opened more doors for me than anyone else I had worked with. I had been willing to ignore what I had written off as quirks.

Sal drank. Not every day, but enough that I knew what signs to look out for. When Sal drank, you could never quite be sure what he would say. But again, I wrote this off, because who didn't have a family member who kept everyone on their toes at Thanksgiving? And yes, he often brought up how he had given me a chance when the industry favored men—but that was more of an annoying character flaw.

"Bonne is going to call you any minute," he continued, ignoring my question. "They're going to make you the athletic director. Congratulations." With that, he hung up.

I sat in a state of shock. His congratulations felt cold. He might have taken a chance on me years before, but everyone in the industry knew that he was also protecting himself. The beauty of hiring a woman as his assistant athletic director was he didn't have to worry about the university replacing him with me. It ensured a layer of job security. While hiring a woman as the second-in-command generated great press, and the school was praised for hiring a woman for a leadership role in such a male-dominated field, promoting her over a male counterpart would guarantee backlash. Renton fans, at least according to Sal after a few glasses of whiskey, were not ready for a female to lead the program.

So hiring me, hiring a woman, had guaranteed a *ton* of good press. For Sal, for the university. For everyone but me.

As soon as the announcement had gone out, every career choice I had made in my entire life was suddenly under a microscope. I was the face of women who loved sports. A poster child for success, for diversity. Of course I was accused of sleeping my way to the top. Multiple sources claimed that I couldn't even name more than two positions on a football team. If I cited one wrong stat, I was scrutinized to no end.

And now, as AD I'd be scrutinized even more.

I tried to focus on the positive. I was finally going to get my dream job. I thought of my ten-year-old self. How I told my teacher that I wanted to be a coach when I grew up and my teacher said that it was a boy's job; had I considered being a journalist? I was pretty and had a face for the camera. That's what my teacher told me.

In high school I decided to be more realistic. The AD route, while still a stretch for a woman, was more realistic than a coach. The more I learned about what an athletic director did, the more I knew I was made for the job.

And all of a sudden, it was becoming a reality.

Despite my shock, tears of joy welled in my eyes. I was going to be an athletic director. At a Division I university.

But then, just as quickly, I felt the glass ceiling shattering, and the shards falling on me. Taking over for Sal would not be easy. The athletic program treasured him. The media loved him. He always said the right things to fans and reporters alike. No matter what this scandal turned out to be, it would never take away his seven eleven-win seasons in a row. And now I had to fill his shoes.

I couldn't imagine what Sal could have done to get himself fired. Had he broken university or NCAA rules? Yes, he drank too much and often said crude things, but that wouldn't be enough to get someone as successful as him fired. Those eleven-win seasons were a security blanket. He must have really messed up.

My phone rang once again. I didn't need to check the caller ID; I knew it would be Joel Bonne, the university's president.

"Hi, Nora?" His voice sounded like he had already worked a full day.

"I just got off the phone with Sal," I said, deciding to spare him the pain of having to break the news.

"In that case, I will cut straight to it. Nora Bennet, on behalf of Renton University, I would like for you to step in as our interim athletic director." He spoke in a monotone, as if someone had put him up to it, as if he never would have chosen me for AD.

I didn't care. Joel Bonne would just be one more person that I would have to win over by proving my competency. I gleefully accepted his offer.

"Can I ask what happened with Sal?"

"There's an investigation, I'm sure that more will come out soon. Sal has been accused of coercing professors to give preferential treatment to athletes and some potential money laundering."

I could feel my phone buzzing against my ear. Almost as soon as he explained what had happened, he was off the phone. I could only imagine how many calls he'd have to make this morning. When I hung up with Joel, I found hundreds of messages had flooded my inbox. The news was already spreading.

I logged on to Twitter. There it was, at the top of my feed for the world to see.

Renton University fires beloved athletic director, Sal Higgins. Assistant AD, Nora Bennet, to replace as interim.

I scanned through the comments. I knew it was a bad idea before I started scrolling, but I needed to know what people thought.

Most people complained that Sal shouldn't have been fired. There wasn't enough evidence. But there it was, the third tweet from the top.

> Well, here is another team I won't root for. Who wants
> to tell Renton University that you're not supposed to
> promote the diversity hire?

All my hard work condensed down to two words.

Diversity hire.

I finally found the courage to click on the report that had started this wildfire. I recognized the name on the byline, Mason Pont. He had reported on most of our games last season. I always thought that he was fair in his reporting.

About halfway through the article, my door swung open, and onto my bed plopped Margo, blissfully unaware of all that had taken place in the last thirty minutes. I looked at her tiny ringlets that overflowed onto my lap as she snuggled closer to me.

For the first time since getting the news, I felt courageous. I wasn't just doing this for me. I was doing this for us.

After all, the world was watching.

3.

ANNE

August 10, 8:30 a.m.

My entire wardrobe had seemingly made its way from my closet onto my floor. I should have laid out something last night but had been too jittery. I knew one thing for certain: I was not going to wear khakis. I made a point of asking about the dress code at my interview. But honestly, I needed the job so badly that I would have surrendered my sense of fashion. That's how desperate I was.

I needed an internship to graduate. Any internship as long as it somehow related to my field of study, business administration. When I was a freshman, this didn't seem like a big deal. It felt light-years away in the future. However, three years later, the closer I got to the requirement, the bigger deal I realized it was. More specifically, how expensive getting an internship can be.

Something no one tells you when you're a wide-eyed freshman is that most internships expect you to work for free. And most internships are likely in a city far from campus. So you not only have to work for free, but you also have to pay moving expenses and rent in a city that is not yours.

So when I saw the internship for the athletic department on the school's job board last spring, I knew that I had to get it. Even if I didn't care about sports, I wanted the internship. I needed the internship. It was paid. It was within walking distance of my apartment. And I wouldn't have to wear khakis. It checked all my boxes. Win-win-win.

I, of course, didn't mention my lack of fan affiliation during the interview. When they called to offer me the position, the woman from HR informed me that the fact that I wasn't a sports management major would bring a needed level of diversity to their team and that they particularly loved my attention to detail. This led me to believe that most people applying only wanted the job because it was in the athletic department and they liked sports. They probably didn't have business administration experience, and they probably didn't come to the interview equipped with ideas to improve the department's data and information management. I tried to focus on my business skills and not their comment about diversifying their team. No matter the industry, the nuances of business administration remain the same.

There was no time to overthink their decision to hire me now. I gave myself another once-over in my mirror before heading to the kitchen.

"Are you already on cup number two?" my roommate Noel asked, gesturing toward the full coffee cup I was holding. She daintily sipped an herbal tea. She was the one college-age person I knew to have resisted a caffeine addiction.

"Oh my gosh, you scared me." I hadn't noticed her as I walked into the kitchen.

"I'm sure that has something to do with the unnatural amount of caffeine currently in your bloodstream."

"Yeah, yeah, but I need it. I was up most of the night panicking about this job."

"Relax. It's just an internship. No one takes these things seriously."

Noel's parents had paid her tuition in cash. She had the freedom to not take these things seriously. Not that she had taken advantage of her privilege; she took school more seriously than any of our friends. And not because her parents put extra pressure on her. On the contrary, when her mother visited, she always told Noel that she was working too hard and that she should enjoy her college years. Her mother seemed convinced that Noel would just marry rich, eliminating her need to make an effort in her classes.

This was in stark contrast to any advice my parents had given me. In their eyes, I never worked hard enough. They constantly reminded me of the value of a dollar and what was at stake. They were convinced that years from now, prospective employers would ask about a stats class that I got a B- in. Being around Noel's family was refreshing. That was why after I met her our first year, I clung to her. I needed someone like her in my life. She, like me, viewed college as a magical door that would open up all future opportunities, just as long as you worked hard enough, and we both tried desperately to tune out our parents' voices.

"Okay, but last night I had the realization that I should probably know something about the athletic department, so I spent hours googling information instead of sleeping. I mean, I know nothing about sports. I think I went to like one football game freshman year? I can't be the one ignorant person in the office. I want to make a good impression."

"What happened to business is business no matter the business?" she asked. I glared as she poured herself another cup of tea. "Okay, what did you learn about the athletic department?"

"A whole lot of nothing. But I now have enough base knowledge to at least fake my way through a conversation. Like, I know the major highs and lows, so I won't smile or frown at the wrong moment. And my boss, Sal, seems nice. My late-night internet search had nothing but good things to say about him. He coached for a few years before moving his family here." I had stayed up until almost 2:00 a.m. researching the school's history. Most of the recent articles were about predictions for the upcoming season and reporters praising off-season choices made by the football coaching staff.

"All good signs then! You know that interning for an athletic director is a big deal, right? Like, this is going to look so good on your résumé!"

I couldn't help but smile. "I know! It'll be worth it."

———

The walk to the athletic complex was supposed to take fifteen minutes. I'd timed it the day before. I didn't want to be awkwardly early, but I didn't want to feel rushed, either.

But nerves had turned me into a speed walker, and I stood in front of the athletic complex five minutes earlier than I had intended. The large, looming building looked a lot more alive on a Monday morning than it had been on the lazy Sunday afternoon before.

The lobby echoed with voices. People frantically ran around. It looked like half of the people were on their phones, no one using proper phone voice etiquette.

"Well, George, what are we supposed to do about it?" one man yelled.

"I said no comment!" barked a woman in a crisp pantsuit.

"No, I don't have any more information, and if I did, you know that I can't share it."

"As I said, that's confidential."

When I had been here a month ago to interview, the atmosphere had been much calmer. But that was during the height of summer. The fall sports season was starting in a few weeks. It made sense that things were livelier now.

"Who are you? If you're from the press, you know the rules. You're not allowed to be here." It took a moment to register that this person was talking to me.

"No, I'm sorry, I'm not with the press. I'm a new intern, Anne. Today's my first day." I stuck out my hand and instantly regretted it. The man in front of me had a cup of coffee in one hand and a stack of papers in another. He was clearly not in a position to shake hands with the intern. I felt myself blush.

"I'm sorry, who're you interning with? I can point you in the right direction. Obviously, it's a madhouse this morning."

"With Sal Higgins's office."

I thought he was going to choke on his coffee.

"Is that supposed to be a joke?"

I shook my head.

"Wow, you're kidding me." After he recovered from almost dumping his coffee on both of us, he said, "Okay, well, I'm Graham. I work in compliance. Let me walk you to the office."

"Is it normally this hectic?"

"No, I'd say that today is the exception. Wait, did you not see ESPN this morning?"

I panicked. I hadn't thought about checking the news that morning. I'd done so much research the night before I had thought that would be enough. Who knew that the sports world had so much news to constantly keep up with? I mean, the season hadn't even started yet.

"No, I was online last night, but I didn't check this morning."

"Well, there's been quite a shake-up. We're not supposed to say more than what's already been reported. So basically, if and when you're asked about it today, please just say that you have no comment."

I figured that that would be extremely easy to do as I had no idea what he was talking about.

"You got it, no comment, lips sealed."

"Okay, you just need to go in through that hallway and then the first door on your right. Good luck. I'm sure that this will be a first day you'll never forget." He flashed me a warm smile. I felt the urge to beg him to be my friend, to help me figure all of this out.

"Thanks for your help!" Before I could finish my sentence, he was gone. I wasn't 100 percent sure what it meant to work in compliance, but he seemed busy.

Walking down the hallway, I experienced my first quiet moment since entering the building. I didn't pass another person on my triumphant stroll to my new office. It almost felt eerie, abandoned. Maybe everyone in this part of the building started their day later?

I found the door labeled "Sal Higgins, Athletic Director" and cautiously pushed it open.

"No! No press! No unauthorized visitors!" a voice harped as soon as I cracked the door, slamming it back in my face.

"I'm not with the press," I yelled back at the door. "My name is Anne. I'm the new intern. I'm supposed to start today."

From the other side of the door, I heard a slew of curse words. A few seconds later, the door opened.

The feeling in the room matched the energy in the rest of the building: chaos. Papers were strewn everywhere. The woman who greeted me looked as if she had slept there. The room smelled like coffee and fatigue.

"Well, you picked quite a day to start. I'm Helen, the assistant to the athletic director." Helen attempted to tuck a chunk of hair back into her bun before reaching out to shake my hand.

"Oh, I didn't mean to pick a bad day to start. It was actually HR and my advising professor that picked my start date because I'm doing this internship for credit." I could hear myself rambling. It was clear that Helen wasn't really paying attention to what I was saying. None of those details actually mattered.

"It's fine, it's fine. How could you have known? How could any of us have known?"

"Known what?"

"It's Sal. He's gone."

4.

The Times
August 10, Sports Page
RENTON'S ATHLETIC DIRECTOR SAL HIGGINS ACCUSED OF
MONEY LAUNDERING AND MORE
MASON PONT

In one of the most shocking events of the off-season, Renton University has fired its athletic director, Sal Higgins.

Higgins took over as the university's athletic director eight years ago and completely turned the program around. Many credit Higgins for putting RU's football team at the center of the national conversation. Under Higgins's leadership, the team went from years of 0-12 seasons to leading the conference. The team's success is considered to be the biggest and quickest shift by any NCAA football program in the association's history.

Higgins's success was not just a victory for the football program. In addition to guiding the football team to seven eleven-win seasons and three national championships, almost every one of RU's athletic teams was more successful during Higgins's tenure. Higgins also improved the school's recruiting efforts and raised the annual budget by securing significant gifts from the school's athletic fund members.

Higgins began his tenure at Renton after a DUI incident that led to an internal investigation at the university, where he served as the head football coach. At the time of Higgins's hire, Joel Bonne, Renton University president, assured RU that the board had looked into Higgins's background and saw no grounds for further investigation or concern.

Higgins's history with alcohol is not the only cause for concern. New information has implicated Higgins in a series of scandals at RU, which prompted the university to terminate his contract early this morning.

An independent investigation led by our team at the *Times* uncovered that Higgins was involved in academic fraud and laundering donations to the program for his personal gain. Several professors have come forward claiming that Higgins coerced professors into giving preferential treatment to athletes. We expect that the NCAA will launch a formal investigation within the week.

As this story develops, we will bring you more information. The school is expected to appoint Assistant Athletic Director Nora Bennet as interim athletic director.

At this time, Higgins and his team have no comment on the ongoing investigation.

5.

ALEXIS

August 10, 9:30 a.m.

Our departmental staff meeting was a waste of time. All anyone could talk about was the firing, or "mutual departure," of Sal Higgins, the athletic director.

Finally, one of the professors said, "None of our jobs are at risk, so why are we still talking about this?"

Unless you were one of the professors in his pocket, I thought to myself. But I didn't dare say that out loud. My palms hadn't stopped sweating since I read the news that morning.

Everyone acted so surprised at the meeting. It was as if no one believed that someone at our school, a school that worshipped the athletic department, would ever compromise their morals to give a student-athlete an advantage. As if no one in our beloved English department would betray academia for athletics. I wondered if they knew how naive they sounded.

I had many surprises when I started working here. For one thing, I had assumed that people would behave like adults. Instead, I felt like I was back in the cafeteria of my middle school. As the conference room buzzed with gossip, I was reminded that no one could make up a story quite like an English professor. We had minimal details as to what Sal Higgins had done, yet the professors around me were slinging theories like they were entering a short story contest.

I had just wanted the meeting to end. I didn't want to spend all day faking my surprise at what was the university's worst-kept secret. We had the new semester to prepare for. Speculating on Higgins's crimes shouldn't be a priority.

"If you've ever felt pressured by the athletic department, or Sal Higgins himself, we invite you to come forward and share your experience with us. We want to ensure you all feel safe," Nathan Bennet announced. "As the dean of the English department, I take these accusations extremely seriously. The other deans and I have been in communication with President Bonne, and I know that he takes them seriously as well. We are all united on this."

I nearly choked on my coffee. Of course Joel Bonne, the university's president, and Nathan Bennet, dean of the English department, would say that they sided with academic integrity. They couldn't outwardly say that athletics were the most important thing to the school. Where the university invested its money spoke volumes. The air-conditioning in our building had been broken for at least a year, and nothing had been done to fix it. Meanwhile, if a light bulb burned out in the athletic complex, there would be talks of rebuilding a newer, better facility.

There was no way Nathan actually wanted to hear about our experiences. He and the entire faculty were primarily worried about keeping the department's reputation clean. Nathan was surely worried about how this would affect our funding. Everything was somehow connected to our budget, or the lack thereof. But he needed to look like a good boss. He needed to at least imply that he cared. In a room full of people with advanced degrees, I was sure that everyone understood this was just semantics. I had joined the English department wide-eyed and naive three years ago. The three-year-ago Alexis might have welcomed

Nathan's invitation to share our experiences. But I knew it was just a script. If someone came forward, it wouldn't help anyone. The information would be neatly filed away, and the whistleblower would find themselves without a job the following semester.

When I had taken this job, I envisioned myself like Rory from *Gilmore Girls*. I had spent my whole life buried in a book. I was a writer. Finally I had a chance to put all that nerdy knowledge and hard work into practice and pay my bills. It wasn't by any means my dream job. But it had its perks. A university professor. I loved the way it sounded when I told people what I did.

When I was hired, I was so young and inexperienced. I never once considered that university politics would become part of my everyday life. But I soon learned that interdepartmental rivalries and conflict were unavoidable. I anticipated some sort of annoying political hierarchy within the department. What I didn't anticipate was university-wide politics. It was like reliving high school. And I again found myself at the bottom of the social pyramid. At the top, the athletes. Only now these athletes were on TV, and the fame had made them even more unbearable.

I would bet that every single professor had been asked for preferential treatment by an athlete or a coach at one time or another. I was sure Nathan, the very person asking us to report anything suspicious, had been asked for multiple favors by multiple athletes or coaches. It was like a rite of passage. After three years on the job, I had heard hundreds of excuses from coaches as to why some player should be exempt from whatever it was I had assigned. It was sickening. I didn't fool myself into believing that everyone taking my class wanted to be there. Especially English 101. But I at least imagined they'd have some level of respect for the class. Time and time again, I was proven wrong.

As soon as the meeting ended, I rushed back to my office, desperate to find something to distract me from the news.

But the walls in my office seemed to be closing in on me. I felt antsy staring at my laptop, willing myself to do some work.

"Knock, knock!" I was startled out of my angry daze. Talia stood at my door. She and I had been hired the same semester and had instantly gravitated to each other. We had a sense of solidarity. We found comfort knowing that we both were trying to learn the ropes. Everyone else in the world of academia seemed to have everything figured out. A few weeks into that first semester, Talia had come into my tiny office crying. She had no idea what she was doing. She felt out of her depth. In truth, I did, too. But up until then I had been too scared to admit it. It was nice to know that I wasn't alone. We'd been joined at the hip ever since.

"Hi, sorry, you startled me."

"There's no way you're actually getting any work done. I know for a fact that you've had your syllabus done for weeks and have read all the required reading like five times by now."

She was right. I closed my laptop. There was no point pretending to work.

"What's up, Talia?"

"Is your head still spinning from the meeting this morning?" She seemed genuinely concerned for the welfare of the school. I was doing everything in my power to forget the meeting had ever happened. I wanted to just keep my head down and do my job and never think about Sal Higgins again.

"Yeah. My head's spinning in frustration. I can't believe that we had to spend our whole meeting talking about that man. It's a waste of time. It's not like we all didn't already see the story and didn't know they fired him. I don't see why it needs to affect the rest of the university."

She sat down in the chair facing me, curled her feet up under her, and leaned forward so that both of her elbows rested on my desk—her favorite gossip posture.

"Do you think that they know who they're looking for?"

"What do you mean?" I tried to force my face not to redden.

"Like, do you think they already have names of the professors who were a part of it? Or do you think they're truly on a witch hunt?"

I pondered that for a moment. I honestly hadn't thought about it. Maybe they already knew whom they were looking for and it was a formality, something they were just doing for appearances. Maybe it was all already over.

Talia went on. "I read a little bit more about it this morning. There's no way the school doesn't know more than they're letting on. They have to have names, or at least some hard evidence to prove that Higgins is guilty. They can't just terminate his contract over hearsay." I wasn't surprised that she had done more digging; Talia always was a researcher.

I tried not to overthink the implications of all of this. If someone was found to be involved, they'd lose more than their job. They'd never get hired at a university again. No one wants someone tainted by scandal. But I wasn't going to make this into something that it wasn't. I had worked too hard to get my position. I was involved with projects I loved. I had been assigned classes that I was genuinely excited to teach in the coming semester. I wasn't going to let that all slip away because of a rumor.

I grounded myself in reality. I reminded myself what was true. I had a job I loved, a supportive boyfriend, great friends, a great town to call home, and a living houseplant. But that list just reminded me of everything at stake. Of everything I could lose.

I wiped my palms against my jeans.

"I wonder who it was," Talia continued. "Like, if anyone in our department was involved. I mean, I know that many athletes take English classes, but English doesn't have the same reputation as geology or something. There's a reason Geology 101 is called Rocks for Jocks."

"I've no idea." I wiped my hands again. I loved my friend, but I wanted to be alone. I wanted to be out of this office. I wanted to escape the walls that felt like they were caving in on me.

"It's madness. Did you hear that they hired a woman to be the interim for Higgins? And she's Nathan's wife! Honestly, when I heard that, my first concern was that her connection to Nathan would cause the English department to be investigated more. But now I'm thinking we must be okay, because why would they promote someone married to the dean if they were suspicious of our department?"

"I bet she's really feeling the pressure." I felt myself cringe on her behalf. "I hope she doesn't mess this up."

As all women vying for a leadership role know, it only takes one woman making one small mistake to ruin the chance for the rest of us to get a promotion.

6.

NORA

Parking was a nightmare. Parking was always a nightmare. Whoever designed the athletic complex didn't take into account that people have to drive to work. Sure, it was beautiful, but beauty doesn't equal parking spots. And that morning the lot was crowded with news vans.

I wasn't mentally prepared to face the press. I was barely prepared to face my coworkers. I'd been on an emotional roller coaster the whole morning. One minute I was filled with hope and joy, and the next, dread and panic.

No wonder Sal drank so much. I was only four hours into the job, and I could already feel the pressure mounting, hyperaware that my every move would be watched.

I waited in my car, hidden behind my sunglasses. The university had offered to send security, a police escort or something. But I wanted to sneak into the office under the radar. A police escort would advertise my arrival. Instead, I called the one person in the department I knew I could trust, Helen. I fidgeted anxiously until I saw Helen's messy hair bouncing through the parking lot. She looked tired.

Poor Helen, I always liked her.

"Nora, I'm so glad you're here. It's madness in there. I've never seen such upheaval." Her eyes darted around as if looking for a reporter hidden behind a car.

Though the architects had failed to account for everyday parking needs, they did think to build an underground tunnel from the basketball arena to the main building. I wasn't the first person to try to avoid a run-in with the press.

"How're you holding up?" I asked Helen once we were safely inside the tunnel.

She stopped and started shaking, sliding down the hallway wall until she was slouched on the floor, hysterically sobbing. I couldn't help but join her on the ground.

"Nora," she managed through the tears, "I need you to know that I had no part in any of this. HR called me this morning with a ton of questions. They seem to think that I had a role in this whole thing. I really didn't know anything." More sobs.

Anyone who knew Helen would know that she wouldn't be involved in any illegal activity. Helen was the perfect picture of purity. She was kind and dedicated to her job. She loved rules and was a terrible liar. Helen was always the last to know if we were planning a surprise party for someone in the department because she couldn't keep a secret for more than five minutes.

If I were to make a list of coconspirators, Helen would never make the list.

"I know, Helen. None of us knew." I added the last sentence to assure her that I also didn't know. "I hope that you'll stay on as assistant. I can't imagine moving into this job without you."

She took a deep breath. "It would be an honor," she said, slowly pushing herself up off the floor.

We walked for a while in silence. We both needed a bit of calm.

I wondered what the day ahead would look like. If someone like Helen feared for her job, I could only imagine the state of the rest of the department. I was sure that everyone who thought they were anyone would want assurance that they still had a job after this Sal shakedown.

If any of them were left.

I hadn't thought about other people in the department being fired, too. The article had claimed that professors were involved. I wondered if Sal had other people inside the department helping him out as well.

I wouldn't have been surprised. It would have been hard for him to pull the crimes off alone.

But there was also a good chance that people might leave because they didn't want to work with me. Change in leadership is hard. People were loyal to Sal. He had a way of making everyone feel as if they owed him for their careers. That made it hard for his colleagues to consider working for anyone else.

Sal often began his meetings by reminding us that he had hired us. He was the one who plucked our résumés out of the pile and believed in us. Why would we look for employment anywhere else? He once told me that no one else would consider hiring me. The fact that my name was Nora was a nonstarter. "You can't take someone with the name Nora seriously. There will never be a president named Nora!" he jokingly said to me once. Without him, I was nothing. With him, I was Nora Bennet, assistant athletic director.

Sal was different from other bosses. Or at least he led people to believe he was. He hired based on ability. He believed that his team was capable. No one else, or so he said, would even give me a chance, not without a glowing reference letter from Sal himself.

"I forgot to mention," Helen said, interrupting my thoughts, "Sal had hired a new intern, Anne. She started today."

7.

LAUREN

August 10, 9:15 a.m.

I had decided not to leave my bed. At least not for the foreseeable future. The walls of my room, my house, felt like they were collapsing in around me. My bed felt like the only safe place.

He was gone, but for some reason that didn't make me feel any safer.

I sat up slowly, spotting my phone on the floor across the room. Earlier that morning I had thrown it. Not at Sal, I would never be so reckless, but into the nothingness between us, as if the act of aggression would mend the pain welling in my chest.

The morning's events came back to me. I had gone to bed before Sal. This was not unusual, especially so close to the start of the football season. Before dawn he woke me by screaming, "Damnit! You have got to be kidding me!"

"Sal?" I called out. The screaming came from his home office, which shared a wall with our bedroom.

His feet hit heavy on the floor as he stormed into our room.

"This, did you know about this?" He waved his phone violently in front of my face.

"Sal, what are you talking about?"

"You knew about this. You knew about this, and you didn't think to warn me. You didn't think to warn your husband. I thought we were a team. Damnit, Lauren, how could you be so careless?"

"I don't know what you're talking about!" I said.

"Then google it," he growled.

I found my phone on the nightstand, unsure of what I was supposed to be googling.

"Just open Twitter, Lauren; stop playing stupid."

Slowly my feed began to load. And there it was, a story from the *Times*. An exposé detailing my husband's alleged crimes. The article hit on all the high points—excessive drinking, bribing professors, and money laundering.

"Sal . . ." I didn't know what to say. What does one say to such things?

"Lauren, how could you let this happen?"

"How could I let this happen? How could you—"

"Do not accuse me of anything. You're no better than the rest. If you cared about me, if you loved our family, you would have figured out a way to stop this story. What, Lauren, did you decide to just sit this particular battle out? You're the one who insisted we move to this godforsaken town in the first place. You and your connections. This was all your idea. Well, look how that turned out."

He started frantically pulling things out of his dresser drawers, throwing them into an old duffel bag.

"Where are you going?" It was too early in the morning for my brain to comprehend what was transpiring.

"I have to get out of here. I need to take care of this, save my reputation, since you couldn't seem to care less."

"Sal, what is going on?"

"Did you really think that good old Joel Bonne would let this one fly? Did you think that once the story was published, you could call in another favor? Well, it's too late, Lauren. They're firing me. Or we're mutually parting ways or some bullshit like that. Are you happy now? Is this what you wanted?"

It wasn't. But that didn't matter. He truly believed that it was all my fault.

I wished that it had been my fault. That way I would have at least had a heads-up that my entire world was about to crash down around me.

I wished that he had given me the chance to fix things.

Had it all been a lie? Every time he promised that he would get help. Stop drinking. See a therapist. I wanted him to be better. I wanted him to be the person I had fallen in love with. And so, I believed him.

I thought of Sal, the years that we had spent together. All that I had sacrificed to get him to that point in his career. I had known as soon as I married him that saying yes to Sal would be saying no to my own dreams. But I had believed in him. We were a team, and I had always prided myself on being a team player.

When we met, I had wanted to be more than just someone's wife. I had gone to business school. I was going to get my MBA. But once we got married, studying and holding down any job long enough to advance my career became impossible. Sal's world had a bigger gravitational pull. We moved for him. We pivoted for him. For him. For him. For him.

I knew that he'd be successful. He wasn't just one of those guys who was all talk. No, not Sal; he had a plan. He studied the careers of athletic directors and coaches. He used his never-ending charisma to network, never forgetting to call someone and wish them a happy birthday and always showing up at the right moment. He knew what steps he needed to take and the people he needed to connect with to become an AD.

And he did it. Of course, he did. But ask anyone who has gotten what they wanted, and they'll tell you it is never enough.

Not that any of that mattered. Not when I was alone in our bed, realizing I had been just as blinded by his charisma as the rest of the world.

There was nothing to do but bury myself deeper into the safety of my comforter.

8.

ANNE

August 10, 9:30 a.m.

The first day of any new job is awkward. I knew that going in. I just hadn't imagined that it would be *so* awkward. Helen reminded me of a bumblebee—circling, surveying, but unsure where to land. She hovered over me, trying to explain to me my job while also trying to figure out if either of us would actually have a job by the end of the day. I imagined that life was extremely stressful inside Helen's brain.

After settling me in, she left the office in somewhat of a rushed panic, leaving me alone, instructing me to wait and not touch anything. She said she would be back soon with answers.

I was uncertain which questions she was trying to answer.

In the interim, I had no idea what to do with myself. I fished around in my bag and found my phone. I had turned it off, at the advice of Noel.

"You should always look as professional as possible, especially on your first day, and nothing says unprofessional like scrolling through Instagram at work," she had lectured me that morning. Noel was made for a professional environment. She was one of the few people our age who actually enjoyed talking on the phone instead of texting. She always dressed up for class, and even on the weekends, she refused to wear casual clothing because she didn't want to risk coming off like she didn't care. Not that this caused her to put more effort into her studies outside class, but she made sure to keep up appearances in the classroom.

I'd almost forgotten I had my phone with me. As soon as it came back to life, I was flooded with messages, most of them informing me of what I already knew: Sal Higgins was fired.

If it weren't for this internship, I would've filed this information away in some deep corner of my brain and honestly not given it a second thought. Likely, I wouldn't have even found out that he was fired until after the school year started. I had nothing to do with the athletic program, and it wasn't something my friends and I talked about. But today, my position had shifted. The messages I was getting asked me about the firing as if I had some insider knowledge. I remembered what Graham from compliance had instructed me in the lobby. No comment.

It didn't take long to figure out what Higgins had done. Bribing professors. I felt myself let out a sigh of relief that he hadn't been fired for sexual misconduct.

The internet, as usual, was full of opinions. The more I scrolled, the less I understood. Instead of talking about Higgins and what he had done, everyone was analyzing Nora Bennet. Half of the internet was overjoyed that a Division I school was going to have a woman athletic director, and the other half was furious that she even existed in the first place.

Her promotion overshadowed Higgins being fired. I was sure that if they had promoted a man, the new appointment would not be the hot-button topic of the day.

I felt bad for Bennet. The ink hadn't dried on the contract, and people were already either putting her on a pedestal of perfection or planning her funeral. Literally, multiple tweets held death threats if the team lost one football game this season. It seemed like overkill to me.

To think I felt worried about my first day of work. At least I didn't have the whole world watching my every move, planning my death.

I heard the door open behind me and almost fell out of my chair. I'd been so consumed by the article's comment section, I'd forgotten where I was. In shuffled Helen and a woman who I assumed was Nora Bennet.

"Hi, Anne?" she said calmly, reaching out her hand.

"Yes, hi," I said, fumbling to get out of my seat, and shook her hand.

"I'm Nora Bennet, your new boss." Her voice sounded calm, in control, as if this had been the plan all along. "What a day to start a new job, am I right?" she said with a wink. "Helen here is going to show you around. I promise you, it's not always this chaotic."

"Thank you so much. I'm really excited to be here. I—" I realized I had started launching into the "thank you for hiring me" speech I had prepared for Sal. But Nora wasn't the one who had hired me. She knew nothing about me. She wasn't going to find my khaki joke funny, because she wasn't the one who knew that I had an aversion to khakis. Instead, I should have thanked her for not firing me for being a member of the previous administration.

The next thing I knew, I was back in the eerily quiet hallway, chasing after Helen, who walked surprisingly fast.

"Nora is great," I heard Helen say. "I obviously haven't worked with her a ton, but every time I have, she's just been so kind and sure of herself." I wasn't sure if Helen was talking to me, or assuring herself that everything was going to be okay.

"This whole hallway is for the athletic director and staff." She snapped back into conducting my orientation. "The deputy directors and their assistants also have their offices here. Most of them are either working from home today or dealing with their department. That's not normally the case, working from home, but with everything going on, it's in the best interest for some staff to stay out of the way. No one wants to be ambushed by the press if they can avoid it. And you saw the lobby, working from the peace of one's home might be the only way to get anything done today."

Her eyes flashed quickly to me as if she just realized the gravity of what she'd said.

"Also, you have to remember as a staff person here, you cannot say anything to anyone who doesn't work in athletics. You have no comment. Because even if you're just an intern, they will use you as a source. You can't be too careful about what you say outside the walls of this building."

"Yes, got it. My lips are sealed." I hadn't realized that this job would require so much secrecy.

She gave me a look as if to say I didn't fully understand the importance of my silence.

"Right, so your desk is in here, this is our public-facing lobby. The hallway you came in through is mostly used by employees. If someone has a meeting with the AD or a deputy director, this is where they come. Part of your job is to be the gatekeeper of that door." She motioned to the door we had just walked through. "Especially now, only people with a confirmed appointment or security clearance are allowed in."

It was hard to imagine anyone trying to sneak in. But I nodded along. I wanted Helen to know that even if I thought it all was ridiculous, I would take the job seriously.

"I sit out here as well." She motioned to the desk across from mine. "Especially now, it's really important that one of us sits out here at all times."

I couldn't help but think of *The Devil Wears Prada*. I wondered what would happen if I needed to go to the bathroom. I regretted drinking two cups of coffee this morning.

"Most lunches are working, at least in the fall with the football season and basketball right around the corner. On your desk is a list of basically everyone you need to know. This list, obviously given what happened this morning, is subject to change. But it's accurate as of this morning. Anyone from top donors to senior staff will call asking to speak to Nora. I earmarked a few donors in particular who think that because they give hundreds of thousands of dollars, they have earned the right to talk to the AD whenever anything goes in a direction they don't agree with. I'm assuming today we're going to get a lot of phone calls from these people thinking they have the right to an inside scoop. Again, we have . . ."

"No comment," I said authoritatively.

"Yes, perfect. The phones are currently turned off, but I think by ten we should be ready to start taking calls."

I checked my watch. Ten o'clock was less than fifteen minutes away. I felt my palms get sweaty. I didn't think I was ready to explain the situation to someone on the other end of the phone line.

Helen rolled her chair over to my desk. "Okay, here's our plan."

9.

NORA

Deep breaths. Inhale, exhale. Do not get on Twitter. That was my mantra for the day. It turned out, the entire internet should be avoided.

For my whole life, I had dreamed about this day. I imagined walking triumphantly through the lobby of the athletic complex with my head held high. At the welcome interview, I would be asked if I knew how much of an inspiration I was to girls everywhere. No one would question whether I deserved the job. No one would wonder if I slept my way to the top (I was so thankful that Sal's scandal had not involved sexual misconduct). No one would ask who would take care of Margo while I worked long hours.

But that was all a fantasy. The memo for my first-ever interview as athletic director said the following:

> Date: August 10; 9:02 a.m.
> To: Nora Bennet

From: Jake Finn, deputy athletic director—communications
Subject: Morning Press Conference
Priority: Urgent

I'm writing to inform you of this morning's press conference where we'll introduce you officially as our interim athletic director. Below you'll find a list of the subjects we will be covering in this press conference and some questions that we predict you will be asked. Joel will escort you to the conference room at 10:15. Please wear something red to show your support for the school—if possible, something with the Griffon logo. If need be, someone in equipment can bring you something.

Subjects to be covered by the department:

- *The departure of Sal Higgins—Joel Bonne, university president*
- *The appointment of Nora Bennet—Joel Bonne, university president*
- *State of the department—Nora Bennet, interim athletic director*

Possible questions to prep for:

- *How do you feel about being selected as interim AD?*
- *Who else, if anyone, from the department was involved in the scandal?*
- *How long did the university know about the scandal without acting on it?*

- *How much money was lost?*
- *Will this affect bowl eligibility?*
- *What qualifies you for this job?*
- *What are your thoughts on Title IX?*
- *How will you handle being a mother while being an athletic director?*

See you at 10:15.

I noted that Joel planned on walking me to the conference. If I was having a rough day, I could only imagine how overwhelmed his office was. Nevertheless, I felt grateful that he cared enough to walk me to the conference. Up until that point, I had had few interactions with Joel, but everyone who worked closely with him spoke highly of his intentionality. Walking into the meeting with the university's president would signal that the university backed me and that we were a united front.

I looked again at the list of questions. I knew that a man in my position would have a much different set.

At my first sports-related job interview—a marketing intern for my town's local hockey team—the first question I was asked was, "Can you name any hockey players?" I could. I did. And I didn't say anything snarky. The second question asked about my favorite hockey play. I put on my biggest smile and mentioned a play I had seen the team run during their last game. I got the job. I didn't think twice about these questions until midway through the internship when my co-intern told me that during his interview, he had spent the whole time recounting his most recent spring break. He wasn't asked one question about hockey. They just wanted to know if he was a good time.

So I did what most women in my position do. I outworked him. I was funny. I always laughed at the jokes my boss told, even when they were at my expense. I showed up early. I didn't cringe at locker-room talk. At the end of the internship, the other guy got a full-time position and I got a free T-shirt.

That was just how it was. I knew early on that I could either stomp my feet and cry, or I could work harder. The woman who works harder is the one who has a chance to get a job. Especially if she remembers to laugh at her male colleagues' jokes.

Most of the time, I didn't think about it. I just kept quiet and did my job. But most of the time I didn't have to prep for the sort of questions I was about to be asked. I can guarantee that Sal, in his entire tenure, was never asked how he'd handle being an athletic director and father. But there was no time for bitterness. An emotional woman wouldn't prove to the men they were wrong. My only choice was to shut up and do my job.

And avoid Twitter. And definitely not cry in front of the camera.

10.

ALEXIS

August 10, 11:00 a.m.

I don't know what I had expected Nora to be like. The internet hadn't sold her very highly. She spoke in a way that made it clear she had media training or worked with a voice coach. Her cadence was even and steady. It was a voice of leadership, commanding but calm. Every word she spoke sounded calculated without seeming overly rehearsed. I wondered if she used a teleprompter. But she didn't look like she was reading a script.

I understood why she was chosen as the interim athletic director. She appeared to be the polar opposite of Sal—everything that he was not.

Sal spoke zealously and made you feel like the most important person in the room. He remembered details about your life that you didn't remember telling him. He was a politician disguised as an athletic director. He was smooth, ensuring that you knew he was on your side.

Nora wasn't a sweet-talker. She wasn't trying to charm the press. She was concise and direct—the opposite of a politician.

It was impossible to get any work done that day. People in our department couldn't stop talking about it. Our school had never gotten so much media attention. Not even when one of our professors had been nominated for a Pulitzer. I guess as an English department, the thought of journalists writing about us was exciting, no matter what the story was about. I could barely go for five minutes without someone coming into my small office to ask me what I thought about the whole thing.

It seemed like everyone had begun their own investigation. Forty-two professors now imagined themselves to be Nancy Drew. No matter how they phrased their questions to me, it was clear that they all wanted to know the same thing—was I involved? Everyone was a suspect.

After the fifth professor plopped down on the chair across from me, asking me if I had any insight into what happened in the athletic department, I realized I had to get out of my office. It was suffocating. Didn't these people have work to do?

So I ran as far away from the building as possible. After a year into the job, I started keeping a pair of running shoes in my office for moments just like this. My first year I had felt trapped as the demands of this job had quickly mounted. So I kept a change of clothes in my desk drawer for when I had a short break and needed to sneak in some exercise.

Walking down the unusually quiet hallway, I thought I could feel eyes peering at me from behind computer monitors. It was as if my colleagues were waiting for me to step out of line, to do something suspicious, something that made me look guilty. I had to get out of there. I needed to run.

I made my way to the trail that looped through the most scenic parts of campus. After a few minutes, I realized where my feet had carried me. I hadn't given one thought to where I was heading. I ended up there out of habit. The path had led me straight into the eye of the storm.

It was a beautiful building. It towered high, overlooking the rest of the campus. A status symbol, it loomed in solitude as if saying, "Look, but don't touch, only the elite will be granted access." As I approached, I saw that the entrance of the building was blanketed with reporters.

"Professor Baily?" A voice snapped me out of my daze. I had stopped running. I didn't even realize what I'd been doing. The fog and fatigue of the day had taken over.

"Hi," I said and paused. I knew this girl had been in my upper-level creative writing class last semester, but I couldn't remember her name. She'd sat near the window. Or maybe the door? I knew her name hid somewhere in the far corners of my brain.

"It's Noel!" she said without missing a beat, as if she didn't expect me to remember her name. "I was in your creative writing class last semester. I just saw you're teaching my senior seminar as well! I really enjoyed your class last semester."

That's right—she was the rambler who always brought the smell of herbal tea into class.

"Of course. Hi, Noel."

"Are you trying to see the madness for yourself?" She motioned to the crowd of journalists.

"Oh, no, just out for a run!" I tried to force my voice to sound casual yet rushed. I didn't have time to stop and talk to a student.

"You picked a crazy route this morning. My roommate is interning for the athletic department, and today's her first day. I thought I'd drop her off a coffee, but I had no idea that it was going to be so chaotic. I can't even get into the building."

"Well, put it in the fridge so she can drink it later." I was only half listening to her. But if they had the building on lockdown, the situation was more serious than I thought. "Who does your roommate intern for?"

"Well, that's the crazy thing, she'd gotten a job with Sal Higgins, but obviously he's out. I'm not sure what's going to happen, but this must be quite a crappy first day of work, if you ask me. I figured it would be crazy here today, but I hadn't thought about all the additional security. There's no way they'll let me deliver this coffee. So much for that friendly gesture."

I looked at the coffee that Noel gripped and realized that she could be my reason to go into the building. I had a keycard, but I had no real reason to be there. Noel, on the other hand, presented the perfect excuse. I'd just be the friendly, clueless English professor helping a student out. I hadn't meant to go to the building, but now that I was there, I felt like I was being pulled inside. I had to see for myself what was going on inside the sacred walls.

"I remember when I started working here, knowing I had one friend in the department, Talia, made all the difference. She made those first days so much better. It's nice to know that you're not alone." I wanted Noel to believe that I had no ulterior motive for going into the building. I wanted her to think I was someone who understood the pains of a first day of work, rather than someone who was calculating all the ways her life could be on the brink of falling apart. "My keycard gets me into the building. I'm sure your coworker would love to see a familiar face."

"My roommate. Sure, that'd be great, if you don't mind interrupting your run?"

"Not at all, let's go to the basketball arena, there's a better entrance over there."

And just like that, we were like moths to a flame.

11.

ANNE

August 10, 11:00 a.m.

Every day won't be like this. I repeated that to myself over and over. This was not going to be forever. The first day of any job is overwhelming. Sure, no one could have predicted the way this day was going. But it wasn't anyone's fault.

Well, other than Sal Higgins, who'd caused all of this commotion in the first place. And maybe the journalist Mason Pont, who had the gumption to expose Sal's crimes to the world. Not that running the exposé was Pont's fault—that was his job. But I did fault him for the timing.

To say that the phones had been ringing off the hook would be the understatement of the century. We'd had a momentary reprieve, at least from reporters wanting a quote, during the press conference, but nothing seemed to deter the donors and fans. It was insanity. I honestly never would have guessed that people could be so invested. Or could feel so entitled to believe that they deserved an insider scoop.

"At this time, we have no comment, but I invite you to check back with the department's website, rentongriffons.org, where we'll post updates as we have them. See you on August 29 for our home opener!" I had said these words on repeat all morning. My mouth was dry. I had no idea that this job would involve so much talking. I had no idea that this job would involve so many angry people. Sports were supposed to be fun! I thought fans liked the team they rooted for.

The worst part was that these people directed their anger at me. It was as if they actually thought I had something to do with the whole mess. As if I had any say in the decisions of our former athletic director. It took all my self-control not to break down after one particularly rude conversation.

"I'd like to speak with your boss," he demanded after I gave my spiel.

"I'm sorry, she's unavailable at the moment." I looked over at Helen, who was also drowning in phone calls.

"Then I invite you to look up my Athletic Number." He said this as if it were a proper noun. "I think once you see my ranking, you'll change your mind."

I typed his information into the system I had learned how to navigate only an hour before. He was ranked 2,562. As in, he gave the 2,562nd most to the Griffon Athletic Fund that year. According to the ranking system, 2,562 equated to about $15,000. At the start of the day, this number would have dropped my jaw to the floor. Now, after fifty-plus phone calls, I was unfazed. I had already talked to the 100th, 268th, 756th, even someone in the double digits. They all had one thing in common. They had all been kind to me, understanding when I said that I was unable to give them additional information.

In my two hours on the job, I found that it was people who gave enough to be ranked between 1,500 and 3,000 who were the most difficult. They carried more of a sense of entitlement than those who ranked higher. It was a really interesting paradigm.

"I'm sorry, sir, I'm still unable to provide you with additional information. I'm afraid everything I told you is all that I can disclose at this time." I made sure to enunciate. I wanted to sound as professional as possible.

"Do you not see who I am? Did you know that I was in a fraternity with Sal Higgins? Does your little computer tell you that? Do you know what that means? That means I can call my good friend Sal up right now and get the details from him myself. But I thought that I'd give this school the benefit of the doubt. The school's going to lose donors, and it's going to be your fault for not sharing information with supporters like me. I hope that you know that. You know, this whole thing is un-American." Clearly, I was not as good at hiding my Moroccan accent on the phone as I thought I was. I reminded myself over and over again not to take his comment personally. But tears still welled in my eyes. He rambled on for at least three more minutes. The conversation finally ended when he called me a tight-lipped un-American shrew before abruptly hanging up.

I didn't understand what people expected of me.

I wanted to tell him that this was my first day on the job. That I honestly had nothing to do with the firing of Sal Higgins, and if he was such good friends with him, please call him and tell him to sort this all out because it was making me want to scream. I also wanted to inform him that despite my accent, I was an American citizen, and I would happily conduct this conversation with him in French or Arabic if that was more convenient for him. What an *espèce de merde*. But, instead, I politely repeated that I had no comment.

I thought about my interview with Sal, the only time I had actually met him. That portion of the interview had lasted maybe fifteen minutes. He had seemed nice. Like a lovable uncle. The uncle who drinks too much and uses the occasional profanity, but an uncle whose kindness made it easy to write off that behavior. I had fallen victim to Sal's charm. Words rolled off his tongue like candy, sweet and full of promise.

I was looking forward to working for him. He made the whole world of athletics sound so exciting. If he knew this hurricane was coming, he hid it well, behind his air of confidence.

I wondered what it would be like to walk through the world like that. I never had that luxury. I doubted I ever would. But talking with him that one time made it feel like a possibility.

There was a rap on the door. People had been knocking all day. Helen got up to shoo the person away when I heard a familiar voice.

"Anne, I brought you coffee!" Noel yelped as if she was trying to get the words out before Helen shut the door on her foot.

"Helen, it's okay, it's my roommate, Noel." A woman I'd never seen before trailed Noel. She looked more like a professor than a student. Noel had a way of making friends with anyone who crossed her path, so this wasn't surprising to me.

Almost every evening, she came home telling me of the people that she'd met. "If you go into every conversation believing the person that you're talking to is interesting, you'll meet interesting people!" she had assured me once when I asked her how she met so many fascinating people. I couldn't help but wonder what she would say to the queue of angry callers. I wished that I had her people skills.

"I don't want to stay long, obviously you guys are super busy, but I brought you a coffee, I thought that today of all days you'd need it. Man, what a madhouse out there." Her friendly tone brought levity to an office that had been bogged down by hours of negative interactions.

Helen cleared her throat. She clearly was not in the mood for an interruption. I noticed Noel instinctively look back toward the door, but her friend's eyes were darting around the office, as if looking for something or someone.

"Thank you so much! I should be home tonight by six, I think?"

"Perfect! Stay sane!" I watched her subtly elbow the mystery woman as if clueing her in to the fact that their short visit was over.

And then, coffee in tow, I returned to my desk where another four calls waited in the queue.

12.

NORA

August 10, 12:05 p.m.

I was determined to make it through my first day. The press conference was over, but I could feel the adrenaline high wearing off. I allowed myself to exhale just a little. But, even with that major event checked off my to-do list, I still had a stack of papers a mile high on my desk. I had no idea where to start. Everything seemed equally important, and everyone believed that their problem should be my top priority. I had never seen so many memos marked *urgent* in my life.

I had the next thirty minutes free. I checked my email. Equally as overwhelming. Same for my voice mails. I had several messages from Nathan. I needed to return his calls, but I just wanted to crawl under my desk and have a moment of quiet.

"Nora?" I almost fell out of my seat as my phone's intercom went off. Helen. Precious Helen, who also hadn't expected her Monday to be like this. I needed to get over my self-pity.

"Hi, Helen."

"Hi, Nathan's here to see you—oh, I guess he's already on his way back, sorry I couldn't stop him."

I sighed. That seemed like Nathan; he had a way of just assuming he would be let in wherever he was.

A few seconds later there was a subtle knock on my door.

"Hi, Nathan." I tried to conceal my stress.

"Your majesty?" he said as he entered the room with a dramatic bow. I noticed he held a take-out bag. I suddenly realized why I had the next thirty minutes free; it was lunchtime. As much as I had not been expecting his surprise visit, Nathan always had a way of lightening a mood. And he brought me lunch.

"You can call me Queen Nora," I said with a laugh.

"So, I heard a rumor that you had a new office, and I wanted to come and see for myself."

I had yet to talk to him about everything. By the time I had gotten off the phone with Joel, Nathan had left for his morning run and I had rushed to get Margo and myself ready and out the door. I had been in survival mode. I hadn't had a chance to return his messages. How could I have not warned him of the media onslaught he was about to endure? That our daughter was about to endure. I was a terrible mother.

"Nathan, I'm so sorry I haven't been in touch. I was in such a hustle to get Margo to daycare, and then it's been nonstop since I walked into the building."

"Relax," he said with his typical breezy smile. "It's okay. So, you had no idea that this was coming?"

"None. You would've known if I had." I let out a sigh of relief. He wasn't mad. Of course, he wasn't. Nathan was the most easygoing person I'd ever met. "That call this morning was from Sal. All he said was that a story had run and that he was mutually parting ways with the university—"

"Great, so he was fired," Nathan interrupted while pulling a french fry out of his bag.

"Mutually parted ways," I corrected with a wink. "And he told me that I should expect a call from Joel appointing me as the interim AD."

"Wow, Nora, I'm so proud of you." He sounded impressed. I knew that he was being genuine.

"Thank you." My voice was tired.

"Have you been working a lot with Joel today?"

"He walked me to the press conference, which was, by the way, an onslaught of questions they never would've asked a man in my position. Afterward we talked a few things through. He seemed equally frustrated that the media chose to focus on the fact that I'm a woman. They didn't seem at all interested in the future of the program. Anyways, we talked briefly about next steps, that sort of thing. He mentioned that he also reached out to all the deans?" I knew that this news impacted the rest of the university, Nathan and his department included. I didn't want to mention Joel's cold tone on the phone this morning or how he'd barely made eye contact with me at the press conference and I had to pull him aside afterward to talk with him. He was tired, and it had been a long day already. I didn't want Nathan reading into his behavior as well. One person overthinking their boss's actions was enough for our family.

"Yeah, I'm sure that there will be a lot of meetings about it in my future. We spent half our departmental meeting talking through everything. But meetings aside, I'm proud of you, Nora. I always knew you'd get this job. They would've been crazy not to promote you."

Talking with Nathan was refreshing. He'd known me longer than anyone else in the building. He'd never once questioned my ambition or my desire. He'd never once told me that I wouldn't be able to do the job. In fact, my career was the reason why we'd moved around as much as we had. And he always did so joyfully, never mentioning the reversal of typical gender roles. That was why I loved him.

"So, what's for lunch?" I asked.

"Well, I wasn't sure what to bring, this is my first time dining with royalty, but I know that Nora Bennet likes a classic hamburger and fries."

"Hmm, funnily enough, Queen Nora does as well," I said.

We sat in comfortable silence, both enjoying our lunch.

"Do you need me to drop off and pick up Margo this week? I can. I have everything prepped for the next semester."

"Nathan, are you sure?" We normally traded drop-off and pickup duty. I thought of the list of questions I'd prepped for this morning's press conference—Where is your daughter? What will your daughter do while you're at work? They felt like accusations. I didn't want to be the type of person who took advantage of her husband. I didn't want to be the type of mom who abandoned her child for her career.

"Nora, these are clearly extenuating circumstances. My school year hasn't even started. Maybe you don't know this, but our daughter is pretty great. I really do like hanging out with her. If things get too overwhelming, we can always hire a nanny. A lot of people do it."

"She's great, isn't she?" I ignored his nanny comment. I could only imagine how the press would react if it got out that I couldn't do it all, that I had to hire help.

"No matter what, no matter what stupid questions they ask you, I can personally attest, you're a good mom."

I could no longer hold back the tears.

13.

ALEXIS

August 10, 3:00 p.m.

My run around campus hadn't been enough to calm my nerves, so I made an appointment to get my hair done. The next best stress reliever was a fresh color.

Helen had clearly recognized me. Of course, she had. It had been reckless for me to go to the athletic complex in the first place. I don't know why I had offered to escort Noel inside. I should have just pretended not to know her, kept running. I knew that it was risky to go inside. Did showing my face in the building prove that I had nothing to hide, prove that I was innocent? Or did it just make me look reckless and stupid?

I took a deep breath, my head fully covered by the hooded hair dryer. I felt invisible. Safe. Protected. At the moment, I was just a normal woman getting her hair done before the start of the new semester.

But I couldn't stop thinking about Noel. Her eyes were full of promise. It seemed like she really meant it when she said she enjoyed my class.

To be honest, Noel reminded me of myself when I was her age. Back then I believed that the world was good.

Twenty-one-year-old me had her whole life planned out. I was going to marry my college boyfriend, Curtis. We would move to some beach town, probably in Maine. Not because either of us had been to Maine, but it sounded like a great place to have a little cabin and spend our days writing. He would write bestselling presidential biographies, and I would pen the next great American novel. We would be a power couple. In between our writing deadlines, we would travel. To France, Portugal, Bolivia, India. Places we had read about but never visited.

We would spend Thanksgiving with my family, Christmas with his.

We would never be rich, but we would be happy.

As it turns out, you can plan your future as much as you like, but there's absolutely no guarantee that any of it will actually happen. Especially if the plan involves the cooperation of another person.

A month before we graduated, I had been expecting a proposal, but instead I found out that Curtis had accepted a job with a major publishing house and would be moving to New York. I'd already committed to the MFA program at Renton.

I wanted a long-distance relationship. He wanted to break up. So, we broke up.

I swerved. I vowed to myself that I would channel the breakup into the plot of my book. Out of deep feelings comes great creativity. Or so I told myself.

I graduated with my master's. I had two degrees. One earth-shattering breakup. Zero novels written.

Being a writer who didn't write wasn't sustainable. No publisher will pay an advance on a book that has yet to be written, let alone outlined.

I didn't have a backup plan to my backup plan. I was broke and out of options.

So, I took a job as an assistant professor.

Thirty-four-year-old Alexis had a new plan. She had a new boy-friend. Faithful friends. A job that allowed time to write. That was until the news about Sal broke and I was reminded of everything I had to lose. All I wanted to do was remain invisible under the protection of the hooded hair dryer.

I thought about the other professors in my department, who for the first time since I took this job seemed very eager to talk to me. I told myself that they didn't suspect only me. They suspected everyone.

I pulled out my phone. I had it set to "do not disturb" because I didn't want to see everyone's reaction to the news. I didn't want them to ask my opinion. I didn't want to repeat my answer like a broken record all day.

I saw a text from Beau. I felt a pang of guilt that I hadn't reached out to him. We both had a lot at stake. He wanted to know how I was, if I was okay. Of course, he wanted to know if I was okay. That's why I loved him. He was thoughtful and intentional even when things were spiraling out of control. I cursed the stupid athletic department and ignored his message. He deserved a more eloquent response than my frazzled brain could offer him right now.

I really needed to talk to my cousin, MP. He was the person who knew me the best. As a journalist, he was also the person who happened to know this story the best. He would know what my next move should be. At the very least, he would listen without judgment. He had spent years listening to me. The same age as me, he had patiently helped me navigate high school. We had a special bond and had spent almost every waking minute of our childhood together, only returning to our own houses at the end of the day.

I noticed that MP was among the seventy-two people who had tex-ted me. I didn't even realize seventy-two people had my phone number.

Are you okay?

I responded, I mean, this was not how I thought my semester was going to start. MP, what do I do?

I waited. I saw that he had sent his message a few hours ago. It was just after three o'clock. He'd still be at work. To my surprise, he responded almost instantly.

Lay low. You're O.K.

He was right, of course. I shouldn't do anything to draw attention to myself. I shouldn't do anything rash. I needed to keep my head down and keep working.

Every professor I knew had had at least one less-than-pleasant experience with someone in the athletic department. And there was the reality that the athletic department got the money. Money that many departments could use to fund research or, at the bare minimum, pay their professors a living wage. It felt like a never-ending power struggle. The world of academia and the world of athletics. Pitted against each other in an endless battle for resources.

This was the unpleasant reality of working at a university. But at the end of the day, it was just a job. I needed to take a deep breath.

How are you? I responded.

Fine, the fall is always the busiest time regardless of what stories I'm reporting. Phone has been ringing off the hook . . .

My reply was interrupted by my stylist returning to check on my highlights, removing my helmet of protection.

I needed a drink.

14.

ANNE

I had survived my first day. I felt more exhausted than I had in weeks, possibly years. Helen and I had both stayed at the office an hour after we turned off the phone lines. We both had other responsibilities to catch up on. Items that had been put on the back burner as we answered the constant calls. The soundtrack of a ringing phone continued buzzing in my ears. I thought it might be hours before the sound stopped playing itself on repeat.

The most surprising thing about the day was I'd actually enjoyed it. True, nothing about the day had been easy. I had never been cursed at more in my entire life. I had cried multiple times in the bathroom. But I had survived. I had done it. And the rush of adrenaline that came with it felt good. I'd enjoyed telling people that I didn't have a comment. I liked that people thought I had insider info. I loved the hustle, trying to make sure that we were as prepped as possible for whatever bomb would be deployed next.

Helen and I walked slowly out of the office, back through the lobby. Though crowded, it was still quieter than earlier that morning. Things were starting to calm as we all adjusted to this new reality.

"Anne!" I heard a voice call out from behind me. I saw Graham jog to catch up to us.

"I'll see you tomorrow? Great job today," Helen said with a weary smile. I imagined that the last thing she wanted was to be sucked into another conversation with a coworker.

"Yes, see you tomorrow, thanks for all your help today, Helen."

She smiled in appreciation and then turned in the direction of the parking lot.

"You made it through your first day! How'd you hold up, or the more important question, will you be reappearing tomorrow?" he said with an easy laugh. I was thankful for a friendly face, for a familiar face. Even if we only had one previous interaction, it felt like I was running into an old friend. It seemed like years ago that I had run into him in the lobby. I had learned so much since I had walked through those doors just hours earlier.

"You know, I liked it way more than I thought I would. I would dare to say I even had fun." I still felt the energy of the day buzzing through my veins.

"You had fun telling people all day that, no matter how important they think they are to the university they have given thousands of dollars to, they're actually nothing?"

"Well, when you phrase it like that, yep, pretty much! I can't imagine your day was any easier, I imagine that about a thousand compliance rules were violated with all of this?"

"You've no idea. I think it would be a violation for me to tell you how many violations were committed." He laughed.

We walked toward the parking lot. The stairs of the building were littered with evidence of the reporters—crumbled take-out wrappers, business cards, a pen. That debris was all that remained of the mayhem of the day.

"I guess this means the story is over? A new day, a new news cycle?"

"I doubt it, not with football season just around the corner. I imagine not a game will go by all season where this isn't at least mentioned or some commentator questions if Nora's appointment as AD was the right call," he said with a tired sigh. "Hey, want to go out for a celebratory first-day-of-work drink? We can talk a little bit more about all of this."

I thought for a moment. I was exhausted. But also, I knew I couldn't talk to Noel about what had happened today, and I needed someone to talk it through with. Graham, as a coworker, was safe.

We walked to a bar near my apartment. The bar was all but empty—one of the joys of spending the summer in a college town. In a week, it would be impossible to find a chair, let alone an open table. But that night, there was peace. It felt like the quietest room I had been in all day. I tried to breathe it in. When I was a freshman, the thought of spending the summer in Renton seemed like a nightmare. No one stuck around. What would I do in my free time? But now, a few years older, and a lot wiser, it felt like a welcome reprieve. I suspected that I might like the summers in Renton more than the normal bustle of the semesters.

It felt like I had keys to the castle. Free to go to any restaurant or bar without a reservation. I could bring a picnic lunch to the quad and find a space on the grass—and eat peacefully with no fear of being decapitated by a Frisbee.

"Okay, so now that we're not in the confines of the athletic complex, you can tell me the truth, how was your first day?" Graham asked as he returned with our beers.

"I was being serious, I actually liked it! It felt like everyone around me also had the first-day jitters. Like we were all in this madness together!"

"You're kidding me?" He leaned back in his chair, taking a long drink from his beer.

"Okay, so if it's not the joy of dealing with a major crisis that keeps you coming to work each day, what is it?"

"I just like rules. Compliance is like a rule-follower's dream. My job is basically to make sure that everyone follows the NCAA's rules and regulations. I wish that I could tell little five-year-old me, self-proclaimed recess rule enforcer, that there was a job like this. I would've enjoyed school a whole lot more, knowing that this was waiting for me on the other side."

I laughed. "Wow, you make your job sound so exciting. I imagine that today would've been your dream day then—so many rules to enforce."

"You would think, but today was like rule enforcement overload. I spent my whole day trying to keep wildfires under control while my boss spent his day in meetings. I'm the lowest rung on the compliance ladder. Normally, I only work with women's volleyball in the fall. I don't have to worry about the machine that is football. I mean I still work the games, but it's not my main focus. The more important people worry about that monster."

"How long have you worked this rule-enforcing dream job of yours?"

"This is my third fall season. I started as an intern and then a grad assistant. This is my first season as a full-time employee."

"Look at you working your way up."

"Yes, I'm the picture of what you can expect in two years!" he said with a wink. "So, what about you, are you a sport management major? What made you want to intern in the athletic department?"

"No, it had nothing to do with sports. This was a last-ditch effort to fulfill my internship requirement. Plus, it's paid and I didn't have to move to another city."

"What do you study then?"

"I'm majoring in business administration and minoring in psychology."

"And what would you like to do with that combo?"

"I'd love to help businesses shape their culture. Help with employee well-being."

"So basically, a fancy HR person?" he teased.

"Ha, ha." I sipped my beer. "Okay, I need to talk about this with someone, because none of my friends care about sports and I was instructed by Helen to not talk to anyone outside of the department about the whole Higgins thing. I want to, no I need to, hear all of your thoughts."

"All of them, huh?" I watched him look off into the distance as if weighing his thoughts, deliberating what he could and wanted to share. He took another sip of his beer. "I think Nora will be a great athletic director. I think the university made a really smart move appointing her. She's who I would've picked." His response seemed like that of a politician. I could tell he left much unspoken, and there was even more between the lines I didn't know how to read.

"You make it sound like she was a contestant on *The Bachelor*," I said with a laugh. "Did you ever work with Higgins?"

"Not a ton, I think I only interacted with him like four or five times in a professional capacity. He was always really nice, but he had no reason to work directly with me. Especially if I did my job, there was no need for him to even remember that my division of the compliance department exists."

"And in a nonprofessional capacity?"

His smile faltered slightly.

"Oh, I'm not meaning to imply you were implicated in all of this!" I quickly corrected.

"No, no, it's fine. I was in about twenty meetings all day trying to figure out how I might be implicated in all of this. Sal's my uncle."

15.

NORA

August 10, 10:58 p.m.

My feet had swollen to twice their normal size. Walking hurt. Keeping my eyes open hurt. As soon as possible, I needed to see a chiropractor; otherwise, I worried I would never be able to walk normally again. I wouldn't have made it through the day had it not been for my team. I felt such deep gratitude for them. Even that poor sweet girl who started today.

Even Joel had made a point of checking in on me. He had also called and emailed me multiple times in the afternoon. Any coolness I had detected that morning had melted away. I was just being paranoid, reading into his tone, when really, he must have been exhausted. I could tell that he was trying to make it clear that I was the one he wanted to lead the athletic department. He'd told me multiple times that I had the university's full support; whatever I needed, I just had to say the word, and he'd be there.

What I really needed, although I could not admit it to the university's president, was a full night of sleep. Maybe I'd take a bath when I got home. Most likely I would fall straight into my bed.

I turned the key in my front door, the warmth of my home calling me inside.

I padded cautiously down the hallway to my kitchen and was greeted by Nathan, sipping a scotch, reading the day's newspaper. It felt surprisingly normal.

"I sent Sandra home." Sandra was our emergency after-school babysitter, a Hail Mary if neither of us could pick up Margo. She wasn't a nanny, a point I often reminded myself of. Every family used a babysitter now and then. "And, I have some pizza for you in the fridge. Sorry, I broke into the scotch cabinet without you, but it was just there staring at me."

I let out a sigh of relief.

"Can you pour one for me?" My voice sounded tired and worn out. It vaguely occurred to me that Nathan said he'd pick up Margo. He had told me that it would be no problem. But I was so desperate for help and a conversation with someone I trusted that I didn't question him, and I put the dream of falling into bed on the back burner.

He grabbed me a glass and poured my drink.

"How's Margo?" I asked with a pang of sadness, realizing I hadn't seen her since early morning.

"She had a good day. She and Sandra went to the park, and she made sure to shout to anyone who would listen to her that her mommy now ran the school."

"That's my girl." I was proud to be her mom.

"How was your first day? Was everyone nice to you? Did the kids talk to you?" He quizzed me like he did our daughter.

"Ha, ha. The first day was as smooth as it could have been. But was everyone nice to me? That's a hard question to answer. Half of the internet is waiting for me to fail, while the other half is holding me up as if I'm their savior. It's very confusing. And yes, the kids talked to me—too much talking in my opinion. The press hung around outside the building all day long. Helen and our new intern, Anne—poor girl, this was a terrible day to start—anyways, the two of them spent most of the day answering the phone, and every spare moment they had in between calls was spent shooing people out of the office."

"Oh man, nightmare."

I thought back through my day, remembering our lunch.

"Didn't you tell me at lunch today that you could do school pickup all week?" I hadn't meant to bring it up. I especially didn't mean for it to come out as an accusation. As soon as the words were out of my mouth, I wanted to pull them back. Something had probably come up. As the dean of his department, the days leading up to the start of the semester were busy. At least he thought to contact Sandra. At least he saw our daughter today. I should be grateful, not trying to pick a fight.

"Something came up. I told you, you must not remember. Which makes sense, with the day you had. But don't worry, I'm around the rest of the week. Super Dad, reporting for duty!"

"No, you told me that you'd pick her up." I didn't have the energy to have this conversation, this fight. Nathan was always jovial until you questioned him.

"It's okay, Nora. You've had a crazy day. The rest of the week, I'm on it, no Sandra."

"Thank you," I said, still feeling as if I was having a déjà vu moment. "That would be so helpful, Nathan."

"Of course, anything for my daughter and her high-powered mother." He gave me a proud gaze.

"How was your day?" I desperately did not want to spend any more time on a conversation that could inadvertently make me feel like I was failing as a mother.

"Not nearly as eventful as yours. I imagine you were in meetings all day, trying to get to the bottom of all of this?"

"On and off. The NCAA is sending in an investigation team. I can't talk about it. But the goal is to leave no stone unturned. They're trying to figure out how much money was stolen, if any gifts were given to players, which professors were bribed. The whole thing's a mess. And then there is of course dealing with the inevitable sanctions we'll be handed. I don't know what to think."

"It sounds like you don't have to be involved too much then?"

Had he been listening to me at all? I was the athletic director of a school that was being investigated by our governing body. If anything, that made me the most involved. I, of course, could not say that aloud. That would be asking for a fight. He was right, I was exhausted. I wasn't going to let this impossibly long day cause me to pick a fight with my husband. He was clearly doing the best he could.

"I mean, I'm not conducting the investigation, but I'm the figurehead of the department. I do have to cooperate with them. It says something that Joel trusted me enough to give me the job, but that doesn't mean that I'm exempt from the investigation or questioning." It felt like the more mature response. The whole thing was giving me a colossal headache.

"Man, what a mess this guy left behind." We'd never spent much time with Sal and his family. Between Nathan's schedule and Margo, we were just too busy. I wondered, if Nathan had known Sal as well as I did, how he would react. Would he feel the mixed emotions I was feeling? I'd known Sal as a person. We spent thousands of hours together inside the athletic department.

"From the sound of it, it's a very extensive investigation. And since I was in a leadership role while all of this was going on, they're going to look into all my connections, meetings, travel, etc., just to make sure that it was all by the book. Oh, that being said, you might also be contacted. As someone who is connected with me. But maybe because of the English department as well? I know that they're planning on interviewing professors, but I'm not sure to what extent."

"Man, I'm sorry. They're really going no-holds-barred on this thing. What are you going to do about Joel and Richard?"

I'd yet to have a full conversation with Richard Ross. The football coach had sent me a curt email explaining that he was deep in the throes of prepping for the upcoming season and wouldn't have time to meet until later in the week. I had reminded myself that this was true; he was preparing for the season, though I couldn't help but wonder if he would have delayed a meeting if Sal needed to speak with him.

"Well, I assume that Joel will remain the university's esteemed president, and Richard is hopefully preparing to win some football games."

"Well, I meant do you think that they're going to be fired?"

I was taken aback by his question. I didn't have the headspace to think about another major player at the university being fired. I had spent a good amount of time working with Joel throughout the day and couldn't see a plausible situation where he would be let go. Suspicions that I might not have been his first pick for this job aside, I had nothing but respect for him; everyone at the university did. I'd heard many alumni say that he was the best president in our university's history.

On the other hand, Richard was known to have issues, but it was nothing new and nothing brought to light because of Higgins. He was successful, and because of this he acted as if he was entitled to behave however he wanted. Frustrating to work with, yes, but as far as I knew he'd done nothing that would get him fired.

"I don't think so, Nathan. Joel has an entire university to oversee. I already feel bad that he had to spend so much time in athletics today. At the end of the day, we're just one of many departments. And Richard, I mean everyone knows he's a jerk, but I don't think there'd be any reason to fire him, especially so close to the start of the season. He's a good coach, and there're still a few years left on his contract. Which means, Sal drama aside, we can't afford to fire him right now."

"So, you don't think either one had a hand in all of this?"

"Nathan, I can't talk about this anymore. I'm just trying to do my job, and I trust that the investigation team will do theirs. That's all anyone can hope for at this point." I realized that I was on the brink of crying. I needed to stop talking about work. I needed to go to bed.

As if on cue, Nathan glanced at his watch, the time approaching midnight. "It's late. You need to get some rest. I'll clean this up."

I was finally alone. I had survived.

16.

LAUREN

August 11, 7:05 a.m.

I made it. August 11. A new day. A blank page. A fresh start.

Although this fresh start didn't erase the previous day's events. Nothing would.

I wanted to pull the covers back over my head for the second day in a row. Bury myself in the safety. But I didn't. Or more accurately, I couldn't.

I've always been a planner. I love a schedule. Ask anyone who has ever gone on vacation with me—every moment is planned to a T. Life is better experienced when every moment is perfectly calculated and planned. Every minute of every day accounted for efficiently. I'd implemented schedules to keep my family in line, to keep everyone safe and on the straight and narrow.

These calculated systems were how I'd ensured that everyone made it to baseball practice wearing the correct uniform and had extra snacks to share. It's how I'd made sure dinner was always on the table. It's how I could always keep track of where everyone was. Where the away games were. Which team we played that weekend. Keeping a strict schedule was the only way to keep a busy family afloat.

I thought about my son, Hunter. I'd not heard from him since the news broke. Or, more aptly, I hadn't checked my phone. For all I knew he'd been calling me hourly. I didn't want to be rescued. He had his own life to worry about. I didn't want to be the poor fragile mother who calls her child back to her from his own adult life. I was supposed to be emotionally stable enough to save him. Normally, I was.

I had to reach out to him. If I didn't, an even worse fate awaited me. He could just pop in and visit. I didn't want him to see me in this state.

I had to get it together.

I pulled on the sweatshirt that I had haphazardly thrown at the foot of my bed and made my way down the stairs.

The house was quiet, eerie. Not that I had expected anything different.

The late-summer sun was already high in the sky. It was my favorite time of August. The days felt endless. Waking up in the morning felt like walking into a day that had already begun, waiting to greet you with hope and promise.

I made a cup of coffee. I thought about enjoying it on the front porch and then instantly thought better of it. I had no idea what the world outside the safety of my house was like, and there was a good chance something unpleasant waited for me on the other side of the door.

I had to text my son. Confirm that I was still among the living.

I walked back to my room and found my phone, next to a pile of laundry. I reflected on the previous day. I had acted childish, immature. What adult woman throws her phone?

Slowly it powered on, coming back to life. I wished I could ignore everyone but my son's messages—fake condolences, people trying to get an inside scoop on Sal, people I hadn't spoken to in years resurfacing from the shadows, the press.

But as soon as it powered on, it started buzzing with notifications. An unwelcome song of ringtones echoed through the quiet house. Text messages, missed calls, emails, ESPN notifications—all confirming that this had not, in fact, been a terrible nightmare.

Predictably, there were also messages from the university. They wanted to know if I'd be willing to participate in the NCAA's investigation. The coordinator had taken the liberty of scheduling a meeting for nine thirty. I felt pathetic that they had correctly guessed that I had nothing on my schedule. My full-time job had been to be Sal's wife, my calendar dictated by the sports season and his travel. My stomach dropped at the thought of the meeting. I should have checked my phone yesterday. That would have given me more time to prepare, more time to cancel or reschedule. I didn't want to reveal how little I had known. Most people, I imagined, would have cheered their own innocence. I just felt shame.

Shame that I had missed the signs—despite all my tightly managed schedules, shared calendars, routines. How could I have been so stupid? How could I have missed clues? And now, I'd have to admit my naivete in a formal investigation. The whole world would see my blind spot. A stereotypical self-absorbed, ditzy housewife. It would confirm the idea that I knew people had of me.

I came across a message from Helen, sending just a few *x*'s. A sign of solidarity. I'd always liked Helen.

Hundreds of messages from other wives, all of whom I am sure were grateful that this was my life and not theirs.

Joel had also reached out. His message said that he was so sorry. He offered to bring over dinner, groceries, and asked if I wanted to get lunch this afternoon. I felt a rush of relief. Even after everything, he was still on my side. He was one of my oldest friends and had always been a part of our family. To our children he was Uncle Joel, and to his, I was Aunt Lauren. I felt a sting of regret for involving him in all of this. He was just trying to run his university. He wanted what was best for

Renton. I was relieved to see his message, but I didn't have the energy to respond back other than to say I was free for lunch.

Predictably, there were a few dozen messages from Hunter, ranging from threats to make an appearance if I didn't respond soon to denial that this whole thing was actually happening.

There were zero messages from Sal. Not that I thought I would hear from him. Not after yesterday morning when he made it clear that he blamed me for everything. I was the one who had made us move to this town. I was the one who had failed to protect our family. If I would've been a better wife, I would've heard whisperings of this story, and then I could've found a way to stop it. Catch and kill. His accusations rang in my ears. I didn't know how he expected me to see this coming. There was no logic to his anger. He just needed someone to blame.

And I was just a clueless housewife.

I called Hunter. He was always my fiercest ally. He'd always been a mama's boy. He picked up on the second ring as if he'd been waiting by his phone.

"Mom?" He sounded like he hadn't slept.

"Hi, honey, how are you holding up?" I did my best to sound as if I had it all together, positioning myself as the one who had called to comfort him.

"Thank God you finally called. I've spent the last twenty-four hours trying my best to believe that this is all some terrible dream. Or maybe we're on that TV show, *Punk'd*." I heard him laughing. He was always quick to laugh, an instant mood brightener. "How are you?" He sounded as if he was measuring out the weight of each word.

How was I? I had no idea. More importantly, I had no idea how to talk to my son about everything.

"Blindsided." It was the best word I could come up with, encompassing the array of emotions I had felt in the last twenty-four hours.

"When did you find out?"

"When your father woke me up at four something in the morning yesterday to tell me that the story had been published."

I heard him take in a quick breath, trying not to sound like he was taking sides, but it was clear, he was angry with his dad.

"I saw the story on Twitter. I thought it was some stupid clickbait. It was hard to believe it was real. Then I called Dad, and he didn't deny any of it. He just ranted about how careless and unethical the writer of the piece was."

Poor sensitive Hunter. Always trying to see the best in people. He'd probably assumed that his father would deny it all. Hoped that he'd have a reason to believe that these rumors were just that, rumors.

There'd been no denying it because it was all true. I knew as soon as I had seen Sal's face, screaming at me the day before.

"Mom, do you want me to come home? I can take time off work. It's okay."

"No, honey. I'm fine."

"Please call, I mean it. I don't want to go through this alone. I don't want you to, either."

I realized that maybe Hunter wanted to come home not just for me, but for himself as well.

"Honey, do you want to come home?"

He paused. "I think I might look at flights today, just to see if there's anything."

I mentally rummaged through my pantry, already planning what I'd make him for dinner.

17.

ALEXIS

August 11, 7:45 a.m.

It all felt overwhelming. Every interaction yesterday was somehow tainted by Sal Higgins. Nothing seemed to stop the conveyor belt of anxiety running through my brain.

So, I had taken my freshly done hair to the nearest liquor store and bought the first bottle I saw. I just needed something to help tune out the noise. But I didn't even make it through my front door in peace. As soon as I got home, the bottle waiting to be cracked open, I saw him there, sitting on my steps.

"Austin, get off my porch." I tried to fill my voice with confidence, self-assurance.

"Alexis, I have to talk with you. I've been calling you all day. I have to talk with you," he repeated as if he wasn't sure I had heard him the first time.

"No, I have nothing to say to you, and do you seriously not know how this looks, you hanging out on my porch? Do you think that they won't keep tabs on the athletes, to see how you all are taking this news?"

He looked at me as if he hadn't considered that.

"This whole town is dripping with press; do you really think such a public meeting is the best move?" I continued my lecture. I had been his professor, after all.

"You didn't answer your phone?"

"So, that led you to believe that the best thing to do would be to show up at my house?" My pulse raged.

"I didn't know what else to do."

"You have to get off my porch."

"Can I come inside then? Alexis, I'm really worried."

"You absolutely cannot come inside. You were my student; I don't fraternize with students." With that, I pushed my way past his huge frame and into my house, making sure to bolt the door behind me.

And then, like the college students I was surrounded by, I drank my weight in cheap liquor to deal with my bad day.

Now, with every pulse of my headache, I remembered why that was not the way adults handle their issues. I hadn't drunk that much since I was a student myself. Clearly, my tolerance had changed in the last decade. I felt old.

I couldn't help but wonder what my mother would say about all of this, about my behavior. She surely would not have approved. I could hear the lecture playing out in my head. I was throwing away my life. Nothing was set in stone, and did I want to risk the few good things I had?

She of course wouldn't have been referring to my career. All she really cared about was securing her chance of future grandchildren. She would be agonizing over how this would affect my relationship.

I forced myself out of bed. My freshly cut and colored hair was a wreck. No one would guess that I'd just spent $150 on it. Lines of mascara ran down my cheeks. I looked like a mess. I was a mess—who was I kidding?

I don't know why I thought checking Twitter would be helpful. I didn't realize that so many people I followed cared about sports.

Everyone was appalled, and everyone wanted their opinions known. Those who worked at Renton claimed they couldn't believe that something like this could happen here. Everyone else said nothing like this would ever have happened under their watchful eyes.

I knew that everyone was lying.

It was impossible not to believe that something like this could happen at Renton, or anywhere with a high-powered, big-budget athletic department desperate to look good on the national stage. And to assume that anyone could have prevented this? Also ridiculous. People who have power and money will do anything they can to keep it. Money and power turn us all into Gollum. It's an unavoidable fact of life.

I wanted to believe that everyone else was just as scared as me. That their feigned shock was an attempt to prove their innocence. Or perhaps they tricked themselves into believing that they were safe. That even if they had done something wrong, someone else, someone like me, had surely done something worse, making their job safe. Renton University surely couldn't fire all its professors. Not this close to the beginning of the school year.

When I finally peeled myself away from Twitter, I saw I had received an email from the university asking me to come in this afternoon for an interview with the NCAA's investigation team.

I read between the lines. They were trying to figure out who to fire. I must have done something to get on their radar.

The sweat returned to my palms. I forced myself to keep taking slow breaths. I tried to convince myself it was just a part of their process. A request for an interview alone was no reason to panic. They were most likely interviewing hundreds of professors. They were being thorough. There was no need to be scared. There was no need to worry. There was no need to worry. There was no need to worry.

18.

ANNE

August 11, 8:22 a.m.

My workday was technically supposed to start at eight thirty, but after the events of the day before, I figured getting here earlier would be better. Even though there had been nothing more I'd wanted to do than call in sick. My throat was hoarse, I realized, from talking so much the previous day. My feet were tired, and my back hurt. It felt like one day of work had taken years off my life.

I tried to call up the excitement I felt the previous evening. But it felt like I had an excitement hangover.

I took my time walking to work. The sun was shining, already hot. I was thankful the office had air-conditioning.

I hoped I would bump into Graham again in the lobby, but no such luck. It had felt great, after the stress of the workday, to go home and tell Noel that I had made a work friend. I left out the fact that I found him very cute and that his uncle was Sal Higgins. I hadn't had the energy for all the questions Noel would surely have asked.

When I entered the lobby of the building, it seemed considerably less chaotic than the day before. It felt almost peaceful. When I arrived at our office area, I found Helen already there, buzzing around our small lobby.

"Nora's been here since like six," she said to me in place of hello. I wasn't sure how to respond.

"What time are we normally supposed to get here?"

"Sal would only get here that early on game day. I think she's really feeling the pressure of the job," she responded, not actually answering my question.

It didn't take much scrolling on Twitter last night to get a sense of the multitude of people rooting against her. That, along with the reality of so many people clocking her every move, would add an unsurmountable amount of pressure to an already stressful job.

I could only imagine how Nora felt.

"Our inbox is overflowing," Helen said in a frazzled huff. "And there're still things we need to do to prep for the start of the season."

I could tell that her thoughts were starting to spiral. The to-do list was overwhelming.

"What's the most helpful? What if I spent the morning responding to emails and answering the phones, and then you can focus on what needs to be done to start the season?"

Gratitude washed across her face.

"That would be wonderful. Only respond to the emails regarding Higgins's departure, I'll take care of the rest. You should have the form response from yesterday still. Thank you." And with that, she went on frantically moving around the lobby.

I grabbed a cup of coffee from our office machine. This might be the best perk of the job, in my opinion. Noel nearly fainted when I told her that I had complimentary tickets to every game of every sport at the school. That didn't seem as big of a benefit as unlimited free coffee. I honestly doubted that I would go to many games. Most game days, I would have to work until halftime, and then it was unlikely I'd want to spend the rest of my Saturday at work.

But free coffee, that was something I could get behind.

I settled back into my desk, almost afraid to power on my computer and see the mass of emails waiting.

"I thought I heard another voice in here," Nora said as she entered the lobby. "Good morning, Anne!" She smiled warmly. I wondered how much sleep she had gotten the night before. "Thank you for coming back today. After the day you had yesterday, I'm impressed that you didn't leave running."

"Well, when Sal hired me, he'd told me that it was a fast-paced environment. So, I can't say I wasn't warned." I paused; I had barely spoken to Nora the day before. I realized I didn't know how to talk to her. I also realized I had just brought up the man whom she'd just replaced. It felt taboo. "I'm sorry, I didn't mean to mention Sal," I quickly added.

"Better to say Sal than Macbeth," she said with a wink. "Did you study at Renton?"

"I still do. I'm in my senior year. I have to complete an internship in order to graduate."

"Are you in the sport management program?"

"Business. But I wouldn't be opposed to a job in sports." I felt myself blush. She was now the second person to ask me that question. I don't know why I felt so much embarrassment about not studying sports.

"Well, that's good, since you're doing your internship in the industry. What caused you to apply here?"

I thought about telling her the full truth, that this internship was one of the few I could afford because it was paid. But I didn't want her to think I had taken the job out of desperation. I thought about lying, telling her that I was a huge Griffons fan and had always dreamed about working in the department. But I suspected she'd easily see through my lie. Instead, I found a middle ground.

"I saw the job posting on the university's website, and I thought it'd be a great practical way to apply a variety of skills." I tried to sound diplomatic instead of like a twenty-two-year-old desperately trying to get all my credits squared away before I walked across the stage in May.

"So, are you a Sports fan then?" She said *sports* like it was a title, a proper noun.

"I—uh." I was unsure how to answer.

"You don't have to like sports to work here. I was just making conversation." She smiled reassuringly.

"I'm not opposed to liking sports!" I said hurriedly. As if for some reason that comment would improve the situation.

"In every game, there's always more than meets the eye. Working in athletics will either make you fall in love with the institution or curse it." She glanced at her watch.

Helen took the opportunity to cut in. She'd been so quiet I'd almost forgotten she was still at her desk.

"You have a meeting with tickets at eight forty-five," she said knowingly.

"Right, thanks, Helen. I'll see you ladies later."

I couldn't help but notice how she carried herself with confidence. She didn't speak like she was trying to prove herself. She simply commanded herself in a way that made you want to listen. She knew that her opinion was valuable. I doubted that she blushed when she answered questions.

"I have my meeting with the investigation team at nine," Helen said, pulling me out of my daze. "They're interviewing everyone who worked with Sal and a few professors. I'm not sure how long it'll go. They told me the initial conversation would only be thirty minutes. On top of everything else going on, I'm not sure how much I'll be pulled out of the office to deal with this. You're lucky you didn't start a day earlier, or you'd be in the same boat."

"Are you nervous?" Helen had spoken about the interview as if holding it at a distance, seemingly removed, as if she truly hadn't been involved. It would be hard to imagine that Helen was wrapped up in all of this. There was no way she'd be that calm if she were. Or perhaps she just had an incredible poker face?

She pondered my question.

"No, I'm not. I don't have anything to hide. I'm just a woman who loves her job. I just don't want to have to waste hours repeating the same answers to different people."

"Well, I can hold down the fort while you're gone. We have no comment, and no one is allowed past the threshold," I said with a diplomatic nod.

19.

Lauren

August 11, 9:27 a.m.

I hated the athletic complex. I had hated it before Sal betrayed our family. I remember when he first showed me the plans, beaming with pride. It felt cold. The walls covered in metal like it was some sort of modern art exhibit instead of what it actually was, an overly pretentious gym and office space.

I'd made it a point to go there as little as possible. Everything about it made me sick to my stomach. It was state of the art, brand new, which of course to most people seemed like a good thing, but to me, it just seemed like money that could've been spent on more important things, like making sure students who needed it had access to financial aid.

I had shared my opinions with Sal, in private of course. He'd laughed at me like I was a little kid, clueless about what made the world go round. I never expressed my misgivings to anyone else. I presented as the perfect wife. I showed up at games early, donors in tow. I cheered louder than anyone else in our box. I remembered the players' names. I followed the team when they traveled.

That part of my charade wasn't difficult. Growing up, I'd always loved sports. They felt magical. Sports have the power to bring people together, people who would normally never associate with one another, and sports give a community something collective to cheer for. I saw neighbors who hated each other on Friday, hug in pure joy on Saturday under the stadium lights.

I saw the magic work within the walls of my own home. My parents spent most of the week screaming at each other. Blaming each other for everything that had gone wrong. But then, on Saturdays, our whole family would crowd in front of the TV and in one communal voice cheer on my parents' alma mater.

During the commercial breaks, my parents would romantically share the story of meeting on the college's quad. On their first date they'd gone to a football game. My father would brag about how my mother called plays better than the coach.

It was a love of the game that had brought them together, and it was a love of the game that kept them together.

I didn't mean to fall in love with Sal. I had never sought him out, unlike some of the other women I watched, who swooned over his athletic looks. We had just become friends. He sat next to me in our Comm 106 class, simply by chance; Sal Higgins and Lauren Hill, alphabetical serendipity, we used to joke. I didn't even know that he was on the football team. He had red-shirted our freshman year and never mentioned it. One Friday, his seat was empty, and I asked him on Monday where he'd been, and if he wanted my notes. It was only then he laughed and said he'd been traveling with the football team. I secretly believed that he assumed that I had always known he was on the team and was just playing dumb.

He'd known even then that his playing career would end when we graduated. He was good but would never make it to the NFL. Instead of going out for the draft, he made the easy transition into coaching.

I loved being a coach's wife. I was friends with all the other wives; our children played together, and we would complain about our husbands' travel schedules. Most of the wives didn't care about the sport or even watch the games. That was never me. Before we had Hunter, I traveled with the team every weekend. The players knew me on a first-name basis, and they introduced me to their families. I became a mentor to countless athletes. They were like an extension of our family.

We had several good years. And then, that chapter ended. Sal transitioned from coach to athletic director—with my help, of course. But he only acknowledged my help when he needed someone to blame. Transitioning to AD was a good thing, I constantly reminded him. It gave him more responsibility. He helped shape the program, advocating for all athletes—not just his own. It was a more stable position, less in the limelight. It was the right move for our little family.

I didn't realize, before I became a coach's wife, how often people criticize a coach. Every decision is on display. In what would be his last season as a coach, he got pulled over and cited for a DUI. I had told him that his drinking was a problem. He assured me that I had no idea what I was talking about. That I was being paranoid.

I didn't even have a chance to get mad. Instead, I spent every waking minute warding off the press. Denying rumors that he had a long, troubled history with gambling and alcohol. I was too preoccupied with protecting my husband and reorienting our future to get angry at him.

I knew he needed to find a job out of the public eye. Becoming an athletic director would be perfect; it was a natural next step. I didn't care that he would make less money. After the DUI, I knew there would be an investigation if he stayed on as coach. I wouldn't put my family through more public scrutiny.

He surprised everyone by accepting the job at Renton. Everyone except me. We would settle down, and my life would be stable for the first time in years.

I'd grown to love the town of Renton. As much as I hated the athletic complex, I couldn't fault the town itself for that.

If anyone, I should blame my husband. He was the one who had secured the funding and convinced the board of trustees to build it.

"Mrs. Higgins?" a voice queried, pulling me back from memory lane. I turned to see a tall man professionally dressed in a suit, despite the hot August day. He looked much more put together than me. I wondered if I should've dressed up for the meeting. The man gave the impression that he took his job on the investigation team very seriously. I wondered if he was trying to intimidate me.

"Hi, yes, that's me."

"Can you follow me, please?"

We walked in awkward silence down a hallway I had never ventured down before. I could hear the squeaking of shoes against the volleyball court a few hallways away. On the floor beneath me, it was likely that football players were coming in from morning practice. I thought about not just the football players, but all the university's athletes and the consequences that my husband's actions might have on their lives, their futures. Championships stripped, bowl game eligibility removed. It wasn't their fault. I highly doubted that someone on the women's softball team had been a part of this.

I was honestly still uncertain exactly what "this" fully entailed. I was sure that more details would come out. The truth was, the details of what he'd done didn't matter to me. My worst fears about my husband had come true. I didn't need specifics. I knew who Sal truly was.

As we walked down the long hallway, I heard a familiar voice and spotted a woman I knew well.

"Helen!" I called after her.

I watched her spin around and smile in recognition.

"Lauren, hi! I was wondering if I'd see you here today."

"Yes, here I am! I guess they're trying to strike while the iron is still hot? The NCAA really isn't wasting any time on this, are they?"

"No, that's for sure."

An awkward moment passed. There wasn't much we could say. I had a million questions, but I knew this wasn't the time or place.

"It was really good to run into you," I said with a smile as the man in the suit led me into the room Helen had just emerged from. I couldn't risk messaging or calling her. I didn't want to do anything to risk her job. I didn't want to give anyone a reason to investigate her more than she already had been. We were both dangerously close with the common enemy. This would most likely be the extent of our communication for the next few months. We were safer that way.

The room looked sterile. Not in the same way as the rest of the building, though. This room felt sterile in a never-been-used way. I had the impression that we were the first people to sit at the table. It was anything but inviting. The walls were bright white, almost reflective in their cleanliness.

A row of tiny, narrow windows lined the outside wall. They let in light but were too high to see out of.

It was clear that the interviewers had picked this room on purpose. There were no signs of the Griffons' successes from previous years, normally on display all over the building. No plaques celebrating famous athletes from the program, no pictures of students cheering their team to victory.

The room was meant to be a neutral, blank space waiting for a confession.

"So, Mrs. Higgins," the suited man said as he sat across from me, his eyes narrow and dark, "I'm just going to ask you a few questions about our ongoing investigation into Sal Higgins's conduct."

I nodded. I wasn't sure what I was supposed to say, what he expected from me.

"Sal Higgins is your husband, correct?" he asked. I had assumed that he would start the interview with an easy question. I had seen cop shows; I knew how it was supposed to go. He was trying to prime me.

"Yes," I said without much emotion.

He wrote something down on the pad of paper in front of him and then launched into the next question.

"How did you feel about the move to Renton?"

This wasn't where I thought the conversation would go. The question threw me off. "I mean, we moved here years ago. It's hard to recall my exact feelings." That was a lie. I remembered everything about the move. I remember fighting to keep my family safe. The lengths that I had gone to, to make sure that our future didn't crumble away.

"I would imagine being married to Sal Higgins, you moved around quite a bit. I've heard that's common in this profession. And oftentimes the spouse isn't fully on board. How big of a say did you have in your family's move to Renton?"

"I'm not sure that question is relevant."

"I'm just trying to get to know you as a person and learn about your relationship with Mr. Higgins. That's relevant."

He meant my relationship to Sal's misdeeds. He wanted to know if he could trust me. He wanted to know if Sal had trusted me.

"Have you seen your husband since his termination yesterday?"

All the blood rushed out of my face. I felt like I was going to faint. I kept replaying the moment, over and over, of when he had told me. When I found out that our world had shattered.

"I'm sorry, Mrs. Higgins? When was the last time you saw or talked to your husband?"

"Yesterday morning." I silently pleaded that he wouldn't make me recount the moment.

"And did he tell you why he was fired, or were you aware of his dealings?"

I felt wobbly in my seat. I was going to faint. The edges of my vision moved in and out of focus.

"Should I have a lawyer present?" Why hadn't I asked this question before the interview? I mentally kicked myself, frustrated by my own ignorance.

"Only if you want to obtain counsel, which you're welcome to do. We're still uncovering the extent of your husband's wrongdoings, but you currently have no formal connection with the university, nor did you ever receive financial compensation from the university. At this time, you're not a suspect. That is, unless the university sees the need to take legal action against those involved. You're here of your own volition. We're just doing a preliminary investigation."

"Okay." I weighed my options. "Well, I can assure you that I was in no way involved in my husband's actions. If you find yourselves in a position where you need to speak with me again, please contact my lawyer."

With shaky hands, I pulled a business card out of my wallet. Our next-door neighbor Joan was a lawyer and had mentioned a while back that she was always available if I needed anything. I prayed that this qualified as the type of situation she was talking about.

I pretended confidence as I stood up from the table and walked out of the room. I had confirmed my lunch with Joel, but I wasn't sure that I could even make it to my car. He would think I was avoiding him, but I couldn't see him like this. I couldn't talk to anyone who knew. I wanted to hide. I needed to hide.

I scanned the hallway. No bathrooms. What building doesn't have bathrooms on a major hallway? I quickly made my way back toward the lobby until I finally found one and ducked inside, bolting the door behind me. I collapsed against the locked door and sobbed.

20.

ANNE

I was not alone.

The phone lines in the morning hours had been madness, and I missed Helen's supportive smile to reassure me. The thirty-five minutes she was gone for her interview felt like an eternity. I wasn't sure if I needed another cup of coffee, a punching bag, or a walk. My ear felt sweaty from having the phone glued to it for so long. I didn't even know that ears could sweat.

When Helen got back, she pushed me out the door, telling me to take a walk around the block and come back. I couldn't believe the things people said to me on the phone. The callers were much meaner than they had been the day before, as if they were furious that more information hadn't been released overnight and were coming for blood.

The lobby had reverted to chaos. As soon as I saw the crowds of people milling around, I turned on my heel and headed down an unfamiliar hallway.

The white walls felt blinding and like they were closing in around me. I saw a women's restroom and quickly retreated inside, splashing water on my face, trying to make the tears stop. The situation was not my fault. The things people screamed at me were not true. Their reactions were rooted in anger, not in fact. Their words said more about themselves than me. I looked at my tired face in the mirror and repeated that mantra, forcing myself to believe it.

I escaped into a stall to grab toilet paper to wipe my eyes when I heard the door slam, and lock, followed by the all-too-familiar sound of someone crying. Unstoppable sobs. I didn't know what to do. I had no idea how long her crying session would last, and I needed to rejoin Helen. She'd told me to take a walk around the block, and I had already been gone ten minutes. As much as I wanted to hide in the stall, I needed to make my presence known to the crying woman.

"Hello?" I said timidly from my stall.

"Oh my gosh, sorry, is someone in here?" I heard the tearful voice ask.

I emerged from my hiding place.

"Hi, sorry, I think I came to this bathroom for the same reason." I held up my crumpled wad of mascara-stained toilet paper in solidarity.

"Rough day?" she said with a halfhearted laugh.

"It's my second day on the job, I picked quite a week to start," I said, repeating the joke that at this point felt very tired and old.

"Oh, man. Tell me you haven't spent the last two days fighting off the attacks of entitled season ticket holders? You must be working in ticketing to be crying tears like that."

"I had no idea; these people are so mean! I'm interning in the athletic director's office. Which department do you work in?" I made a mental note to try to befriend someone in tickets so I'd have someone else to commiserate with.

I watched her face twitch oddly.

"Oh, um, I actually don't work here." She quickly wiped her face again, standing up abruptly from where she had been sitting on the cold laminate floor, her back leaning against the door. "I should be going. For reference, the only bathroom that keeps tissues stocked is the one near the volleyball courts." The woman unbolted the door and hustled off.

I wandered back to my desk, wondering what could have possibly caused this woman so much distress to hide out and cry in a bathroom in a building where she didn't even work.

I took some comfort in knowing that ours was not the only department at the university to drive people to tears. I wondered if it was just part of having an adult job, crying in the bathroom. My parents had always told me that the real world was a stressful place. I hadn't believed them until I ventured out on my own.

I couldn't help but think about my parents. They had been so proud when I had told them about the internship. They were impressed that there was a lot of competition for the job, and I had beaten out the other students in the interviewing process. When I told them it was a paid position, they let out a sigh of relief.

I honestly can't imagine how my parents would react if they heard how some of the fans acted. That sort of entitlement was unthinkable for them. They kept their heads down and worked hard, expecting little, working harder nonetheless, chasing the ever-elusive American dream. I couldn't imagine a situation where they'd feel they had the right to make a phone call and talk to someone the way these callers were talking to me.

The realization made me both miss and respect my parents even more.

My parents had moved to America from Morocco so my father could pursue his doctorate. Nothing about the experience had been easy. I had been four at the time. I cried as I clutched my grandmother's legs at the airport. My parents didn't know when they would be able to afford to return to see our family. My father was the only one in our family who could speak English. In the wake of 9/11, he knew he had taken a risk moving to America. But neither of my parents complained. I never saw my mother cry when someone made fun of her accent or pretended not to understand her broken English. They had told me repeatedly that if you put your head down and work hard, good things will come.

It wasn't until I got to college, when my classes were challenging or I worried that my financial aid package wouldn't come through, that I realized how thankful I was for the lessons they had taught me. I worked hard. That didn't mean things were perfect, but it meant that I could take care of myself.

"How was your walk?" Helen asked politely when I returned to my desk.

"I didn't get very far." I decided against telling her that I had spent most of my "walk" crying in a bathroom. I didn't want to be the woman who got too emotional and cried on the job.

"You were right about people being meaner today. I can't believe the gall of some of these callers. It's embarrassing that they're associated with our university." Helen huffed. "I wish that my voice was deeper, then maybe I'd be treated like an actual adult and not like I'm still a student. No offense," she added quickly.

"None taken, I get it. I was thinking the same thing this morning after the fifth person accused me of being incompetent and too young to know anything."

"Honestly, this is not a new problem. Sal treated these people like gods, and now that he's not here, they expect the same treatment and they're surprised to hear *no comment*." I could tell she was trying to figure out how much to share. This was the first time she'd brought up Sal conversationally.

There was a pregnant pause.

"How'd your meeting with the investigation team go?" I asked, unsure if I was overstepping or not.

Helen sighed. "It was fine. They're clearly still in the early phases of the investigation. I'm sure it will be one of many conversations. I have nothing to hide and I don't mind talking with them, I just wish that this wasn't happening during our busiest time of the year. That reminds me, I have to attend meetings with Nora most of the afternoon, so I'll be in and out. But hopefully, the calls will die down soon."

Since I had come back to my desk, we already had seven calls waiting in the queue. I doubted it would slow down, but I nodded to assure Helen that she could trust me with the office.

"Just so I'm not leaving you all alone, one of the other admins will help you answer phones. I mean, it's not like you have all afternoon to just sit here and answer phones, there're other responsibilities to this job."

I looked at the huge stack of cards sitting on the corner of my desk. The department had decided that it would be smart to send out a postcard from Nora to every Griffon Athletic Fund member, expressing her gratitude for their continued support during the transition. I was supposed to stamp all of them with her signature and attach the address labels. The athletic fund had sent me a very detailed email saying that this should be my top priority. The stack of address labels looked as thick as a book. It was going to take me more than an afternoon to finish, especially if I spent most of my time on the phone.

"I'll order us both delivery for lunch," Helen said as she noticed me eyeing the postcards. "Courtesy of the department."

21.

ALEXIS

August 11, 11:35 a.m.

I'm not sure why I had thought it would be a good idea to meet my colleagues for coffee before my interview with the investigation team. It'd been planned weeks ago, a celebration to the end of summer before our schedules filled up when the new semester started.

Everyone seemed to have had the dream summer. Vacations to the ocean, backpacking in the mountains that surround Renton, and even a trip to Europe. It seemed as if everyone had come to coffee ready to show off their best-of list. I wondered if I was the only one who couldn't sum up her summer in a perfect Instagram-worthy post. Sure, I had spent a week with my family, and Beau and I had gone on a few weekend trips, but that felt like nothing compared to what these women had done. I enjoyed the peacefulness of Renton in the summer. It may not be as glamourous as a trip to Europe, but it was enough for me.

Their stories made one thing clear: I couldn't admit that my life was on the verge of falling apart. I couldn't tell them about Austin's visit yesterday, or how I was summoned to campus by the investigators. These weren't the type of issues I could talk about with them.

These friends only wanted the highlight reel.

I thought a lot about Austin's visit. I thought about how he went from having the lowest grade in my class to passing with flying colors. I was sure that he had read the article. He knew Sal was fired for pressuring professors to change athletes' grades. Austin was lazy with his schoolwork, but there was nothing he cared more about than football. Anything that might come between him and playing this season was a threat. I was sure that he was just as scared as I was.

But after catching up on what everyone had done over the summer, it seemed that all my friends wanted to talk about was Sal. I'd assumed that this group of friends would want to spend our time together solely bragging about the summer's activities. Even though they were linked with the university, we normally avoided talking about work when we got together. If I'd known this was all they would want to talk about, I would've canceled, especially given the hangover that still plagued me.

"Alexis, you've been quiet," Marcy keenly observed. "You're the one always saying how much you hate how athletics control so much of university life. You have to have some thoughts on this?"

"I think it's ridiculous how much energy has been spent on this already. I mean, it's as if the university cares more about getting to the bottom of this than they do about us preparing for the fall semester." It was all I could muster.

"You know what I heard?" Jill piped in. "I heard that the NCAA wants to interview any professor who had athletes in their classes the past few years. I don't think they realize how many professors that is! What a waste of money and everyone's time."

"Really?" I asked. My voice sounded more hopeful than I had intended. "They're interviewing everyone who taught student-athletes?"

"That's what I heard. I haven't been called in yet, maybe they're working alphabetically or something. Or maybe the fact that I only taught girls on the tennis team didn't really raise a red flag. I imagine that they only care about the moneymaking sports. Who really knows, now that Sal's gone, I would guess others aren't too far behind him." Marcy spoke so fast that her words almost ran together as one.

"Oh, like Richard Ross, that guy always gave me the creeps," Talia said, her face filled with disgust.

"I never met the guy," Jill said quickly, as if trying to prove to us her lack of association.

"I did." The words came out before I thought about them. Every head at the table pivoted in my direction.

"And . . . ," Marcy prompted.

"Talia's right. The guy is a creep. We didn't talk long, but he spent the entire conversation staring at my breasts. I doubt that he heard a word I said. He came off really entitled, like I should be so thankful that our paths happened to cross. Like I owed him something because of all he's done for this university."

This got a round of scoffs from the table. If there's one thing professors hate, it's a pompous athletic department staff member.

"The English department gets so many athletes. I think their coaches tell them that our classes are an easy pass," Talia offered.

"I got a call. I'm supposed to go in this afternoon." I hadn't intended to confess this to my friends. I didn't want to incriminate myself.

"What? Why didn't you say something! Are they interviewing you because you interacted with Ross?" Marcy's question came out more like an accusation than an actual question. I regretted mentioning that I had met him.

"Well, as Jill said, they're interviewing everyone. I've had so many football players in my classes." I gave as few details as I could manage. I didn't want anything I said to raise more questions.

"What time is your interview?" Marcy asked, still sounding accusatory.

"Twelve thirty." I glanced dramatically at my watch. "I actually should probably head to campus. I have to meet them at the athletic complex, and I have no idea what the parking is going to be like. When

I ran by the building yesterday it was a madhouse. There were reporters everywhere."

I left out the key detail that I had ventured into the building to see the chaos for myself.

"Well, you'll have to report back. I taught a few basketball players last semester. I'm sure that my number will soon be up. I want to know what to expect," Talia said with a smile.

———

Parking was fine. The disarray of the day before had calmed. I was almost twenty minutes early. I took a few laps around the building to kill time, and subconsciously realized I had gone to my favorite spot, the balcony that looks out over the football stadium.

"It's beautiful, isn't it?" a voice asked from behind me. I nearly jumped out of my shoes.

"Yes, it is." Even if someone didn't like football, it would be impossible to deny that the stadium was impressive. It overlooked the lake. From my spot, I could see beyond the stands to where boats casually drifted by, like little dots in the distance, families enjoying the last few days of summer before the school year started again. Farther still sat the foothills of the mountain range. The mountains weren't visible but for their hazy glow. They loomed in the distance, casting their glory on the rest of the valley.

"This is my favorite spot on campus. It's the reason I took the job after all. There was no way I could give up the chance to look at this view all day."

"Your astronomical coach's salary wasn't what sealed the deal?"

"Alexis, are you okay? We haven't had a chance to really talk since—"

I turned to face the voice, cutting him off. His eyes looked tired, as if he hadn't slept in weeks. He had called me last night. I hadn't called him back. I was afraid that it would make me look guilty if anyone tracked my calls.

"The investigators called me in for an interview today. I don't think it's a good sign, Beau, that they called me in on the first day of the investigation." I hated that my voice sounded wobbly.

"You should've called me."

"Yes, that would've helped me look more innocent."

"Alexis, you did nothing wrong," Beau answered firmly.

"That's easy for you to say. But how do you think this looks to the investigation team? I was secretly dating you, the assistant football coach, and then half of your players end up in my English 102 class?"

"Most of them had signed up for that class before we even met. Every student has to take English 102. It's not your fault that your class just happened to be the best timed in relation to practice. You did nothing wrong," he repeated, as if that would change the situation.

"Austin showed up at my house last night."

"How does he know where you live?" he asked, almost forcefully.

"I have no idea. Google, probably. I told him to leave. I can't be seen with him, he went from being the worst student in my class to one of the best. Something happened with his papers, I know it. He was scared, and he knows that there are professors talking to reporters."

"Alexis, you're going to be fine." He took a step toward me. I couldn't help but lean into a hug. "We're going to be fine." I couldn't tell if he was trying to reassure me or himself.

We stood there for a few minutes, taking in the peaceful lull of the lake. The sound of touring students on the field below, taking selfies as if they were players on the football team, echoed through the otherwise quiet corner of the campus.

"Are you okay?" I asked Beau reluctantly. If they had called me in for an interview, it was likely that he'd been questioned already.

"I'll be fine. I rarely interacted with Higgins. I just had my interview. They have no evidence that I was involved. I wasn't involved." He added the last sentence as if to assure me. Everyone seemed to assume they'd be considered guilty until proven innocent.

I took a deep breath. We were going to be fine.

"I should probably go. I have my interview soon."

He squeezed me closer. "You're going to be okay. You did nothing wrong." He let me go, and I could feel his support bolstering me as I walked away.

I tried to stride confidently into the stark athletic complex. There was something about the architecture that made me feel small, insignificant. I wondered if that's why they chose to conduct the interviews there.

I made my way to the interview room, knocking tentatively on the door. A man in a plain suit ushered me in and pulled out a chair for me. Another man loomed in the corner. It looked like they were trying to play "good cop, bad cop." The room smelled like sandwiches. I wondered if they had just eaten their lunch.

"You found the room okay," the man stated. It was not a question.

"Yep, the building's easy to navigate."

"You're the only person we've interviewed today who has said that. Everyone else complained they got lost."

"What can I say, I'm good at reading a building map," I said dryly, feeling like I had fallen into a trap.

"So, you wouldn't say you have previous experience navigating the halls of this building?"

"Are you asking about my attendance at school sporting events?" I asked, not wanting to give them the answer I knew they were looking for.

"No, Ms. Baily, I wanted to ask about your relationship with Beau Kennedy."

I said nothing. I didn't know what they knew. I didn't want to give them more leverage than they already had.

"Ms. Baily, is it true that you and Mr. Kennedy are involved? Are you, or were you at some point, in a relationship with Beau Kennedy?"

The rephrased question felt like a punch in the gut. I don't know why I felt as if I had suddenly been sent to the principal's office. Neither Beau nor I had done anything wrong. But I couldn't help overthinking and imagining every worst-case scenario that could possibly unfold.

"Yes."

"Were there any particular reasons as to why you kept your relationship a secret?"

"I'm a private person. Beau is in the spotlight a lot. His job is not a secure one, we didn't want to make a big deal out of our relationship until it became something serious. As a coach there's always a high likelihood of being moved around." It was starting to feel like a conversation with my mother. I was almost sure the next question would be about my commitment issues and if my college relationship had left permanent scars.

"Do you and Mr. Kennedy talk about his job often?"

"Not any more or less than other couples. He tells me about his day, and I tell him about mine. We don't spend hours dwelling on the minutiae, if that's what you're asking?"

"You mentioned that you didn't want to get serious in case he took a new job. Was there a reason Mr. Kennedy would think he should look for a new job?"

"Do you know much about a coaching career?" I could feel my blood pressure rising, and I was getting defensive.

I watched the suit nod, only slightly. Of course he did; he worked for the NCAA.

"Have you noticed, from their first coaching job, how often they have to move around and fight for promotions? Beau's young, he's still proving himself. There's a high likelihood of him moving, not because he's covering something up or running away from something, but because he's good at his job and will be promoted. And a promotion would most likely mean moving away from Renton. That's the coaching world."

"Interesting." He scribbled on the yellow legal pad. I wondered if that was an old habit. The whole interview was being recorded, so there was no need to take notes. "Let's leave Mr. Kennedy on the bench for a moment." I saw him smile at his own joke. "Did you ever have any interactions with Sal Higgins?"

I felt my face flush. This was why I could never play poker. I realized I needed to contact MP. I needed to figure out what the investigators knew. MP was a great poker player. Our mothers had always said that he was born to be a spy. He kept a straight face no matter the hand he was dealt. And he knew how to get others to fold.

He had to know more about the story than what had been printed. I knew my cousin well enough to know that he would wait until the best moment to play his cards. He wouldn't let anything go public until he was ready.

But what I needed then wasn't that version of MP; I needed my cousin. I needed my lifelong friend and confidant to tell me how in over my head I was. I needed to know for my sake as well as Beau's. MP would tell me. I knew that reporting was important to him; he loved his job. But I was family. That had to be more important.

22.

Nora

The job was aging me. I felt like the "after" picture of a president. At inauguration, a new president has a spring in their step. Their face tight, hair minimally gray. But four to eight years later, it's a whole different picture. Wrinkled and aged exponentially from the stress. Only two days into the job and I felt like I had three times as many wrinkles. Before the football season opener, I'd need to touch up my rapidly sprouting gray hair.

I wondered why my gray hair seemed to grow so much faster than my normal-colored hair. It felt unusually cruel.

My last meeting had ended at 9:15 p.m., a conference call with other athletic directors in the conference. As the football season grew closer, everyone's schedule became more and more packed, and meetings were held later and later in the day to accommodate. I just felt grateful that I wasn't on the East Coast.

Helen had left hours ago. I nearly had to push her out the door, convincing her that she would only be helpful the next day if she had a full night of sleep.

I walked across my spacious office and made the mistake of sitting on the couch. I'd replaced Sal's couch with the one from my old office. I wanted to make the office feel like my own. Plus, for some reason, his old couch felt grimy to me. This new couch had the amazing ability to suck me right into it. I shouldn't have sat down. I doubted if I'd be able to get myself back on my feet.

I reflected on the day. It was remarkable how much had been crammed into a fifteen-hour period.

I had met with the investigation team. There had been no briefing to cue me into what I should expect from that meeting, so I'd spent most of the night before lying awake, running through every possible way that conversation might go.

Though I'd sat in that conference room hundreds of times, during the interview it felt bleaker, void of any joy I usually found in the athletic complex.

"Mrs. Bennet, I'm not sure you're aware of how seriously the NCAA is taking this investigation." This had been the investigator's opening line. No platitudes, no small talk, straight to the point.

"I've a pretty good idea, and my team and I are also doing everything in our power to cooperate. I want what's best for the department. As you can imagine, this comes as a shock to us all, so we're doing our best to sort through all the details."

The interviewer barely looked up from his notes. I don't think he truly heard what I said. Or if he did, I doubted that he believed me.

"How well did you know Sal Higgins?"

"I worked with him every day for four years. We didn't have much of a relationship outside of work, but I spent a significant amount of time with him." Suddenly I was second-guessing every word. I worried that my answer made me sound either guilty or stupid for not picking up that anything was amiss after spending so much time together.

"And during the countless hours that you two spent together, did you notice anything about his behavior that was of question?"

I took a breath. What would Sal say? This felt like a terrible moment to channel him, but he'd always been better at answering questions than me. With the press he spoke like a politician. Never showing his cards.

"I'm sorry, can you be more specific?"

"Sure, while you worked alongside Sal Higgins, did you see him engaging in any inappropriate relationships with professors or athletes? Did you see him solicit favors from other members of the university staff? Did you hear any rumors of money laundering? Or inappropriate workplace behavior, excessive drinking, anything of that nature?" The interviewer checked his notes as if to ensure he hadn't left anything out before he nodded at me, waited for my reply.

The room spun. I wasn't sure if I could continue. There was too much on the line if I said the wrong thing, if I did the wrong thing.

"Sal had a DUI years ago, but that was well documented and before he took the position here at RU."

"What about anything recently?"

"Nothing that went beyond locker-room talk." I cringed as I said those words. I hated that expression. I hated that it was used as a euphemism for inappropriate behavior. But it was what Sal would have said. It was a politician's answer.

The interviewer nodded as if I had given him what he was looking for. I was sure he'd heard plenty of locker-room talk in his day. If the NCAA started policing it, almost no employees would still have jobs. He knew that as well as I did.

"Thank you for your time today, Mrs. Bennet. We will be in touch."

He didn't reach for my hand as he showed me to the door.

That meeting had been hours ago, and I was still replaying everything in my head. Had I said enough? Had I said the wrong thing? Would they believe my story? At this point, did it even matter?

Since the meeting, I'd surrendered all my passwords, emails, and documents, all to be searched to ensure that I was as clean of a candidate as they had believed when they hired me.

I had a meeting with every coach, assuring them that their sport was important to me. I guaranteed each one that their job, investigation pending, was secure and I wouldn't be conducting a staffing overhaul. The thought of finding a new coaching staff right now made my stomach hurt. It wasn't like these people were strangers to me; I had been working alongside them for years. But now, everything was different.

Helen helped me organize my schedule and make travel arrangements as far out as possible. I felt guilty leaving Nathan to handle the childcare, but I didn't have a choice. I wanted Margo, and those who doubted me, to see that a woman could have both a career and a family.

In between meetings, I sat through what felt like a never-ending stream of press interviews, saying the same thing over and over again. Every reporter wanted a direct quote from me. Not surprisingly, most of the questions seemed more related to gender than to sports.

I spent too much time reassuring reporters that being a woman wouldn't prevent me from doing my job well. I would treat every sport fairly. I didn't plan to only focus on women's sports and cut funding from men's, as some reporters seemed to believe. These reporters knew that, but they didn't care. They'd run their stories anyway.

I doubted these sorts of questions were ever posed to a new male athletic director. The world doesn't watch you in the same way it watches a woman. An outsider.

All day long I felt the eyes of the world, watching, waiting for me to fail, waiting for me to do something that would turn me into a meme or a funny one-liner. If I was going to be successful, I needed to figure out how to do my job without living in that fear.

From my place on the couch, I used my foot to pull my purse to me and dug around until I found my phone. I figured I might as well find out what was going on in the world, seeing as how the couch was holding me hostage. In addition to more congratulatory texts and some messages from concerned donors, I saw Nathan had messaged me a few times.

He and Margo had spent the afternoon at the park. I tried to ignore the twinge of guilt I felt for not being there with them. Margo would be fast asleep by the time I got home. He was a good father. I knew I would never survive the week without him.

I had no time to feel guilty. This situation wouldn't last forever. A time would come when things would return to normal. When I could do school drop-off and pickup. When I could see my daughter for more than just a few minutes as I rushed out the door. In the meantime, I reminded myself that it was such a gift that she got time with her father. Not many kids got that. It would be good for her.

Margo would be okay. I needed her to be okay.

23.

The Times

August 28

NORA BENNET IS OFFICIALLY ON THE CLOCK
MASON PONT

Renton University has been in a scramble since the departure of its ill-fated athletic director, Sal Higgins. His replacement, Nora Bennet, the conference's first female athletic director, has now been at the helm for over two weeks, and it seems the Griffons have been so consumed by the scandal that some supporters worry she hasn't had time to prepare for the upcoming football season.

Recently, several high-profile donors have either dropped support completely or decreased their annual donation to the program.

Most of these donors state their change in support is due to the promotion of Bennet, not the actions of Higgins. "The whole thing screams Title IX," one donor, who requested that their identity be kept anonymous, noted. "I won't support a program that fires an innocent man to fill the woman quota. There's no hope for the program after a stunt like this."

Bennet and her team would not comment on this story, but from her actions the last two weeks, anonymous sources close to Bennet worry that she is more concerned about cleaning up after Sal than ensuring that the program is ready for tomorrow's home opener. Those close to Bennet say that she is spending more time with the NCAA's investigation team than she is in meetings with coaches. They commented that the meetings she is prioritizing have more to do with ensuring the school's reputation is in good standing, instead of meeting with those on her staff to ensure trust and understanding about the direction of the department.

As per our initial investigation, it is clear that a number of university faculty participated in the scheme, as well as some key people within the athletic department. Though the investigation is ongoing, it appears that, at minimum, Higgins had coerced professors into giving special treatment to athletes. There is also evidence that Higgins was involved in a money laundering scheme. Bennet has been pressured to release the names of others involved, but the university has yet to make an official statement. At this time, everyone who works in the athletic department has been questioned by the external investigation team. It is unclear if anyone else within the department will resign or have their contract terminated in light of any findings.

The College of Liberal Arts is currently being investigated for involvement, a source close to the situation reported. Multiple professors within the department have been questioned. A source stated that many athletes enroll in English courses because English is considered an easy major. It is unclear if this is due to additional "help" from professors within the English department or not. It should be noted that the dean of the English department is Nora Bennet's husband, Nathan Bennet.

Several coaches have also been under more rigorous investigation, including head football coach Richard Ross. As this story goes to press, Ross will continue coaching and has made no indication that he will step away from the team.

Tune in to West Coast Network Saturday, August 29, at 3:00 p.m. to watch the Renton Griffons play the Golden University Tigers.

24.

LAUREN

August 28, 9:10 p.m.

I had my favorite people under one roof—my son and my nephew. If it wasn't for the current circumstances, I would be absolutely elated. Hunter had been staying with me since Sal vanished. I was still unclear about where things stood with Sal and me. Hunter had been in contact with him, but it had been spotty. Texts at random hours of the day. Sal never answering questions posed.

From what I could gather, the investigators had been unsuccessful in reaching Sal. I wasn't surprised. The man would only make himself available if he wanted something. If he held all the cards, he made himself an open book. But as soon as the power shifted, he was elusive. He was good at going dark. I doubted that I would hear from him. Not now that I was an enemy.

Hunter and I were almost positive that he was hiding out at our lake house, waiting for things to calm down. I wondered if I should change the locks, in case he decided to reappear in the middle of the night. Was I supposed to file divorce papers? His absence left a thousand unanswered questions. But this was who he was. Sal always ran from his problems, leaving them for me to clean up.

And now, he'd run away from his family. Of course he did. He wouldn't want to face the press camped out on the front lawn since the story broke. Instead, he left that dreaded task for his wife and kid to handle. It made my blood boil. Some people don't change.

I was sure that wherever he was, he was just fine. He was an adult. He was an adult with a limitless credit card. I fought all of my instincts to fix things and take care of him. It helped that I wasn't ready to talk to him yet. Our dirty laundry was strung up for the world to see. As the shock slowly dissipated, I got angry. Angry that he put us through this. Angry that he got to disappear while I had reporters on the doorstep. Angry that, in his mind, I was to blame. Angry that, once again, I had to clean up his mess.

Multiple people—friends, my child, the press—had asked if I would attend the opening game. The question made me want to laugh out loud. It was my first free fall Saturday in years. Why would I want to use it to show my face at the place where I was most likely hated? I suspected that no one wanted to see the wife of the man who had just betrayed the university. Plus, I wasn't sure if I even had tickets. I'd always used Sal's comps and sat in his box, but now his box belonged to Nora.

I tried to focus on the good, the few good things in my life that were left. My boys were home. We were together, sitting around the table, drinking a beer.

Graham was not technically mine. He was my sister's son, but because of proximity, I saw him more than she did. He was just a few years younger than Hunter. The boys had grown up spending weeks in the summers together. They always acted more like brothers than cousins.

By sheer coincidence, or because he wanted to follow in Hunter's path, Graham had decided to attend Renton University. Since then, Graham came over for dinner at least once a week.

Hunter had moved away, but Graham had stuck around.

Sal had been so proud when Graham set his sights on working in the compliance department, although since the scandal broke, I wondered if it was more that he was happy to have someone in compliance to potentially help right his wrongs. I didn't want to believe that Sal would've done anything to compromise Graham, but what did I know? I was just the wife who had been blind to everything going on.

It was hard not to question everything that had happened in the last few years. It was easy to believe that we were all just pawns in Sal's scheme.

I sipped my beer and tried to be present, to listen to the boys talk about their jobs, the upcoming football season. The conversation felt so normal. It seemed easy for them to separate Sal from their love of the game.

"So, Mom, are you going to go?"

I snapped to attention, not realizing at first that the question had been directed at me. "Sorry, what?"

"I was asking, Aunt Lauren, if you wanted a ticket to the game tomorrow? I have one set aside for Hunter, but I wasn't sure if you'd want to go as well?" Graham asked.

"No, I think I'm going to sit this one out."

"I get it, I'd do the same if I was in your position. I can't tell you how much of my day has been taken up by managing the press. It's ridiculous. I'm worried that no matter how the game goes, the only story reported will be about Uncle Sal or Nora."

"People will always see the story they want to see," I said solemnly.

"So, what are you going to do with your free Saturday?" Graham asked. I wondered if he minded working the weekends. I imagined that his schedule made it hard to date or have friends outside of athletics. He worked the events that most people went to for fun.

"I'm not sure yet. Nothing too crazy, I don't want to do anything to draw attention to myself. I'll probably just garden or finally read the books collecting dust on my shelves." I longed to do anything normal, anything that didn't remind me of the mess my life had become. I wanted to do something that made me feel capable, instead of like a victim.

The boys nodded as if they were trying to pretend they didn't think I was lame. They were too young to understand that a Saturday without plans was actually a glorious gift.

"Have you seen the stats on the new quarterback? They found him at some junior college," Hunter said, pivoting the conversation back to football.

"I remember when Sal found out the transfer was going through," I said, not realizing that their eyes had locked on mine. I had mentioned He Who Shall Not Be Named. "Yes, your father and I talked about who was on the team. I do like football, you know. As a fan, I cared."

"Yeah, Richard had to fly to meet the guy." Hunter was on the edge of his seat. He did this when he was excited about something; he had since he was a kid. "He said as soon as he watched him run a few plays, he knew that he had to get him to come to Renton. This guy is not your normal junior college recruit."

"Can you imagine that arm with Austin at wide receiver? I think we really have a chance this year. And just in time, too. I don't think there's a world in which Austin doesn't enter the draft this spring. He's too good to risk doing another year of college ball." Graham's voice was filled with excitement.

"Totally agree." Hunter nodded so vigorously I thought he might lose his head. I loved watching them talk about football. It made me feel like they were boys again, sitting around the table having an after-school snack. Back when life was simpler. I missed those moments.

I started clearing dishes off the table. By the time I sat back down, the boys had shifted topics away from football, as Graham was saying, "No big deal, her name is Anne."

"Is this a girl you're dating?" I asked with parental curiosity.

"No, no. Not dating," Graham corrected a little too quickly, going slightly red. He at least liked this girl. "She's the new intern in the athletic director's office, her first day was the day the news broke, could you imagine? But I was saying that everyone has been so stressed out, she told me about a woman hiding out in the bathroom sobbing. The woman didn't even realize Anne was in the bathroom and locked them both in there. Like it's such a tense work environment. Everyone's just waiting for the next person to get fired."

I thought about that day in the bathroom. I obviously couldn't share that I in fact happened to be the woman in the bathroom Anne referenced.

"So, how'd you meet her?" I tried to steer the conversation away from that scene. It reminded me that I had another interview set for next week. This time I would be armed with an attorney, but that made me feel more guilty. People only engaged a lawyer if they had something to hide, or at least that was what I had learned from television.

"I met her in the lobby on her first day. She looked like a lost deer. Clearly too panicked to be a member of the press. I felt bad for her. She thought that her first day was the baseline normal of what things are like, so at least it can only get better from there."

"Well, it sounds like she'll have a story to tell for years to come."

I busied myself cleaning up the dishes. Pretending like I was listening to whatever it was they were talking about, trying not to think about the next twenty-four hours and the potential headlines.

25.

ANNE

August 29, 7:05 a.m.

I felt more nervous about the game than I had felt about my first day of this job. I wondered if I'd feel this way every Saturday. Or at least the ones with a home football game. I had stayed at the office late the night before, not because I needed to, but because I wanted to make sure that I had everything ready for the game. I did not want to mess things up.

I worried more about Nora than I did about the players on the field. I knew Nora. She was my teammate. I interacted with her every day. It felt personal for me. And after two weeks on the job, it was clear to me, no matter what happened on the field, the story would be about Nora.

She hadn't said this, of course. She was much too grounded to say something so self-centered. But I could tell everyone in the department was thinking it. I committed myself to doing everything in my power not to mess things up for Nora. It almost felt like a battle cry.

Campus had been completely transformed since Thursday. Not only were there floods of students arriving early for the fall term, but alumni from all walks of life had made the pilgrimage back to Renton.

The most impressive of these alumni groups were the RVers. Graham had warned me about them. They transformed the parking lot across from the stadium into a Renton-themed KOA. In my three years at RU, I'd never paid attention to this spectacle. The business school sat on the opposite side of campus, and I'd never given a second thought to the hundreds of tailgaters who rolled into town each weekend in the fall. As the weekend drew closer, I had an uptick in calls and questions about the RVers' lot. It seemed like the place alumni went to see and be seen. It was the Renton equivalent to the popular kids' table in a high school cafeteria.

Graham had convinced Noel and me to watch their arrival. He had promised that it was the best entertainment Renton could offer on a Thursday night. So we grabbed a pizza and watched the unofficial parade from the top floor of the athletic complex, which had an incredible view of the parking lots.

"Seriously, every Thursday in the fall I feel like I'm chased out of the parking lot by these crazy people and their RVs," Noel complained, chewing on her pizza. "I mean, if the university really believes that the most important part of college is the academics, then I shouldn't have to spend my Thursday afternoon praying my class doesn't run long so I can move my car before being yelled at by drunk alumni."

"Okay, but you can't seriously believe that most people think that academics are actually the most important part of school?" I countered. "Just work the phone line in my office for one hour, and you'll quickly be proven wrong."

Graham nodded in agreement. "These people are a breed of their own. It's as if all the memories they have of their years in school here have been replaced with only those involving sports. They don't remember going to classes. I bet there's not one of them who could tell you where the Smith Building is. But each one could recite verbatim the menu at the Griffon Den." The Griffon Den was the most popular bar in Renton. "This is one of my favorite things to do every year, watch this parade. It brings such different people together. When we walk back through the parking lot tonight, it'll be the friendliest place in the whole town. I bet that at least three people offer us a beer, and everyone we pass will smile and yell *Go, Griffons*."

It was like watching a highly complex dance as a flood of RVs came rolling down the recently vacant street. It was hard not to be in awe of the spectacle.

"This is incredible," I said, watching the RVs stream in. Every vehicle was decked out in red and navy in support of Renton.

"They have it down to a science," Graham said expertly. "These guys that come in on Thursday nights, they all know each other, they've been doing this for years. They respect each other, no fighting over who gets which spot. If for some reason one of them can't be there for a game, his spot remains vacant. It's like an honor code of sorts. You don't see that in some of the lower lots."

"The lower lots?" Noel asked.

"The lots that have a lower athletic fund donation requirement." Surprising myself, I heard the words come out of my mouth before I even registered that I knew the answer.

"Look at you, new kid on the block!" Graham teased.

"If I had a dollar for every time someone called and asked if they could get a special one-game-only pass to this lot, I could afford the donation price required for entry," I quipped.

"Ha, good luck, the waiting list is years for this lot. Aren't calls like that supposed to go to the general line?" Graham asked.

"In theory, I think. But somehow everyone who has donated more than one thousand dollars has Sal's office number, and so they use it. I think he gave it out in a promo or something a few years ago, and people hung on to it. We get some really stupid questions, and I feel like an old-fashioned phone operator. I have to forward so many calls. I mean, not to brag, but I have every department's extension memorized by this point."

"Wow, too cool for school," Noel said with an eye roll.

We watched in reverence for another thirty minutes as alumni hugged, reuniting for the first time in almost a year. Noel left us, branching off to head to a classmate's house for a party, leaving Graham and me walking back to my apartment. Almost everyone we passed had a friendly word, especially when they found out that Graham and I worked for the athletic department. Only a few people mentioned Higgins or Nora, and they were quickly silenced by their comrades. Even still, their comments seemed mild compared to what I had heard on the phone. There must be something about being face-to-face that prevents a person from making rude comments. For the most part, it seemed like the RVers were just enjoying the high of the return of the football season.

The scene somehow made me feel calmer going into the game-day weekend. Maybe our fans weren't as cruel as the ones I'd dealt with on the phone.

"Do you want to be one of them someday?" I asked Graham as we navigated through the packed streets. As we got farther away from the RV lot, the crowds thinned a little, but it was still obviously a game-day weekend.

"You mean an RVer?" He thought about this for a moment. "I don't think so. I love their enthusiasm, but I prefer the magic behind the scenes. If I'm out there with them, sure, I'd get to tailgate and could have a chance of watching without being interrupted with work, but for me, the magic is knowing that I had a hand in helping make this all happen." He gestured to the crowds of people around us.

"That's one of the things I love about sports," he continued. "It represents something special to everyone. To me, the magic is in the rules and logistics. For a wide receiver, the magic is catching a game-winning touchdown. For the RVers, the magic is gathering with friends you only see during the football season. For them, I think there's something magical in seeing you're not alone in your crazy love of a team. And it makes you feel young again."

We walked in silence, taking in all the activity around us. It *was* magical.

I tried to channel that feeling on Saturday morning as I, with trembling hands, got dressed in my Griffons polo. I reminded myself that these were kindhearted people who loved their fall traditions. They weren't as scary as I had built them up to be in my head.

Noel had left me a note on the kitchen counter as well as a bar of chocolate, just in case I needed a midday pick-me-up.

Since I didn't have a parking pass, and because I had to leave my house so early, Graham had offered to pick me up so I didn't have to walk. I felt relieved that I wouldn't have to show up alone. Even if we worked in different departments, it still felt like I had an ally.

"So where are you going to watch the game?" he asked me as we slowly navigated through the morning's congestion. For a town where getting stuck at one red light was considered heavy traffic, the fact that cars filled the roads at seven on a Saturday morning made it seem like we had entered an alternate universe.

"I hadn't really thought about it." I knew I was expected to work until halftime, but I hadn't considered what I would do once I finished my shift. I was more focused on surviving the day. If anything, it was likely I'd go straight home and take the world's longest power nap.

"You should watch the game from the press box. It has by far the best view, a lot of the staff go up there to watch once they're done working."

"Do you work until halftime as well?" I asked.

"No, I have to work the whole game. But normally things at least slow down during the third quarter. It really depends on the game."

We pulled into the parking lot. I forced myself to let out a long breath. It was all going to be okay. I reminded myself that there was no way that anything could be more stressful than my first days on the job.

26.

ALEXIS

August 29, 2:00 p.m.

There was a longer line than usual to pick up my ticket at will call. I couldn't help looking around, nervous, as if expecting to get caught. As if standing in line alone would somehow incriminate me.

I'd started going to games at the end of last season when Beau and I became exclusive.

I would get in the special will call line to pick up tickets left by a player or coach. I was used to the process; it was a part of my game-day routine. When he first started leaving me one of his tickets, I would wait in line worried that one of my students would see me. Like most paranoid fears, it had never happened. At least that I knew about.

We continued to keep our relationship a secret, and I kept waiting in the special will call line, awaiting the day we would be found out.

Since my first interview with the investigation team, things had been rocky with Beau. Most of the rockiness was my fault. I felt like I was on a boat in the middle of a calm lake, standing up, trying to create waves.

Every time we saw each other, I felt like I was committing a felony. It felt like somehow our relationship was unethical. But ending it wasn't an option. For many reasons. Ending it would imply that one of us had something to hide. I had admitted to the investigation team, on the record, that I loved him and that we were in fact dating. And it was true. If I broke things off, I knew it would raise more questions. When we'd had to surrender documents that showed the timeline of our relationship, it felt like handing over my diary for the school principal to read. I felt exposed. And so, I rocked the boat. As if causing chaos would make things any easier.

We were in love. I had no reason to break up with him except some weird, deep-rooted anxiety that we'd done something wrong. And that together we'd cause the other's demise. Either way, we were in hot water together. And I was learning to be okay with that.

So there I stood on another sunny Saturday, waiting in a slow-moving line to get my ticket. To prove to the investigation team that we were ethical. That although our relationship was, at least for now, a secret, we did things normal couples did. Even though the longer I stood in the line, the more I felt like I might be on the verge of a mental breakdown. I wanted to run away. I hated football. I loved Beau, but I didn't want to spend my Saturday at the game.

But, for the sake of love, there I stood.

On Wednesday night we'd had the talk. The "do we announce our relationship to the world" talk. I said that the middle of an investigation didn't feel like the right time for a grand romantic gesture. Beau disagreed. He thought keeping it a secret made us look more guilty.

He was right, of course.

I could hear my mother telling me, reminding me, that I had a fear of commitment. That my reflex was always to run. No matter what, if I got scared, I ran. But today, I wasn't running. After the game, I was going to march myself down to the sideline and stand with Beau. It was the best thing for him, for me, for our relationship, and for our innocence.

It didn't matter how many times I reminded myself that I wanted to be with Beau, I still felt anxious.

"Oh my gosh, Alexis!" An overly eager voice instantly snapped me out of my anxious train of thought. I turned to see Talia. Of course, today was the day that I'd run into someone I knew.

"Hey, Talia!" I tried to sound friendly and not seem disappointed to see one of my closest friends.

"What are you doing here? Just last week you were cursing the very existence of the athletic program." I hated that she had such a good memory.

"Well, someone left me a ticket, so I figured that I shouldn't let it go to waste." I felt instantly bad about lying. I was incriminating myself. In a few hours, she'd know the truth anyway. I'd done nothing wrong by having a relationship with Beau, I reminded myself. I was being dramatic. I needed to get used to people knowing. Telling Talia was a good first step.

I let out a long breath.

"Actually, in all honesty, I'm dating one of the coaches, and he left me a ticket." I hated how quickly I rushed to get the words out. I'd done nothing wrong. Beau and I were adults. And Talia was a safe person to tell. She was always a supportive friend.

"Wait, what!" Her jaw was almost on the ground. "How long, who, I want all the details."

"Beau Kennedy, we've been dating for a while now, but we weren't ready to go public, just with small-town politics and everything. We didn't really tell anyone, but now with the investigation and everything, we figured it looks more suspicious keeping it a secret."

"You. Are. Kidding. Me." She made each word a sentence of its own. "How in the world did you not tell me this?"

"I didn't really tell anyone except my family," I said sheepishly. "Why are you here?" I quickly tried to change the subject before she could make me feel more guilty than I already did.

"One of my friends left me a ticket. The assistant to the athletic director, Helen Markus."

I forced a smile. Of all the people, of course, she knew Helen. "I don't know if I know her. How did y'all meet?" I tried to keep my voice steady, underplay how much I knew about the personnel working in the department.

"Oh gosh, I've known Helen forever! We actually went to college together, and then when I took my job here, we reconnected! I'm sure I've talked to you about her. Anyways, a couple of times a year she leaves me a ticket. Most of the time she can't actually watch the game with me, but it's fun! I'd never say no to a free ticket! Where are your seats? If we're close enough together, we should try to move next to each other."

"Yeah, that sounds great," I responded, on autopilot. I was trying to calculate the potential ramifications of Talia knowing, and apparently being good friends with, Helen.

The line continued to move at an excruciatingly slow pace. I imagined the poor student workers on the other side of the glass, most likely at their first day of work, trying desperately not to mess up. I heard the man in front of us in line, sounding drunk, yelling at a student about his tickets.

"I'm sorry, but I can't give you your tickets unless you can present a valid ID." The student's voice trembled. I imagined she was doing everything in her power not to cry.

"Do you know who I am? If you don't give me my ticket, I will call Sal Higgins right now and he will have you fired so fast your head will spin. Now give me my ticket."

I couldn't help but laugh at his arrogance. Waiting in line brought out the worst in some people.

"Do you have a problem?" I said. The man jarred, spinning to look at me. His breath reeked of alcohol and cigarettes.

"Sir, Mr. Higgins is no longer associated with this university, so a call to him would be useless," I said calmly. From behind the protective glass, the student shot me a grateful look.

"What do you know, lady? Do you really think he simply walked away and has no more influence? He's still calling the shots, you'd better believe it." His drunken words slurred together.

His tone sounded threatening. What did I know? Way more than I cared to admit, truthfully. But I hadn't considered that Higgins might still have influence within the department. It honestly wouldn't have surprised me. In fact, I was shocked that I hadn't thought about that earlier. Beau had made it clear that Sal wasn't the type of person to walk away quickly or quietly from a fight. If he was still in control, then any peace I had started to feel in the last two weeks had been in vain, and I was not as safe as I believed myself to be.

"Sir," a new voice called out from behind the protective glass of the will call booth. "My name's Tucker, and I'm the ticket manager. Amber said that there's an issue?"

The drunken man swung himself around to face the window. "Yes, this kid here has informed me that I can't have my ticket unless I show my ID, and I tried to tell her that I've never had to show my ID before now, I was always just allowed in. Sal Higgins and I go way back, and I was personally informed that nothing would change with his departure." His tone completely shifted when he addressed the manager, someone who he assumed had authority.

"Unfortunately, sir, that's our policy. Even when Sal was the athletic director, that was our policy. I'm not sure who you spoke to, but I'm afraid in order to give you your ticket, I'll need to see your ID. We still have some tickets for sale, if you'd like to purchase one instead."

His body language made it clear that he didn't want to purchase a ticket.

"Tucker, why don't you call Mr. Higgins, and I assure you that he'll quickly straighten things out."

"Unfortunately, sir, I don't have Mr. Higgins's number. He also has no authority over our ticket office anymore. If you'd like to pick up a ticket that was left for you by a member of our staff or a player, you'll need to show ID. If that isn't an option, you can purchase a ticket, or leave. I'm afraid that if you continue to hold up this line, I'm going to have to call security."

I wanted to applaud Tucker. I welled up with pride that he was standing up to the mess that Higgins had left behind. Things were going to be different. There was hope.

The man stormed off, assuring Tucker and everyone within earshot that they would be sorry. When it was finally my turn at the counter, I happily handed over my ID, and in return I was handed a ticket and a field pass.

"Wow, a field pass?" Talia remarked when she saw the large packet. "He must really love you."

27.

NORA

August 29, 2:35 p.m.

The whole day had been a blur. One moment, I was lying in bed, hoping—willing myself—to fall asleep, and the next I was sprinting around the athletic complex managing nonstop meet and greets, smiling and shaking hands with donors.

When my alarm had gone off, I tried to trick myself into believing I'd actually slept. I clicked into my email and was greeted by more messages than I realized my inbox could hold. Hundreds of people requesting tickets or making sure their tickets would be at will call. I scanned the list to make sure that I didn't need to follow up with anyone personally and then forwarded the 99 percent that remained to Helen and Anne.

It had taken all of my self-control to remain in my desk chair and not curl up on the couch in my office. It sat there across the room, daring me to take a nap. I sneaked a peek at my watch.

I'd been at the facilities since six. There had been really no point in lying in bed wishing for sleep. At least at work I could do something productive without waking up Margo or Nathan. Nathan had called me around six thirty, so I probably hadn't been as quiet as I imagined when I left.

"Sorry, I know it's early, I didn't mean to wake you up when I left." I doubted he was calling to complain, but I wanted to at least acknowledge that I'd most likely woken him up.

"Don't worry about it, you know I don't mind the mornings. Hey, I don't mean to bother you so last minute, especially on a game day, but I was wondering if you had room in your box?"

I mentally scanned the list I had approved.

"It depends, Nathan." I felt my body tense, as if preparing for an argument. As much as I loved my husband, I didn't have energy for a last-minute favor if one of his friends wanted a ticket.

"Well, let me rephrase, do you have room in your box for Margo and her daddy?" At this, my heart melted. "Margo crawled in bed shortly after you left and asked if we could go. I hadn't thought to ask earlier because I know Margo normally couldn't care less. But I think she wants to be there to support you, and I think it would be really good publicity."

I hated that he thought of using our daughter for publicity. But I hated myself more for knowing that he was right.

"Of course there's room for you guys. I'll call Helen right now. Will you be okay to stay with her during the game? I honestly have no idea what my day will look like."

"Yes, done, I'll be Dad on duty!" he said proudly. "You're going to do great today, I'm so proud of you, Nora." I could feel the warmth in his voice.

"I couldn't do this without you." I really meant it.

In the last few weeks, I'd received a lot of unsolicited advice from people around the country, all of them assuming that they knew how to do my job or, more aptly, that I didn't. Most of the advice I tossed out. But the only other female Division I athletic director, Kelsie Moore, had called me earlier that week to say she was rooting for me. Not our team, she'd quickly assured me with a laugh, just me as a person. She couldn't betray her own school.

"But the one thing I would advise you to do, I know you have probably received so much advice this week, but this is the most important, woman to woman: make sure you wear the most comfortable shoes you own. Whatever you do, don't try to wear heels or anything cute. Only tennis shoes, your favorite Nikes. Trust me on this."

By 2:30 p.m., my phone informed me that I'd already walked over ten miles.

I had twelve minutes before I was expected in the athletic director's box, where key donors and members of the community were waiting for their chance to meet with me. The honor of having a seat in my box wasn't enough, apparently; everyone also felt the need to share their various misgivings about the department. I was beginning to wonder if I was too introverted for a job that required this much schmoozing. As I sprinted around the facilities, I made a mental note to send Moore a thank-you email; the shoes were a lifesaver.

I would never have survived the day in heels. It didn't matter that my office was on the other end of the complex; I wanted to use the short break to my advantage and have a little moment of solitude. It was the only way I'd make it through the rest of the day.

The hallway leading to my office was quiet. That was my favorite part about working in that wing of the building. No one had any reason to be there, especially not on game day. It made for the perfect midmadness escape.

"You didn't change the locks." I heard the voice coming from my chair before I saw his face. If he was surprised to see me, his voice didn't convey it.

"What are you doing here," I said flatly, not as a question but as a statement, implying that he was in no way welcome in my office. Or anywhere near this building for that matter. He didn't even flinch.

"Haven't you heard the expression, 'Don't bite the hand that feeds you'? Or how about, 'I scratch your back, you scratch mine'?" I knew he'd been drinking. He had the habit of speaking in idioms after a beer or two. And there was no way someone in their right mind would break into my office on a day when there were so many cameras and news crews around.

"You need to get out of my office." I tried to make my voice sound authoritative, to hide that I was shaking with fear. I was afraid to find out what he wanted.

"Wow, you haven't even been in the job a month, let alone won a game, and the power has gone straight to your head." He laughed as he flicked a finger against his temple.

"Sal, this is not a joke, you need to get out of my office. I'm putting myself—my career—at risk just by giving you the benefit of the doubt and not calling security right now." I tried to appeal to the logical side of his brain.

"I don't think you understand the implications of me no longer working here. I just had a few loose ends that I needed to tie up." He said this as if it should be obvious. I didn't want to think about what other secrets could be buried in this building.

That was when I realized why he was in my office. He wasn't there to confront me; he was there to find something. Most likely he thought he'd be able to sneak in without being seen. Though press swarmed the campus, there was also a massive crowd of people, one that he could blend right into wearing a Griffons hat. And once he made his way to the building, well, I was sure that he still had someone in his good graces who helped sneak him inside. Plus, usually no one was in this wing of the building on game day.

"What are you looking for, Sal?" I asked.

"Can't I just come in here and talk with my old pal? I missed you, Nora. We haven't spoken since I left."

"You're right. Gee, I don't know why I haven't picked up the phone to call," I said dryly. I looked at my watch. My short break was quickly being chipped away. This wasn't the peaceful pause I'd imagined.

"You know I could help you. You must recognize by now the size of the mess you have to clean up. I can help you, Nora. I'm the only one who really knows how to fix this."

"You're kidding. Sal, it's your mess that I'm having to clean up. You have to get out of my office. I'll call security."

"You wouldn't do that to your old friend, the one person who took a chance on you, who took a chance on a woman. Everyone said I was crazy. But I scratched your back, and now you scratch mine. We're fighters, Nora. That's why I hired you. You and me, we're one and the same."

"I was the most qualified person for the job, that's why I was hired."

"Keep believing that, if it helps you sleep at night. If that's what helps you fight impostor syndrome, or whatever it is the feminists claim holds them back. They gave you my job because you're clean. But you and I both know, you have to be willing to do anything you can to stay ahead. This is a man's game, after all. You have a lot of track to make up, being slated in the outside lane."

"You have thirty seconds to get out of my office."

"When I called you to let you know what happened, a very generous courtesy to my friend, I told you to do your job. I'm trying to help you do that, Nora, why can't you see I'm helping you?"

"How is this helping me? Helping me would be staying away, far away. Helping me would be never having done anything that would give cause for an NCAA investigation. Breaking into my office, on the first football Saturday of the season, how could you possibly believe that's helping me?" I almost spit the words. I did everything I could not to raise my voice.

He leaned back in his old chair, a posture I'd seen him take many times.

"Nora, Nora, Nora, you want the world to believe you're so innocent. I'm trying to preserve your narrative. I'm trying to remove any additional evidence from this building, from this office. I had left behind a few loose ends. I didn't know Mason Pont would release his story so quickly. It left me with some unfinished business."

"Sal, you're a crook, you cheated to get ahead, and if you left something behind, so be it, this is my problem now, you made sure of that when you so *graciously* hired me. You need to get out of my office now." I took a step forward assertively.

Slowly, he pushed the chair, my chair, back from the desk and stood up. He walked with unabashed confidence toward the door, nearly checking my shoulder as he passed me.

"Watch yourself, Nora. Don't forget I'm only trying to help you. You don't know who you're even fighting against."

I bolted the door as soon as he was on the other side. I rushed to my computer, thankful that I had changed my login password, and typed an email to the facility office, requesting that at their quickest convenience, they change the lock on my office.

My hope of a quiet break had vanished. I had two minutes to make it back to my box. I downed the rest of the coffee that I'd left on my desk and sprinted toward the stadium, thankful once again that I'd worn tennis shoes.

28.

LAUREN

August 29, 4:30 p.m.

There are some things that I'll always love about living in a small college town in the fall. The air takes on a new aroma, and freshmen, leaving home for the first time, arrive eager to see what their lives will look like free from the constraints of their parents. Alumni reappear on the weekends to cheer on their team and reminisce with people who knew them in what they fondly think of as their glory days. A tangible hope fills the streets, no one knowing what the new year could bring.

For me, January never felt like the new year. September was my new year, August a month of New Year's Eves. That's when I made resolutions, looked over my calendar, and set goals for the next twelve months. My life had always revolved around the academic calendar. I went straight from being a student to a coach's wife.

As I moved around my garden, I realized that I could live my life differently now. It didn't have to begin and end when sports were in session. I still had heard nothing from Sal, which I assumed was his way of telling me that our life together was over. I didn't have to stay in Renton. I could go anywhere. But standing in my garden, I could hear the roar from the stadium just a few miles away, and I realized that I didn't want to be anywhere else.

In the past few days, I had cycled through each stage of grief at an hourly pace. Denial, anger, bargaining, depression, acceptance. Acceptance was the elusive stage for me. After everything I had done for my family, I couldn't believe we were in this position. Which, of course, looped me back to denial. I was exhausted.

I loved Renton, but I knew it was impossible to stay and not be reminded of Sal, especially on the home football game weekends. From anywhere in the city, the roar of the crowd could be heard. Every time we scored a touchdown, the ROTC set off their cannon. I imagined that for anyone new in town who was unaware of this tradition, it would be a fear-invoking experience.

I was just one Saturday into the new season of my life, and I already knew I didn't want to be someone who only knew if there was a football game because suddenly the city had traffic. That felt like denying who I was. As much as I hated how my husband acted, I wasn't ready to give that part of me up. I had loved football before I loved Sal. Sure, I followed the Griffons because we lived here and Sal was the athletic director at RU. But I didn't love sports because of who I married. I was a fan with or without him.

When I was in high school, my statistics teacher assigned a paper on using statistics in the real world. I wrote about the importance of stats in making decisions in football. The teacher asked if my boyfriend had written my paper, or if I wrote it to impress him. I said no. He then informed me that I would make my future husband very happy someday. I wonder what that teacher would think of that comment now. I'd never loved sports to make someone else happy, not even Sal.

For some reason, it felt important to draw this distinction. I didn't go to games because I loved Sal. I'd actually wanted to be there.

I couldn't help but think about the other wives who were being dragged into the scandal. There had to be people who would be fired as a result of whatever Sal had been up to. There was no way he was truly a one-man show. Maybe I could start a support group with these other wives, I fantasized. We were the only ones who could truly understand this weird situation. Unless their husbands had told them what they were doing. Maybe their marriages were built on mutual trust and sharing everything. There was a good chance that I was the only one stupid enough to have remained completely in the dark.

I still felt like I was in the dark. I was likely the most useless person the investigators interviewed. I'd not been joking when I told them that I knew nothing. I assumed they just pitied me and figured I'd been lying. Or at least exaggerating my utter lack of awareness. There was no way the wife knew nothing. The wife is always in on it. Or at least they are in the movies.

I heard a roar from College Hill followed by the blast of a cannon. I couldn't help but smile. Despite everything, I still rooted for the Griffons.

I could've gone to the game. Graham offered again to leave a ticket at will call for me. But I couldn't bring myself to go. I didn't want anyone to feel like they had to make awkward conversation with me. I was happy cheering from my garden.

I wondered what my parents would make of this situation. I'd almost worshipped sports for keeping my parents together. And now sports was tearing my family apart. I wasn't going to let it. It wasn't football, after all, that destroyed my marriage. It was Sal. Football, sports, the athletic department—all of that was just collateral damage. Sadly, I was forced to admit that no matter what career he had chosen, he was who he was.

But I was the one who had closed my eyes to the whole thing. I allowed myself to be blinded by the hope that my marriage would not be that of my parents. Sal was different. I was different.

I heard a car pull up and a door slam. My friends and neighbors had been stopping by all day to offer their support on what they imagined was a difficult day. I felt like I was hosting a funeral. I wanted to hide. I wanted to grieve, I wanted to mourn, in private. I wondered how long the parade of uninvited visitors would last.

"I'm in the backyard!" I shouted. I didn't want to track mud through the house.

"Lauren?" a deep, muffled voice called out.

"I'm in the back!" I shouted, this time louder.

I heard an apprehensive knock on the gate of the yard. The thought crossed my mind that it might not be one of my neighbors knocking. What if I'd accidentally invited a reporter into my garden? Then I finally recognized my visitor's face.

"You really should start vetting who you welcome into your backyard. Can we talk?" Joel stood in my garden wearing his game-day suit and looking unsure of himself.

After the week I had endured, I wanted to seem put together in front of Joel. I had known him most of my life, and yet I never felt like I could fully see any vulnerability. I needed to be more calculated than with most old friends. For that reason, I wished that I had had my hair done and been wearing anything other than the gardening clothes I had on. This was the worst-case scenario. I was knee-deep in dirt after a two-week crying binge.

I wiped my gloves on my already dirty jeans. "Aren't you supposed to be over there?" I said, motioning to the hill where the sound of a cannon had just erupted again.

"I need to talk to you, and honestly I thought that if I came over now, I'd have the best chance of catching you alone, and I wasn't sure if you wanted to see me."

I realized that he was nervous. Me, in my gardening gear—I was making him nervous. "Good guess. I was wondering if you would pop by for a visit." I was almost surprised that it had taken so long for Joel to show up unannounced. Since I canceled our lunch after my interview,

I'd gone almost radio silent. I knew that he'd want to clear the air. "Can I get you a cup of tea, something stronger?"

"No, I can't stay long, I have to be back before the end of the game," he said, answering my real question: How long did he plan on staying? I felt relief that he didn't expect to stay long enough to finish a beverage.

"Lauren, I'm not sure what you've told the investigation. I'm not supposed to know, and I don't expect you to tell me." I could tell he was trying to be diplomatic. "But it would be really helpful if I knew where your husband is. I know this is uncomfortable, but I really need to know. Or if you know where any useful information might be?"

I scoffed. "You're kidding me. Do you actually think I know where he is?"

A look of confusion flashed across his face. "You haven't heard from him?"

"Not a word since the morning he quit."

Now it was Joel's turn to scoff. "You've got to be kidding me."

I felt bad for Joel. He had always been kind to me. He had always respected our long-standing friendship. I felt like I owed him something. I probably did.

I watched as he crossed the yard, wiped the sweat from his forehead, and plopped himself into my decrepit lawn chair.

"New outdoor furniture is on my shopping list, now that I'll be spending more weekends here." I tried to make my tone sound light, airy, blameless. But I couldn't. "Joel, I'm sorry, really, I never imagined that something to this scale would happen."

"I know." He sounded years older than he had moments before. "I can't say that you didn't warn me that Sal could be a loose cannon."

"I guess that favor I owe you is going to come back into play now?"

"Lauren, I don't know what else to do. I'm trying to figure out how deep this thing ran. I'm just trying to save the department. My university. I know that this isn't your fault."

"But?"

"But I have no other options."

"What do you need me to do?"

"I need you to talk to Mason Pont. He's in town this weekend reporting on the game." He pulled a business card out of his wallet and handed it to me. "Text him now, please, while he's at the game. He has a big mouth, and he won't keep it a secret if you meet with him. I know you don't think you know anything, but Pont has no idea who knows or doesn't know what, and if word gets out that you're talking to him, then I think others involved might be scared into coming forward."

"Others" meaning Sal. Joel was trying to use me as bait, a threat to get my husband to talk to the press, to deal with it himself. This made me question how well Joel actually knew Sal. Anyone who knew Sal as well as I did knew that it would never work. Sal would never come forward and own up to his mistakes. Not when he had left me behind to deal with them.

I flipped the card over and over in my hands. I felt like a pawn. But I owed this to Joel, as humiliating as the meeting might be. It would at least give me a reason to shower, to leave the house. I hadn't done much of either since Sal left.

I grabbed my phone, trying to hide the exhilaration I felt. Yes, it was stupid, but it was more than a valid excuse to shower. I could actually be helpful. I doubted that it would work, but someone trusted me enough to help. It felt good to be needed.

"What do you want me to say?"

29.

ANNE

August 29, 5:06 p.m.

I felt like I might have the world's coolest job. Sitting in the press box, I felt like I was a part of the inner circle. I was so glad I had listened to Graham and stayed for the game. The energy was contagious. Feeling the excitement in the press box somehow caused the drama of the past two weeks to slip away from my mind.

I was sitting in a superexclusive room, listening to the murmur of reporters around me and watching the game, while we all munched on complimentary nachos. It was impossible not to have school spirit. If I had known that going to a game could be so much fun, I would've paid more attention to football my first three years at Renton.

There was no yelling in the press box. This room held a reverence for the game, unlike the drunken student section.

I knew that the point of watching a football game was to actually watch it, but I found it so hard not to focus on the crowd. Though I had never enjoyed being immersed in the crowd, I couldn't take my eyes off the stands. A collective mob of red and navy bobbed up and down as one. When I had sat there, I had just felt like another body, another red T-shirt, but from my vantage point in the press box, seeing all those fans together transformed the experience into something beautiful.

As the fourth quarter was about to start, I made my way back to the food table in the lobby. I took my nachos and wandered around. I had always been aware of the tower, but I'd never been inside. It loomed over the stadium seats. It was built the year before my freshman year and was surrounded by controversy because professors thought the money should go toward actual education. As a compromise, and in part due to the grant the university received for construction, computer labs took up the first three floors. The rest of the building housed the press box and luxury boxes.

My work pass technically allowed me into any part of the stadium, but I worried about wandering too far. Given the serene silence of the press area, I didn't want to risk leaving for the hope of a better view.

Plus, I doubted that I'd find a seat with a better view. Helen had a friend at the game, so she was down in the stands with her, but still on call in case something disastrous happened. For her sake, I prayed it didn't. The woman needed a break. She had mentioned an open-air stairwell that doubled as a sort of balcony overlooking the field. When the first time-out of the fourth quarter was called, I decided to find the spot. I wouldn't be at risk of crossing paths with any donors, as they weren't allowed on the upper floor. And I could see the door that led to the balcony from where I sat. If the view wasn't as good, I could get back to my seat in less than thirty seconds. I knew that in a few months, watching the game outside would be insane. I wanted to enjoy the summer heat while I could.

"So, my spot is no longer a secret?" I heard the voice as soon as I pushed open the door to the balcony. I recognized the man as one of the reporters I'd seen earlier in the press box.

"Sorry, I didn't mean to ruin your solitude."

"It's okay, I'm one of many people who believe they're the only one who knows about this spot. Welcome to the club, you will never want to watch the game from anywhere else. I've seen a lot of crazy stuff from up here."

"This is my first game working for the athletic department. I'm Anne, by the way." I realized how awkward I sounded. I was sure he didn't care who I was or that this was my first game. He probably wanted to actually pay attention to the game.

He turned to face me. "Hi, Anne. I'm MP. Where in the department do you work?" He held out his hand for me to shake. He seemed friendly, personable, how I assumed a reporter would be. Their job was to make other people feel interesting—like they mattered.

"I work for Nora Bennet. What about you, who do you write for?"

He let out a whistle. "Nora Bennet. I'm sure that your last few weeks have been crazy."

"Ha, yes, I never imagined that a game day would almost feel like a day off. This is not quite what I expected when I took the job."

"Hopefully that will change," he said earnestly.

"I'm not holding my breath."

The door behind me screeched as it opened.

"Sorry, I'm late—Anne?" Graham halted as he walked onto the balcony and saw me standing there. He looked surprised to see me. He did not, however, look surprised to see MP.

"I told you this was a popular spot," MP said to me with a smile.

"Clearly," Graham said coldly. "MP and I grew up in the same town," he added, as if that explained the awkward meetup.

"I didn't mean to crash your reunion. Helen just told me that if I had the chance, I should watch some of the game from the balcony. She wasn't kidding about the view. It's amazing."

"Good old Helen," MP said with a smile. "She's a good one, you can learn a lot from her."

"Want to get a drink after the game?" Graham said quickly, cutting MP off before he could say more. I couldn't tell if he actually wanted to get a drink or if he was just using it as an excuse to get me to leave.

"Yeah, um, sure."

"Great, I'll text you when I'm off."

"Okay. Well, nice to meet you, MP."

"I'm sure I'll see you around," he said with a smile.

With that, Graham practically shut the heavy door in my face.

30.

ALEXIS

August 29, 7:00 p.m.

It wasn't a big deal. Of course it wasn't. My mother always said I made mountains out of molehills. Every small inconvenience, I acted as if it was the biggest hurdle I had ever faced.

No one cared when I made my way onto the field. Well, that wasn't true; the security guard very much cared that I wanted to go onto the field. No matter how closely he examined my field pass, he somehow couldn't believe that it was real. It wasn't until Beau came over and assured him that I actually was invited that he moved aside.

I don't know why I thought that people would care who I dated. All that intense anxiety felt like a waste. Those who noticed that I was there and attached to Beau seemed genuinely happy for us. "Beau's the best! I'm so happy for you!" they said on repeat. I suspected some people had already assumed that something was going on between us.

I couldn't help but wonder how different the investigation would be if we had just admitted from the start that we were dating.

But then there was Richard Ross. Every woman I knew hated being near the guy. Beau had assured me that he was one of the best football coaches in the country. As if this justified his behavior. If a woman made half of her colleagues uncomfortable, she'd be out of a job. Richard Ross was praised for his antics. The press found him entertaining. Analysts predicted that by the time he retired, he would be one of the winningest coaches in NCAA history. This somehow made people look the other way. I did my best to stand as far away from him as possible. But even still, I could feel the daggers that he shot in my direction. It was clear that he was not a supporter of my romance with Beau. I tried to push those thoughts aside.

He had known we were dating since last football season. I wasn't sure how he found out. Most likely Beau had offhandedly mentioned that he was dating a professor in the English department, and by some process of elimination he had deduced it was me.

But I wouldn't let this moment be ruined by Richard. He had consumed enough of my thoughts in the past months. I wouldn't let his glares steal this moment from me as well.

Given the events of the last few weeks, the fact that not one person seemed to care that I was romantically attached to Beau felt like the bigger of the day's two wins. We could finally be open.

Talia had expertly snapped a picture of us holding hands on the sideline after the game, which she promptly instructed me to post.

The pure bliss of the day would carry me through whatever the investigation could throw at us. I realized that for the first time in weeks, I was happy.

I had told MP that I would meet him at his hotel after the game, and so when I left Beau to celebrate with the team, I was riding on a cloud of love and hope. Everything was going to be okay. If our relationship could make it through a nationally televised scandal, there would be no stopping us.

As I walked alone to the hotel, I made my way through crowds of people laughing and cheering, recounting the events of the game. Everyone acted like the win was a huge upset. But Beau had told me beforehand that Renton University had paid the opposing team to come and play; they weren't even Division I.

But, given the recent headlines about the scandal and Nora's promotion, people thought the win was shocking. Prior to the game, it seemed as though the entire fan base had lost faith. But the team had proved them wrong. The story would still be about Nora, even though at this point, wins and losses really had nothing to do with her. She just needed to avoid the spotlight and not fire anyone. She needed to lay low, let people forget that she was there. That was, at least, what I would have done.

The energy from campus overflowed into the lobby of the hotel. People were high-fiving and celebrating, making plans for which bar they were going to head to first. It felt so refreshing to find a little corner of the hotel bar and sit there unnoticed. From what I could hear, most people were heading straight to the Griffon Den.

I enjoyed the peace that came with knowing I no longer cared about being seen at the town's most popular bar. I would take an empty, overpriced hotel bar over a crowded, sweaty "cool" bar any day.

I was lost in people-watching when MP arrived and quietly slid into the open seat next to me. Another great thing about the "uncool bars": you could always find an empty seat.

"What are you drinking?" He motioned to my now half-empty glass.

"Vodka collins."

"Isn't that what you've been drinking since you were in college? When are you going to branch out?" he said with fake judgment.

"Why would I try something new if I know this works for me? Have you seen what they put in drinks these days? There's a drink on the menu with raw egg whites! I don't want to risk it."

"Egg whites make a drink frothy. It's been around for years," he said as he flagged the waitress, which was easy to do, as we were the only ones in the bar area. "Can I have a whiskey sour, please?"

"What'd you think of the game?" I asked.

"It was good, I think that y'all have a real chance this year. That Austin kid's incredible. And the kid they got from the JC, what a find." I tried not to react to the mention of Austin. "Also, I saw someone I knew on the field after the game," he added with a warm smile.

"I'd been meaning to tell you about that." Even if I was blushing, I couldn't help but smile. "We've been dating for a while now, and with the investigation, we thought it would be better to go public with our relationship, so it wouldn't seem like we have anything to hide. Which we don't," I added quickly.

"Your mother told me a few months ago," he confessed.

"Of course she did. If anyone in our family wants news to spread, all we need to do is tell one of the aunts, and then two days later the whole family will know."

"They're dangerous."

"How long are you in town? Would it be a conflict of interest for you to join us for lunch or something?"

"I wish I could. My flight is early tomorrow morning. But I think I'll be covering all of Renton's games this year, given the story and all."

"Oh yes, the elephant in the room," I tried to say lightly.

"Alexis, I wouldn't be reporting this story if I had a conflict of interest. You're fine."

"And Beau?" I didn't know if I was asking to protect Beau, or if some part of me deep down still worried that he was somehow wrapped up in the scandal.

"As I said, I wouldn't be reporting the story if I had a conflict of interest. Trust me."

I let out a sigh I wasn't aware that I was holding in, trying to believe him. Trying to believe that he actually knew the whole truth of what happened between Ross, Austin, and me.

He looked at his phone, checking the time.

"I have to meet someone really quickly. I told them just to come to the lobby, if that's okay? I don't think it will take more than fifteen minutes."

"Is everything okay?"

"Yeah, it's fine. I think it's just someone wanting to make sure they're 'safe,'" he said with overly dramatic air quotes.

I leaned in and said, "Can you tell me who it is?"

He leaned forward, resting his elbows on the table. For a minute it felt like we were kids again, gossiping.

"Okay, only because I trust you. You have to swear you won't tell anyone, not even Beau?" MP had never been good at keeping a secret, a quality he had clearly inherited from our mothers.

"Pinkie promise."

"Lauren Higgins."

It took me a minute to register who he was talking about.

"Wait, like Sal Higgins's wife?"

"Yes, she texted me this afternoon. I have no idea how she got my number, but anyway, she asked me if I had time to meet up before I leave tomorrow."

"What do you think she wants?" It felt like I was suddenly in the middle of a reality TV show plotline.

"If I had to guess, I think she wants to know what all I have on her husband. Or she wants to make sure that she's not going to be put in the middle of this."

"There's no way she didn't know. Like, how could someone possibly keep a secret that huge from the person they're married to?"

"That's the craziest thing. I don't think she knew, like, anything. Everything that I can find leads me to believe that she was completely in the dark. That doesn't mean that her record is squeaky clean. I think Sal somehow kept her away from everything."

"Oh gosh, I almost feel bad for her," I admitted.

"I wouldn't rush to her side to comfort her yet. The more research I do, the more obvious it is that no one's really innocent." He looked straight into my eyes.

Even though he said that he wouldn't be reporting on the story if it was a conflict of interest, suddenly it was clear: he knew.

"MP, why are you investigating this story? Like, what made you even think to look into it?" I knew there had to be something that he wasn't telling me, some underlying reason that he had started to sniff around Renton in the first place. He had yet to branch into investigative journalism. So his connection to this story, to this university, made me question if it fell into his lap by happenstance.

Before he had the chance to answer, Lauren Higgins walked through the doors of the hotel. I couldn't help but notice how out of place she looked. When I had seen her previously, she was always done up. I had never officially met her, but she was a known figure around town. I had seen her several times at the grocery store, and each time, she looked like she was ready for a TV appearance. But today, she looked tired, like she had spent too much time in the sun and gone days without sleeping. Her eyes frantically darted around the lobby as if she was fearful of who might recognize her.

She looked afraid.

31.

LAUREN

August 29, 7:45 p.m.

It felt like I was swimming upstream as I made my way toward the hotel.

As soon as I parked, I had a moment of panic. What if someone recognized me? It was a long shot, but Renton is a small town, and the people staying at the hotel could be some of Sal's loyal donors. I riffled around the back seat of my car and found an old hat. It wasn't much, but I hoped that a hat, in tandem with my dressed-down attire, would be enough of a disguise. Though I had showered, the thought of getting dressed in anything other than my favorite yoga pants seemed like an impossible task.

I had met enough high-profile people in my life that I rarely felt apprehensive about meeting someone new, but for the first time in years, I was nervous.

When we were kids, my sister was convinced that she would be a spy when she grew up. That's all she'd wanted to do. My parents had bought her "spy gadgets" so she could practice—which meant she spent her afternoons spying on me. Even at ten, I was not amused. Here I was, living out my sister's fantasy. It felt annoyingly ironic.

But it wasn't really spying, after all. I was curious. Joel had just given me an excuse to ask the questions that had kept me up at night. I was there on official business. I had a purpose.

After Joel left my house earlier in the afternoon, I googled Mason Pont.

I didn't recognize him. I had half expected to. Maybe not as someone I had talked to, but I had interacted with the press enough that many of their faces were familiar, even if I didn't know their names. He looked like he was in his late twenties or early thirties—young. I wondered if he was too young and naive to realize what a can of worms he had opened. Yes, the job of a journalist is to report a story, but did he know he was ruining people's lives?

No. He was doing his job. But he was also going above and beyond to prove himself early on in his career. It's likely he'd be promoted as a result of breaking the story. Sal had been the one ruining lives, not Mason. However Mason had gotten his hands on the story didn't matter. He had an ethical responsibility to expose Sal for who he really was. Something I had never dared to do. Maybe if I had known about this scandal, I would have done the brave thing. Maybe, had I known, I would have gone to the press, gone to Joel, done something to put an end to Sal's crimes.

It was easy to find Mason in the nearly empty lobby. He stood out like a sore thumb. He was the only person not wearing head-to-toe Griffon gear. He must have seen me first. He left his table in the bar to greet me. The woman he was sitting with looked vaguely familiar, but I was too tired to place her. I wondered if she was one of his sources.

"Lauren?" he asked courteously. He looked even younger in person. I wondered if he thought this was his Watergate. Bob Woodward was only twenty-nine when he exposed Nixon's scandal. Maybe he would be the sports equivalent to Woodward?

"Hi, Mason."

"Call me MP, I only go by Mason in print." What kind of stupid name was MP? "Can I get you something to drink?"

"No, but thanks, I'm driving." I cringed at my own words. I sounded so old.

We sat down and stared at each other awkwardly. He had picked seats in the middle of the lobby, which gave any passerby a clear view of our interaction. I had rehearsed this moment the whole car ride over, but now that I was sitting there, I had no idea where to begin. He took a long sip of his drink.

This was why I had never wanted to be a spy like my sister. I wasn't good at this sort of thing.

"So, I have two theories as to why you got ahold of me," he said after a few moments of awkward silence. "One, you want to know if I have anything incriminating against you—that is, did your husband use your name as a shill for all of this or something? Two, Joel sent you."

"How do you know that I wasn't the mastermind behind all of this?" I felt frustrated that he had read me so well before we even started talking. Was I really so pathetic that he couldn't even fathom that I would have been involved?

"Because I've been following the story for over a year, and I haven't found one shred of evidence showing that you had any knowledge that anything was going on."

For some reason, my eyes welled with tears. I desperately didn't want him to think I was pathetic. Crying would make me look more pathetic, I reminded myself. I wasn't sure if I should feel somehow violated that this stranger knew more about my life than I did.

"I found out about all of this the morning that your story broke."

A look of shock and pity flashed across his face.

"I'm so sorry, Lauren. I really want you to know that I was just doing my job. I'm just doing my job. As a journalist, I have a duty to report what I find." He sounded genuinely sorry. He was barely older than Hunter. He *was* just doing his job, I reminded myself. Talking to him face-to-face, it was impossible to resent him.

"There's a crazy part of me that thinks I should thank you. If it wasn't for your story, I have no idea how much longer it would have gone on, how much longer he would have lied to me, who he would have hurt." I took a deep breath, realizing I was processing these thoughts as the words came out of my mouth. "This isn't your fault."

"So then, are we going with theory number two? Did Joel send you?"

I nodded.

"Does that mean that he hasn't heard from Higgins, either?"

"You don't know where he is?" I couldn't hide my surprise. He already knew so much about my life, I figured that he had somehow kept tabs on my husband as well.

"So, what does Joel want to know?"

He avoided answering my question. "In brief, he wants to know what you know," I said.

"Isn't it the investigation team's job to figure this all out?"

"Apparently they don't work as quickly or efficiently as you do."

"I'm flattered."

"He just wants a heads-up about what's coming. Is he going to have to fire any more high-profile staff within the department this season?"

"So why did he send you?" he asked without answering my question.

"What do you mean?"

"Why did Joel send the wife of the man at the center of the scandal?"

"Joel and I are old friends," I said shortly. I didn't want to tell him that Joel hoped my talking to MP would make its way back to Sal and cause him to come clean. I suspected that MP would have the same opinion about that plan as me.

"Hmm, interesting," MP said as he took another sip of his drink. I could see the gears turning. His pensiveness made it clear that he knew about my deal with Joel all those years ago. It wouldn't be hard to put together.

"Listen, obviously you know I have a history with Joel"—I decided to get out in front of him—"but I'm here because the people at this school are my family. I'm here not just for Joel, but for my family." I tried to sound convincing.

"I'll call Joel tomorrow," he said, as if that would solve everything.

"Okay," I replied rather stupidly.

"Again, as far as I can see, you don't have anything to worry about," MP added as an afterthought as he started gathering his things. "You have my number if anything does come up. Please know, I'm just doing my job."

"Thank you." I wasn't sure what I was thanking him for.

"I'm going to have to cut this short. I have plans with my cousin tonight."

"Of course, sorry to keep you. Thank you again for meeting with me."

"My pleasure. Don't let Joel bully you." With that, he walked back to the bar.

32.

NORA

August 30, 12:33 a.m.

I heard a musician say once that the loneliest moment of a tour was immediately after a concert—the moment you find yourself alone in a hotel room after standing in front of thousands of people, all of whom came out and paid money to see you perform.

I had just had the first game of my athletic director career. We won. Donors were overjoyed. Players exceeded preseason expectations. Our student section stayed for the whole game, even though we never lost our lead. It was everything I could have hoped for. It was an undeniable success.

As long as I forgot about the minutes Sal had sullied in my office.

And now, I was back in my house, standing alone in the entry. Margo and Nathan were both fast asleep. The only noise was the distant sound of celebration coming from the hill. My feet felt like lead. I feared that they wouldn't take me farther than the foyer. I sank onto the bench intended to store Margo's many shoes.

It felt weird that others were celebrating the fruit of my labor, and yet I felt isolated. I didn't want to think about Sal letting himself into my office. I didn't want to think about what he may have left behind. I just wanted to rewind to the moment that the clock ran down to zero. That moment when I scooped up my daughter, who was squealing with delight.

"You did it, Mommy!" she said over and over, as if it meant something, as if this victory was more than just a game, at least to her.

I thought about Nathan and all that we'd been through. I knew that we couldn't keep up this pace forever. It wasn't fair to Nathan. His life and career were as important as mine. He had papers to grade and professors to assess. His world did not stop for mine. I also knew that if the tables were turned, if it were his career that suddenly took up his every waking moment, it was unlikely he would stop to think about how it affected me. Nathan went full speed ahead not thinking about his family. He was an academic, and somehow, to him, that made his work, his accomplishments, more important. Of course, he had never said as much, but his actions made it clear that this was what he thought.

I forced myself off the bench. I longed for my bed.

Nathan stirred as I crawled under the sheets. I hadn't even bothered to take off my makeup.

"I'm buying you doughnuts tomorrow. I'm so proud," he muttered before he rolled back over.

Should I be proud of myself? I wondered. No matter what part of the day I tried to focus on, my brain automatically redirected to Sal, and the memory of him sitting in my office came screaming back to me. *Should I be proud of how I acted?*

The whole interaction made me nauseated.

I rolled over and looked at the clock. It blinked in response, mocking me. The more I thought about the quiet of my own world, the louder the noise from the hill seemed to get.

I suddenly didn't feel tired.

What could I have done differently? Should I have said something differently? Should I have actually called security? I honestly had no idea.

It was too late to change anything, I reminded myself. I was just wasting brainpower replaying the whole thing.

I felt my blood pressure rising. My clock continued its mocking blink. I knew I wouldn't be able to sleep. I realized I felt ashamed of how I had acted, but there was more to it than that.

I was mad. I was mad that Sal had shown up in my office. I was mad that he had the audacity to let himself in. I mean, seriously, what type of person, after being very publicly dismissed, thinks he can just get away with letting himself back into his old office?

I was too mad to sleep. The longer I stayed motionless in my bed, the angrier I got. I was mad at Sal for acting so entitled. I was mad at my thoughts for keeping me from the peaceful sleep I so needed. And I was mad at myself for being so easily controlled by my emotions. Hadn't I spent years of my life trying to keep my thoughts, my emotions, under control?

I needed to do something. I needed to move. Careful not to wake Nathan, I swung myself out of bed, tucked my feet into my slippers, and slipped out of the bedroom.

Clearly, something needed to change. If I wanted things to be different, I needed to do something different. One thing was for sure, I couldn't let Sal stroll back into my office acting like he still owned the place. I needed to figure out who else was involved. Obviously, he still had some pull within the department or he wouldn't have dared to walk into the building on a game day. Sure, he would have known that the athletic director wing of the building would likely be empty, but still, he had to have some sort of insurance to just waltz in like that.

I did not want my career to be defined by his mess. I did not want to spend my entire tenure cleaning up after him. I did not want to worry that he would show up unannounced again.

I had to admit that I had a strange job. It would be a strange job even if I hadn't taken the position after a scandal. It felt as if all eyes were on me, but no one really understood what I did. The way people talked about my job, they made it seem like I could just wave a wand and fix everything. Hire the right coaches who will recruit the next great players who will never get anything wrong. Simple.

I felt lost. For as long as I had known Sal, I had been trying to figure him out. His smooth talking had always felt slimy to me. But he wasn't the first coworker I had felt this way about. So, I swept it under the rug. I wrote it off as another annoying aspect of working in a male-dominated field.

Everyone on the internet seemed to have an opinion about what I was supposed to do. Every time I got on Twitter, I was met with an onslaught of unsolicited advice. But, in the quiet of my house, I realized that I was the sole leader of the department, and I had no idea how to do the job well.

I wandered into my home office. The office was a renovation gone wrong. The previous owners had run out of money before they finished the addition, a third floor that was supposed to have another bedroom, a bathroom, and a bonus area. Instead, it ended up a quirky loft that was awkwardly too big to function as anything other than an oddly shaped office.

It was my favorite room in the house. In fact, it was the reason why we bought the house. From the office, I had a view of the whole town. I saw the light glowing from College Hill. I loved the view. I grabbed a dusty book off the shelf that I had intended to finish reading years ago, and curled up in my favorite chair, which faced the window looking out on the campus.

Helen had asked me recently if I missed being in college. Having Anne around made the office feel younger, in the youthful way only someone on the verge of the rest of their life could. Being a student was something that I thought about every fall as a new group of eighteen-year-olds flooded the campus, full of hope. I think I missed the feeling of vastness. It was like standing in an empty field, the world stretching out in front of you. You can plant anything in the field, and any number of things can happen.

Twentysomething years later, the vast field of my life looked a lot different than I had imagined. I didn't long to be eighteen again, but I wanted that feeling of vastness back. I missed the hope that goes in tandem with sitting around a sticky bar table with friends, dreaming about the jobs we would have once we graduated.

But more than that, I missed the innocence and freedom I had just a month ago. I hadn't planned to stay in Renton forever. Sure, I really did love this town, Nathan had a good position at the university, and Margo loved her teachers. But I was tired of working for Sal. I was tired of the small-town politics, and I had dreams of living closer to my family. I hadn't explicitly told Sal that I was putting job feelers out, but I had a feeling that he knew. Now that dream was far in the rearview mirror. I couldn't leave now. My excuse for leaving—a promotion to AD at another school—had vanished. Supposedly, I now had my dream job. It would look suspicious to leave after only being in the role for a short time. If the university hired me as Sal's permanent replacement, which all signs pointed to them doing, it would mean committing to Renton for at least the next four years.

I turned another page of the book, trying to fool myself into believing that I was actually reading it.

My thoughts wandered back to Nathan. Could I confide in him? Could I tell him I was struggling with the job? He had been affected, too, in a much different way, but I knew the scandal had been hard on the professors as well. I honestly wasn't sure of the best thing to do. I obviously couldn't tell him about everything; I didn't want to incriminate him in any way. He'd had his first interview with the investigation committee last week. I already felt guilty that by association with me, he was involved in the scandal.

The lights from the campus showed no sign of fading. My brain showed no sign of turning off. I doubted that I would be getting any sleep.

33.

ANNE

August 30, 11:20 a.m.

"So, overall, was it fun?" Noel asked me as we ate our makeshift brunch. She had curled her hair and dressed up. As far as I knew, our brunch was her only real plan for the day. I admired her commitment to looking pulled together no matter what. I might find it annoying, except that she let me borrow anything I wanted from her closet.

"Yeah. I mean, I had no idea what I was signing up for when I took this job. It's just so complex, I didn't really appreciate how many moving pieces go into putting on an event like that." I took a sip of my coffee. "Also, you should've seen the table outside the student entrance, it looked like the shelf of a bar, people tried to smuggle in like entire fifths!"

"Were you able to snag us one?"

"I wish. They all go to the compliance office."

"Make sure you get an invite to their Christmas party! Speaking of compliance, how are things going with Graham?" She gave me a very dramatic wink.

"What do you mean?"

"Come on, you know what I mean, you totally like him. Do you know how many times you casually mention the compliance department?"

"I mean, I work with the compliance department!"

"Yes, but you also work with ticketing, and you never talk about them!"

"Do you actually want me to talk about ticketing? Fine, yes, I think I like him. But I think I made things weird."

"What happened?"

I recounted the awkward run-in on the balcony.

"So, we met for a drink last night, but there were so many people at the bar, and he ended up running into his cousin, who by the way is Sal's son, and I felt like the outsider, and he was just being so shady about the whole thing, and I'm worried that he's somehow involved."

"You have to admit that it would be shady if a person working in the compliance department was part of a fraudulent scheme, right?" she asked.

"Yeah, maybe, but it's the perfect cover."

"Do you know who the guy he was meeting on the balcony was?"

"All he said was that his name was MP."

"Can you check the pass list for an MP?"

"Yeah, I think so. I'm sure it's not his actual name. Like it must be his initials." I paused to take a sip of my coffee. "Wait, MP! It could be Mason Pont, the journalist who broke the Sal story! I heard that he was going to be reporting at our games this season. Ticketing handles all the pass lists, there's your ticketing reference du jour, so maybe I could try to see if there's another MP. But it would make sense that Graham would be kind of cagey about it, if he was the reporter that broke the story. Right?"

"Yes, especially given his family connection to the department. Do you feel like every day of your job is like being in a whodunit novel?"

I laughed. "I can tell that no one trusts anyone else. Like, I think Nora is just sitting on the edge of her chair waiting for the next piece of information to be uncovered. I think she figures it's only a matter of days before someone else will be exposed for being wrapped up in this."

"I wonder if we know anyone who was involved? Like, it's weird to think that one of our professors could have been a part of it."

I nodded in agreement. "I know, I've been trying to remember if I took any classes with athletes, or if a teacher ever accidentally let something suspicious slide."

"I mean, I've for sure had shifty professors, but I'm not sure if this is their brand of rule breaking."

This was the sad reality. Even if a staffer wasn't directly involved in this particular scandal, it was likely that they had something in their career that they were trying to cover up. This had been one of the most interesting dynamics to watch play out. I had seen people within the department casually mention something that they had done in their past as if it was suddenly justified because whatever they had done was obviously not as horrendous as what Sal had done. He had set the new ethical standard.

In reality, these people had just avoided being publicly shamed for their transgressions. Last week an older man, who I think worked in equipment, admitted to me casually that when he first got hired, it was perfectly acceptable to make sexist jokes about female colleagues. The times had changed and so had his humor, he said. At least he hadn't brought scandal upon an entire department, he had justified quickly. It wasn't clear from our conversation if he actually regretted the way he had once treated his female counterparts, or if he was just grateful he had changed his ways before it became a punishable offense.

I tried to shake off the memory.

"How was your night?" I felt a twinge of guilt for monopolizing the brunch conversation.

"It was good. After the game, a group of us went to a bar. I'm kind of tired of bars, though. Everyone seems to think that we should spend every spare moment in a bar now that we're over twenty-one. What happened to other activities? Like, I want to go stargazing! Or at least for a walk."

"But was it fun?" I couldn't help but laugh. Just a few years before, we had longed for the day when we could legally set foot into a bar.

"Yes, it was. I love the start of the school year. There's so much to catch up on. Everyone wants to talk about their summer and what classes they're taking."

Noel was one of the few people I knew who found so much genuine joy in talking to people.

"So, what classes *are* you taking?" I realized I had been so caught up in everything that I forgot that the new semester was right around the corner.

The school year had snuck up on me. It happens to me every fall. Although this year felt different. This was the first time in years that I wasn't spending the last Sunday night of summer frantically making sure that I had indeed purchased enough notebooks and that my pens would have enough ink to make it through the following day. This was the first time that the arrival of the new semester did nothing to change my routine.

Noel spent most of the rest of the day running around preparing for classes the next day. I spent most of my day wondering if I should ask Graham about the awkwardness on the balcony, or if there had, in fact, been any awkwardness. It would not be totally out of character for me to imagine the worst in a social situation. But I saw something accusatory in his expression. And I thought I saw something like relief. As if I had uncovered some secret that he had been too ashamed to tell me.

Except I had no idea what that secret could be.

I checked my phone, mindlessly scrolling, trying to force myself to think about anything but Graham. My newsfeed was full of pictures from the day before. It seemed as if everyone I followed had come back to campus early to attend the game. Every post was a reminder of the day before.

Would it matter if I knew what was going on between Graham and MP? Or even with the interworking of the department? I was just an intern, I reminded myself. I was the lowest rung on the ladder. But I really liked my job. It felt almost magical, and I had just received my first paycheck. I wanted to keep the job as long as possible. And I didn't want my closest work friend to be one of the bad guys. I felt a strong urge to know the truth.

I wanted to text him. It wasn't a big deal, I tried to reassure myself. The meeting on the balcony was giving me pause because I was allowing it to. Graham probably wasn't spending his Sunday afternoon thinking about me, overanalyzing the interaction. I mean, he had given me his number for a reason, so it wouldn't be weird to send him a message. Friends texted each other; it's how normal humans interacted.

Hey, how's your Sunday going?

I typed, erased, typed, erased, the same message over and over. Why was I being such a weirdo? Finally, as if moving on its own volition, my finger hit send, and my message went shooting off into cyberspace.

I started pacing around my room. This was stupid. I was overthinking the whole thing. He was my friend, he was surprised to see me on the balcony, there was nothing else going on. I was making something out of nothing. Right?

My phone buzzed across the room. I sprinted to pick it up.

Fine, you? All that panic for two words . . . This was ridiculous. I was being ridiculous.

Yeah, fine, thanks! I had killed this conversation. How are you supposed to text people? How do normal people have normal conversations?

I'm walking my dog near your house, wanna join?

I felt my heart flip.

Sure, I can be ready in 10

I quickly laced up my tennis shoes and applied a coat of mascara. *Be casual,* I repeated to myself over and over again.

"Hey, hey!" I said when I saw Graham waiting for me on the side-walk outside my apartment. When had I ever before uttered the words *Hey, hey*? I could feel my cheeks reddening.

"This is Troy," Graham said, motioning to the small dog running around us in circles.

"Troy? Like the city Troy in Greek mythology?" Living with an English major had greatly changed my perception regarding names. "Or Troy Bolton from *High School Musical*? Or Troy . . ."

He quickly cut me off before I could rattle off another Troy.

"Ha ha, no. Like Troy Polamalu, my all-time favorite football player. He played for the Steelers."

"I know who he is," I said proudly. "I lived in Pittsburgh for a few years. And also, just because I'm not the world's biggest sports fan doesn't mean I don't know anything." I realized I sounded more defensive than I had intended.

"Of course."

We walked in awkward silence for what felt like hours before I finally found the courage to ask the question. "What was going on with the guy on the balcony?"

I had tried to bring it up the night before, but the bar had been too loud and crowded, and then we had run into his cousin. I knew the longer I waited, the more difficult it would be to find the courage to ask.

I watched his face quickly tense and relax again.

"Oh, you mean MP?" I could tell that he was trying hard to not reveal more than he wanted to.

"Yeah, I think that was his name." I pretended ignorance.

"He and I grew up in the same town, he was a few grades above me in school, and now he works in journalism. Our families were friends. I mean, not super close or anything, but we knew each other." It was obvious he was holding something back.

"Does he cover Griffons games a lot?" I tried to sound innocent. I wanted him to be the one to confirm my suspicion that MP was Mason Pont.

He thought for a minute before answering. "I think he moved into covering sports last year. And I'm sure that he worked our games, there's no way he didn't."

"What do you mean?"

"Oh come on, Anne, stop playing dumb, you know who that was."

His comment stung. I clearly wasn't being as coy as intended. "What are you talking about?"

"That was Mason Pont."

"The guy who broke the news about Higgins?" I didn't want to let him know I had suspected this. I didn't want to give him a reason to believe that I was suspicious of his involvement.

"That's the one. Well now you can say you've met the mastermind who exposed the scandal."

We walked in silence for a few minutes before I mustered the courage to ask my next question.

"Graham, why were you meeting him?"

"Listen, there's still a lot you have to learn about the way the world of sports functions. Sometimes the best and most logical answers don't line up."

"That's not a real answer."

He looked around the street as if he were looking for any familiar faces.

"I was one of his sources." He said the words so fast they were almost incomprehensible.

"What!" I shouted, not so much a question but an exclamation.

"I can't talk about this here, can we go back to your apartment?"

"Okay, paranoid much?" I turned on my heel and started the short walk back to my apartment. I could tell I was walking faster with each step, feeling anticipation and also relief in knowing that Graham was one of the "good guys."

As soon as I bolted the door behind us, I rushed to grab a bowl of water for Troy and plopped down in my favorite reading chair in the corner of the tiny living room. I saw Noel's shoes by the door, which meant she was still in her room, most likely trying to catch every word. She was a master eavesdropper. That would at least save me from having to repeat the conversation to her later, though I knew that she would want to go over every detail.

"Okay, spill." I was already leaning forward, ready to hang on each word.

Graham lurked at the edge of the room, looking unsure whether he should sit or stand.

"Sorry, I'm being a bad host. Do you want tea, water, coffee? I think we also have milk if that's more your thing."

"Yeah, sure, I'll just have some water."

I wondered if he regretted his admission and was doing mental gymnastics trying to figure out what to share now. I grabbed a cup of water and set it on the coffee table, gesturing for him to sit. I returned to my chair and kept my mouth shut. I didn't want my enthusiasm to scare him away.

He took a deep breath. And then another. "Okay," he finally said, as if it were a sentence on its own. I nodded encouragingly. "So I just feel like I need to start by saying that this thing is so much deeper than MP's initial story made it out to be. And like I said, I've known him forever, and when he approached me about doing a piece, we had no idea what it would turn into, or that there was any scandal to report on at all."

"Wait, *we*, as in you were like his main source?"

"I was the one who told him to investigate Higgins."

As he confessed, I swore I also heard a gasp coming from Noel's room. We were going to have a lot to debrief tonight.

34.

ALEXIS

September 15, 10:35 a.m.

"You know, the start of the school year was stressful enough before I was involved in an NCAA investigation." I chuckled weakly at my joke, trying to do anything to lighten the mood.

Beau said nothing. He simply squeezed my hand tighter. Our interviewer was running late. We'd been sitting in a conference room for almost ten minutes with the promise that he was on his way.

"This is starting to get ridiculous." I could feel the beginnings of a nervous ramble when the door mercifully swung open.

"Apologies for the delay," said the man in the gray suit. "Shall we get started?"

I saw Beau nod out of the corner of my eye. This was our first joint interview.

"Now, Ms. Baily"—he looked down at his notes before making eye contact—"I would love to know more about your involvement with the athletic department?"

"I've already answered this question." The words came out harsher than I intended. "Sorry, I'm not trying to be disrespectful, but I have a class this afternoon that I still need to prepare for."

"I understand your busy schedule, Ms. Baily. But now that your relationship with Mr. Kennedy is public, our team thought it might be helpful to talk with the two of you together."

He wasn't the bad guy, I reminded myself. He was just doing his job. I'd done nothing wrong.

"If I'm not mistaken, Alexis and I disclosed our relationship during our first individual interviews. I'm unsure why the public's knowledge of our relationship changes anything now."

I shot Beau a thankful look.

"We just had some questions about the timing, that's all. One could say that it looks suspicious that as soon as it was leaked that the former AD was coercing professors for favors, you two announce your relationship."

"That is exactly why we announced it when we did. We didn't want anyone to think that we had anything to hide. Because we don't. We don't have anything to hide. If we did, we wouldn't have told you about our relationship in the first place." I could feel my words running away from me, my palms sweaty. I didn't want to be there. I felt like I was being backed into a corner.

The questions continued on like this for forty more excruciating minutes. Every question they asked always seemed to circle back to the timing of when we announced our relationship. If I had known this was such a big deal, I never would have kept it from the public eye. We had longed for privacy; instead, at least in the eyes of the investigation team, we had acted like people with something to hide. No matter what we said, how we justified our actions, it never seemed good enough. The interviewer appeared determined to make this detail the nail in the coffin for our guilt. The minutes dragged on until he finally relented.

"Well, then, we can be done for the day. We will contact you regarding any further information we might need. Thank you both for your time."

And with that, it was over. I wasn't sure if I wanted to cry or hyperventilate.

"Alexis, are you okay?" Beau asked me once we were outside.

"No, this is too much. I didn't do anything wrong. But there is so much at stake. This is my career. I can't lose everything that I've been working toward. Not over a stupid man with a big ego."

"Come here," he said, pulling me to him. I didn't realize I had been crying until I pulled myself away and saw the wet mascara stain on his shoulder.

"Thank you, I should get back to my office," I said as I walked away.

"Alexis," he called after me. "We're going to get through this."

I smiled meekly at his confidence. He might get through this, but I wasn't so sure that I would.

———

My office was lacking the normal escape quality that it normally granted me. I felt overwhelmed. Overwhelmed by the interview and by the semester's coursework.

I wasn't sure how many years it would take for the teaching to feel natural. Every year, I told myself that I would use my August wisely. I would get back into a good routine. But then September came rushing in like a flood, overwhelming me and knocking me off my feet every time I tried to make some headway.

This year, I felt like I deserved a pass for my lack of preparedness. The investigation had consumed so much of my time. I had to compile documents proving that Beau and I had an established relationship before the scandal. I had met with the investigation team multiple times, both with Beau and alone. And then, when I wasn't being interviewed or scraping through my inbox trying to find any evidence that might incriminate me, I found myself talking about it. It was no secret within the department that I was being interviewed more than everyone else because I was dating Beau. Most people didn't ask me about it directly, but it was clear from their questions that they wanted more information.

My next class was across campus near the physics department instead of in the English department's building. I had to leave my office ten minutes earlier than normal to make it on time. I checked my email once more before making the trek. My heart almost stopped. There, blinking unread in my inbox, was an email from him. A wave of nausea rushed over me. The room started to spin. I felt faint and put my head between my knees.

This could not be happening.

It had been over a month since the whole thing had started. With every passing day, I felt the weight lifting off me, thinking maybe he wouldn't contact me. Maybe I'd make it out of this.

But now, here it was in my inbox. Why was he emailing me? On my university email no less. I was sure that the university had access to this account. There was no way that this message wouldn't be flagged if the investigation team went through my email. Maybe that had been his intention.

I reached for my mouse and with shaking hands clicked the email open.

To: abaily@rentonu.edu
From: rross74@gmail.com
Subject: meeting

A—
we need to talk asap. you have my number. lets meet tonight.

Twelve words, very limited punctuation, and terrible grammar. The English professor in me cringed. Would it really have killed him to use an apostrophe? Autocorrect should've fixed that.

And then, there was the tone. He moved from a suggestion, to a reminder, to a demand. He didn't even sign his note. Clearly, he knew that I would get his point without any additional information. He didn't include his phone number. He assumed I still had it.

My phone beeped, alerting me that it was time to head to my next class. I was going to be sick. I had no time to be sick. I had to do my job. I couldn't miss my class. I didn't want to do anything to give anyone a reason to think I was guilty.

The interviewer was right. Our timing looked suspicious. We should have never gone public with our relationship. Or, we should have gone public as soon as we started dating. But now, not only did I teach classes frequented by athletes but I was closely tied to the athletic department. The only professor with a closer connection was Nathan.

It didn't help that now that my job was on the line, I realized how much I liked it. Losing it was all that I could think about. I was happy, and it could all be taken away from me.

I would probably never teach again.

Things were going so well for Beau and me. And I had put us both in danger. I couldn't drag his career down with mine. He shouldn't be associated with me. I had been so naive to believe that I was in the clear.

Deep breaths, I reminded myself. I still had a job to do. I grabbed my phone and scrolled to Richard's contact, saved under a pseudonym because at the time it felt clever. Now, it just looked suspicious.

My last class tonight ends at 5. I can meet any time after that. I didn't sign my name, but I couldn't bring myself to use improper punctuation. I stuffed my phone in my bag and tried to will myself not to think about it anymore.

I pulled my office door shut, turned around, and almost ran smack into Nathan.

"Oh, hi, Alexis." He seemed distracted.

"Hi, Nathan." I peeked at my watch. I was going to be late for my class. I had no time for small talk with him.

"Which way are you heading?" His tone changed back to his usual friendly demeanor.

"Actually, to the physics department, I have a class over there this semester."

"Oh, I hate when I get classes out in the boonies. I'm actually heading outside, I can walk with you." He said this as if it was a suggestion, but he clearly assumed I would say yes as he fell into step with me. I was trapped. I didn't feel up to a ten-minute walk with my boss.

"How are your classes going this semester?" I asked the most obvious question, hoping that this low-hanging fruit would occupy the conversation for the entirety of our walk.

"They're fine, pretty much as I expected." Nathan was normally a big talker, so his short answer threw me off guard. "Have you checked your email today?" He asked this so casually, nonchalantly.

I had to force myself to keep walking, not to pause, and not to let my jaw drop.

"I'm sorry?"

"I asked if you've checked your email today, like in the last half an hour."

"Of course, I always check my email before a class." Perhaps there had been a department email recently sent out that I had just accidentally skipped over. Maybe he wanted to ask me about it. He was the head of the department, after all.

"Good. Make sure you take it seriously."

"I'm sorry, I'm not sure what you're talking about." I decided playing dumb was still my best strategy.

"Alexis, you and I both know the email I'm referencing. Richard's not joking around. Make sure you take his request seriously."

With that, Nathan sauntered off in the other direction, as if he hadn't just outed himself to me.

I focused on my breathing. In for four, hold for four, out for four, hold for four. I had to remain calm. I would not let this ruin my next class. I would not be the professor who cried in front of her students.

When I was an undergrad, I had cried during a final. The stress of the test had gotten to me, and after the professor ignored my request for help, the tears had poured out involuntarily. I was mortified. The next semester on the first day of class, when my new professor called my name, his face flashed with recognition and he said, almost with joy, "You're the student that cried in Key's class!"

The rest of the class burst into hysterics. I lived out the rest of my undergrad years as the chick who had cried in Key's class. These labels were hard to shake, especially as a woman. Never again would I allow myself to be the woman who cried in class.

In for four, hold for four, out for four, hold for four. I was going to be okay. I just needed to make it through the next hour. One minute at a time. I was going to be okay. I was not going to have a panic attack in the middle of campus, surrounded by hundreds of students, all of whom had cameras on their phones.

I made it to class, and it went by in a blur.

Walking back to my office was a blur.

I felt like I was heading for disaster. Who all was involved? Was Nathan being blackmailed, or was he a willing participant in this game? Did this mean Nora was somehow involved?

Nathan had always been one of the more friendly professors, always kind to me. I couldn't imagine that he would possibly be associated with Sal Higgins.

I was starting to feel like a wannabe Nancy Drew. Here I was, trying to follow the limited clues, receiving threatening notes, sticking my nose in places I wasn't welcome, involved in something way over my head, and assuming everyone around me was a suspect. I was a living, breathing young adult mystery trope. I even had a (very innocent) very popular boyfriend who was on (kind of?) the football team. I embodied every cliché I had warned my students against using in their writing. The irony was enough to kill me.

I wondered if Nathan assumed I was contemplating making a break for it. Leaving campus and never looking back. I suspected Nathan had put himself in my path to make sure that I did indeed keep my meeting with Richard.

Ross had messaged me back while I was in class. It was short and to the point, similar to his email.

7 pm meet me in the tunnel.

I had dinner plans with Beau, but I could tell him that I was behind on grading. He had mentioned that he was supposed to make an appearance at the volleyball game tonight anyway. I could tell him that if I finished grading in time, I'd meet him at the game. It would also work as an alibi if for some reason someone asked why I was at the athletic complex. I could honestly say I was there to meet Beau. I hated that I considered using his position as a cover.

True to my word, I stayed late in my office to grade. It felt impossible to stay focused long enough to actually do any grading. In all reality, I spent most of the time watching the clock, waiting for the arrival of 7:00 p.m. The hands of my clock seemed glued to their position, never moving, until all of a sudden, it was 6:50.

I nervously gathered my belongings, making sure I grabbed everything important, in case I was fired and lost access to my office. With a sigh I closed the door and made my way toward the athletic complex.

I had walked the route so often I could go there with my eyes closed. Beau and I had met in the tunnels many times. I knew all the secret entrances.

But it was not Beau who had first shown me the tunnels. I had visited them once before with Richard Ross.

When I arrived, I saw his recognizable form standing near the entrance that led to the basketball arena. I knew this was where he'd be—in the part of the tunnel farthest away from the volleyball match in the main athletic complex. He wore a baseball cap and a Renton sweatshirt, looking his part as the devoted coach.

As I got closer, I noticed that he had his hands clasped and his thumbs slowly circled each other. He was nervous.

"You're late," he said, dramatically looking at his watch. It was three minutes past the hour.

"I forgot how long it takes to walk here. It's been a while."

"Surprising, seeing as you're now dating Kennedy. I figured you'd be here every spare moment. But I guess since you two have gone public with your relationship, there's no need anymore for secret tunnel meet-ups?" His words felt slimy and accusatory.

"Something like that." I tried to say as few words as possible, not wanting to give him any ammo or be there for a moment longer than I had to.

"How are your interviews going?" he asked.

"As well as any detailed investigation of my life can go, I guess," I said dryly. I was still trying to figure out why he wanted to meet.

"How many times have you met with them?" he asked.

We both stopped as the distant sound of a door echoed through the tunnel. I recognized the young face of Nora's intern as she sprinted past us. I could tell that she was embarrassed to have interrupted our conversation. Her eyes never left the concrete floor, her cheeks reddening.

"Who was that?" Richard demanded once the door to the athletic complex shut behind her.

"She probably just got lost." I didn't want him to know the girl's connection to Nora. It was unlikely that she saw his face anyway. He had, almost comedically, hidden behind a pillar. Plus, we were just two adults talking. There was no reason for her to assume anything illicit was going on.

He shook his head, clearly annoyed.

"Alexis, how many times have you met with the investigation team?"

"I don't know, with the start of the semester it's hard to keep track." This was a lie. I had met with them four times and exchanged countless emails.

"What have you told them?"

"What do you mean? They asked about my relationship with Beau. That's what they've been focused on." This was the truth; the investigators had spent most of the time validating the authenticity of my relationship with Beau.

"I need you to tell me the truth, Alexis, I don't think you understand the seriousness of this."

"I understand the seriousness of this. Do you think I like having random people snooping through every aspect of my life, reading my private messages to my boyfriend?" He was patronizing me, talking to me as if I were a child, with no acknowledgment that my life had been turned upside down. As if somehow, I had willingly been a part of this whole thing. I hated this. I wished more than anything Beau was a professor—or better yet, didn't work for the university. I wished I taught at a school that had no athletic department. Wherever I ended up next, I would make sure the school had no sports to distract from the importance of academics.

"Then tell me what you've told them."

"I told you, they asked about my relationship with Beau." The worried look that he had been trying to hide suddenly disappeared.

"They haven't asked about me or Austin?"

It was then that I realized what was going on. He didn't call me to the tunnels because he needed something from me or wanted me to do his bidding. He called me there because he was scared. He thought that I held the power in this situation.

I realized that I did.

I could tell the truth about what had happened.

But if he revealed anything, it would not only make me look guilty, but it would be an admission of his guilt as well. He couldn't throw me under the bus without bringing himself and his athletes along, too. He was threatening me because he was scared. But there was nothing he could do to hurt me, not anymore. For the first time, I had power.

"Just make sure you have a good lawyer. And don't contact me again, or I will file a restraining order," I said as I pushed past him and walked away down the long tunnel.

35.

LAUREN

September 24, 7:30 p.m.

My house was quiet. I had never been a person to mind the quiet. When Sal was on the road, I relished the peace. Hunter had left weeks ago. The press was all but gone. My neighbors no longer stopped me on the street to try to get the inside scoop on the scandal. My life was once again my own.

But I felt like there was a shadow, a hole, something left behind when Sal disappeared. His absence left more than a quiet house. It left questions about my future. He had gone radio silent. I knew that he was alive because he'd been in contact with Hunter. I wanted to believe that he was ignoring me because he didn't want to implicate me in any way. He didn't want anyone to question my innocence. But that wouldn't be in Sal's character. Normally his thinking revolved around his own self-preservation. I was the one who looked after the needs of the family.

I heard my phone beep in the kitchen. I grabbed my empty wineglass and used answering the phone as an excuse for a refill. Graham had sent a text asking if he could stop by. Since Hunter left, Graham had made a point of stopping by several nights a week. I think he thought he was being sly by informally checking on me. I texted back, responding that he was welcome to stop by whenever. I wanted to tell him that he probably had something better to do with his Thursday night. He had been mentioning the girl who was interning with Nora more and more, and I was sure that he had a crush on her. He should be interrupting her quiet evenings, not mine.

But I know that he thought he was doing me a favor, and I suspected that Hunter had asked him to check in on me.

Less than five minutes after I sent the message, I heard a knock on my door.

"Come in!" I yelled.

It wasn't Graham who appeared in the kitchen, but Joel.

"You really are casual about who you let into your house," he attempted to joke.

"Believe me, I wouldn't have pretended friendliness if I had known it was you." A few months ago, this would have been a joke. But now the words felt true. I instantly felt cold. I didn't get the impression that Joel was making a neighborly visit. "What do you want, Joel? My nephew is going to be here soon." I intended this to be a cue for him to hurry this conversation along, but it came out more threatening than intended.

"We need to talk about our plan going forward."

I had been worried Joel would attempt to involve me again. I had been avoiding him since my conversation with Mason. He had called me several times, but once I reported the details of my short meeting with Mason, I didn't feel the need to return his calls. I'd considered the conversation with Mason as a type of closure. I needed to move on. I knew that Joel would want to rehash the situation from every angle. I didn't have the energy or desire to do that.

"Joel, *we* don't need a plan going forward. I'm working on rebuilding my life. I'm sure Sal will reappear when he's ready, and when that day comes, I'll figure out my next steps. But until then, I'm content to keep to myself. I don't think that you need to involve yourself in the inner workings of my marriage."

"Do you really think it's all that simple? Is this because of something Mason said to you?" He took a step forward. It wasn't a threat, but it was clear that he was trying to assert dominance.

I held my ground.

"Joel, this is your mess to clean up. My reasoning has nothing to do with the fact that you sent me to go speak to a journalist who knew more about my life than I did." I forced myself to hold firm. I was not going to cry. "He'd been investigating Sal for over a year. This was happening right under your nose, and you had no idea. Don't get angry with me because he outsmarted you, too."

"You know that I should never have had this mess in the first place. If you hadn't come asking about a job for Sal, I wouldn't be dealing with any of this. He's ruined the reputation of my university and taken up too much of my time."

"I already talked to Mason for you. It's now between the two of you to sort out the details. He told me that he would contact you. If I recall, that was me clearing my debt to you. We're even."

"You don't seriously think that meeting Pont for fifteen minutes really makes us even? Come on, Lauren, I know you like to play innocent, but you're not that ignorant. After all that I've done to help your family?"

The comment stung, but I willed my face to remain neutral. I wasn't going to give him the upper hand.

"As I told you a few weeks ago, I don't know where Sal is."

"Lauren, I don't care about that anymore, things have changed, I really need—" The sound of the front door opening cut him off. He shot me a questioning look. I shrugged my shoulders in response, grateful for Graham's timing.

"Hey! Sorry, I was running late!" Graham came into the kitchen looking sunburned. He had most likely spent his day outside, getting the stadium ready for the next home game. I made a mental note to send him home with sunscreen and aloe. He quickly looked from Joel to me and back to Joel. It was clear he was trying to figure out what to say.

"Hi, Graham, have you eaten? Have you met Joel Bonne?" I said nonchalantly.

"I think once. Hi, sir, nice to meet you." He reached out his hand. "Graham. I work in the athletic compliance office."

Joel reluctantly took his hand.

"I didn't realize you had company, Aunt Lauren, otherwise I would've come by later." It was clear he was trying to figure out why the university's president was standing awkwardly in my kitchen.

"Oh, this wasn't a planned visit," Joel interjected. "I was just on a walk around the neighborhood and I figured I'd stop by. Your aunt and I go way back." He put extra emphasis on the word *way* as if trying to remind me of our history, of how much I owed to him.

"Isn't that your car out front?" Graham asked. I couldn't help but smile with pride.

"No, it is, I meant I was on a drive. I was just on a drive around the city. It's good for me to get out of the house."

For a few awkward seconds, no one said anything. Everyone knew Joel was lying, but no one knew what to say. The tension loomed over us.

"So how are things in the compliance world?" Joel asked in an awkward attempt to break the silence.

"Well, we've had quite a lot on our plate this past month," Graham said dryly.

"Mm-hmm yes, that makes sense, that makes sense."

"Graham isn't speaking to Sal, either," I piped up.

"What?" both men asked in unison.

"Graham hasn't spoken to Sal, either, so don't even think about trying to ask him anything, Joel."

Joel's face grew red. He clearly didn't think I would say anything that would hint at why he had "randomly" stopped by. I saw a flash of understanding cross Graham's face.

"Speaking of compliance, as Sal is no longer associated with the university, I don't think it looks great from an optics standpoint to try to track him down. As far as I know, he's cooperating with the NCAA. As far as our family is concerned, he's now just an estranged guy. And, honestly, it's something we'd prefer to process as a family," Graham said definitively, protectively.

I added, "Marriage trouble is hard enough without having the press circling every move. Graham's right, we'd just like some space to put the pieces of our family back together, without any interference. If you'd like to speak to me about my role and involvement with the university, I'd happily meet you during your normal business hours. There's no need to trouble yourself by stopping by again, although we do appreciate how much you care." I took a step toward Joel, toward the door, not so subtly hinting that it was time for him to leave.

"Well, if you do find yourself needing help, Lauren, you know how to contact me."

"Thanks, Joel. But like you were saying earlier before Graham got here, you've already helped my family enough as it is."

With that, his jaw opened and promptly snapped shut, and he was out the door.

When the door was almost closed, Graham spun to face me. "What was that about?"

"I told you. Joel is one of my old friends, he was just coming by to check on me."

"Was he coming by to check on you, or to see if you had any more information?" I saw the concern on Graham's face. We both knew how serious this could be for me, for our family.

"Most likely both."

"How did you guys meet, you and Joel?"

I sighed. It was the last thing that I felt like explaining. But better he knew the truth than come up with his own wild theories.

"I've known him since we were kids, our parents were friends and our families spent a lot of time together. He's a few years older than me, and so I didn't really spend much time with him. I knew his younger sister better. But our parents stayed close, and they always kept me up to date on Joel's life and career. Even though he was older than me and your mom, I think they always hoped that one of us would end up with him. But eventually we all went off to college, and we all grew apart.

"Anyway, when Sal started coaching, Joel and I reconnected because we were both in the academic world. And then, when Sal got his DUI, I asked Joel for a favor. I asked if Sal could have an interview. I'd heard that their AD was going to retire, and I knew that Sal needed to be out of the coaching limelight for a while. Joel agreed to interview him, and Sal got the job. It wasn't as if I forced Joel to hire Sal, I just asked him to give Sal a chance. I was simply looking out for my family."

Graham didn't respond. Deep in thought, he walked across the kitchen and poured himself a glass of water.

"So, now is Joel trying to use that favor to get you to do his bidding?"

"He's trying." I saw a familiar look in Graham's eyes; it was the same one that my son had, that they both had inherited from my side of the family. We are fixers. I saw him now, trying to figure out how to fix this mess, how to sweep up the broken pieces, how to glue them back together. "Graham, there's nothing you can do. You need to let me handle this."

This was my mess to fix. I had used my connection with Joel to get Sal a job. At the end of the day, I was the one who would have to answer for that.

Graham looked distressed. I was tired of being pitied, the poor wife, helpless in the face of her husband's terrible actions. Sure, I might not have known what Sal was up to, but I never believed him to be flawless. Just as I was not flawless. Just as Joel was not flawless. Just as no one was. It was how we dealt with these flaws that determined the course our lives took.

"How are you going to keep him from pressuring you?" Graham asked worriedly.

"I'm just going to keep saying no. I've helped him as much as I'm comfortable with. When I called Joel all those years ago asking him to interview Sal, I knew I was asking a lot. I knew that chances were high that I would someday have to repay the favor."

Graham sat down on a barstool, subconsciously spinning, back and forth. I could tell he was measuring his words.

"Is there anything I can do to help?"

"Just do your job. And make sure that your department never hires someone as risky as your uncle again. Always do a background check. Always call references. Always keep digging."

Graham stayed for another hour. I tried my best to steer the conversation away from Sal and Joel. My life had more dimensions than just those two men. I sent him home with leftovers, sunscreen, and aloe, and then finally breathed in the relief of being alone.

Joel's visit had rattled me.

I had no idea what would have happened if Graham hadn't shown up. I knew I needed to do something. I had sat in silence for too long. I was stronger than that. I was braver than that. I grabbed my phone and scrolled until I saw our last conversation.

Sal, we need to talk.

I sent the message and I walked up the stairs, one at a time, reminding myself with each step that I was brave, that I had done all that I could do for my family, and then I tucked myself into bed.

36.

NORA

Whoever coined the expression "There is no such thing as bad press" clearly had never gotten any bad press. No one told me before taking this job that the press loomed everywhere, like an omnipresent force. And the bad press the department was getting staked a claim in my mind that made it impossible for me to recognize any positive press.

Even though our football team was doing better than projected, as was women's soccer, the public's faith in our long history of success was shattered as soon as Sal was fired. Our volleyball team—which had not been projected to be ranked this season—was struggling. People who I doubted had ever attended a volleyball match took the opportunity to heap on criticism. Fans, now latching on to the volleyball cause, called daily to complain about how I was only focusing on football and basketball and I was letting the other sports fail.

If we have so many volleyball fans, I couldn't help but wonder, *why are the bleachers at our matches normally empty?* I worried that I would accidentally slip and admit this frustration to the press.

The claim that I had spent all my time on football and basketball was of course not true. Yes, I spent more time on the football and basketball programs, but this was not unusual. Helen assured me multiple times that I was splitting my time between the sports in the same way Sal had. If anything, I spent more time on the lower-budget sports. Which was also problematic. There seemed to be an unspoken (though sometimes tweeted) expectation that a woman working in athletics would favor the women's athletic programs.

Many donors lived in fear that if I spent too much time fixing whatever issues plagued the volleyball program, football and basketball would suffer. They often reminded me that those were the moneymaking sports.

Both sides were angry and afraid. And both sides were very vocal and loved to use Twitter to make their voices heard. I had no idea what to do, how to balance this disconnect. When Sal had been in charge, not once had I heard a reporter accuse him of having a gender bias. Sure, the volleyball team suffered under him, but everyone seemed to chalk it up to bad recruiting, not some implicit bias he held against women's athletics.

It was ridiculous. But I knew that if I went on the record explaining how ridiculous it was, both sides would unify if only to drag me through the mud.

There was no way to please everyone. The only thing I could do was attend every single home volleyball match and meet with the coach on a regular basis, to assure everyone that I was doing everything within my power to support the program. And I had to do that without taking time or attention away from the high-profile men's sports. This meant working even longer days than I had planned. But at least the fire was being contained, acre by acre.

On top of everything, I spent countless hours working with the NCAA's investigation team to make sure that we were doing all that we could to contain Sal's wildfire. I barely even counted the hours I spent cleaning up his mess as part of my workweek. It was almost another full-time job itself.

I sat at my desk trying to figure out what to tackle next when Helen called. "Hey, Nora, are you in your office?"

"Yeah, I'm here."

"Do you have five minutes to talk with Joel?" It was obviously a rhetorical question. No matter what I was working on, she knew I'd make time to talk with Joel.

"Yes, is he here now?" I tried to sound hopeful, excited at the chance to talk with my boss. I knew that I was on speakerphone.

"Yeah, I'll send him back."

Seconds later, Joel appeared in my doorway, dramatically knocking on the propped-open door. He looked tired, worn down. I knew that he, like me, had more to his job than cleaning up the mess that Sal had created.

"Hi, Joel." I made an effort to sound extra friendly. Ever since the awkwardness on the first day, he had been nothing but supportive. I reminded myself that he was busy, too. I was not the only one with a full calendar.

"Nora, sorry to barge in here last minute."

"No problem, you caught me at a good time," I fibbed. There hadn't been a "good time" in my schedule for weeks. "Have a seat. How can I help you?"

I prayed that it was a friendly call. Just my boss coming in to check on how I was adjusting to my new role. It was clear from his face, though, that it wasn't a lighthearted visit.

"I just heard from the investigation team. They're recommending we fire Ross."

The words hung in the air.

I tried to keep my face expressionless.

I didn't want Joel to know that this news made my heart stop. I took a deep breath.

I tried to gather my thoughts. I had to calculate every word. I couldn't afford to misspeak, to show emotion.

"They have conclusive evidence of his involvement?" My words remained steady. The months I had spent with a speech coach were clearly paying off.

"Yes, and the people who came forward to accuse him are threatening to go to the press if he's not fired this week."

"Who are these people?"

"They're asking to remain anonymous, but their claims weren't baseless." As he spoke, he pulled a folder out of his briefcase and plopped it dramatically on my desk.

I quickly thumbed through the pages of what appeared to be Joel's own investigation into Ross. I wasn't sure when he would have had time to put this together. Did he have questions about Ross before he heard from the investigation team? It didn't matter now. All the evidence we would need to fire Ross was there. "I think we have a little time before they go to press. They'll ask for names. A story like this can't run without at least one name attached."

Joel let out a long sigh. I reminded myself that none of this was his fault. He was probably just as tired as I was. Maybe even more so because he had an entire university to run.

"I wouldn't be so sure, Nora. I think it was a group of professors. And I think that it's a large enough group that even without a name attached it would be credible."

His tone made it clear that he was not guessing. He knew.

"Professors that he had coerced or paid to give his athletes a break?"

"Nora, I don't know who they were. And if I did, I don't think I can say any more. I just know we need to fire Ross. The investigation team has evidence that he blackmailed professors on behalf of his athletes—that's all we need to know. That's enough evidence to fire him. We need to finally get out ahead of this thing. We cannot keep being reactionary. We need to start running the offense here."

I thought about the implications of what he proposed. He was right: we had to get ahead of things. Mason Pont couldn't break another story of unethical behavior before the university took action. I needed to work to prevent another media scandal. I didn't want to appear to be blindsided again.

"Okay, I'll meet with him this morning. If the investigation is wrong, and he wasn't involved, we'll have to pay out the rest of his contract. I don't have that in my budget." After Ross had led the school on a national championship run last year, Sal had extended his contract five years. He was the highest-paid college coach in the country. We literally could not afford to mess this up.

"Do you know if all the other coaches are clean?" I asked cautiously. Before things went public, I needed to figure out whom to promote as the interim coach.

"So far, they all seem okay. If you're thinking about who to promote, I'd go with whoever had the least contact with Higgins. I don't want it to look like we fired one hack just to replace him with someone who was also involved. We need to cleanse this department of Higgins."

He was right. I mentally ran through the list of coaches. It would be hard to find someone who was qualified but hadn't had much contact with Higgins *and* who had worked minimally with Ross.

I had never fired anyone. I had to not only ruin the life of the man I was firing but also face the significant backlash from donors, as well as endure an increase in media coverage. I knew I should preemptively delete Twitter from my phone.

After Joel left, I buzzed Helen. "Helen, could you come here?" Clearly Joel thought this was my problem to deal with. He had done his job by warning me, and now he could wash his hands of it all. Helen appeared at my doorway. I felt grateful to have her as an ally. "Can you please tell Ross I need to speak to him as soon as possible? And do you have any meetings this morning? Would you mind joining me in the conversation with Ross?"

Helen gave me a puzzled look. I motioned for her to come in and close the door. I replayed my conversation with Joel.

"You're kidding," she said once I had finished explaining.

"No. So I just could really use someone at my side right now. Plus, I need a witness in case he goes crazy."

"Yes, of course." She warmly put her hand on my arm. "I'll get Ross."

Throughout my tenure at Renton, I'd tried to limit my interactions with Ross. In the few exchanges that we did have, I'd left feeling small. I was sure that was his intention. Though Ross wasn't known for filtering his words, I noticed that he especially had no filter around women. He was careful not to go too far, to say something that would get him fired. But it was telling that most of his female staff members quit within a season.

The thought of confronting him made my stomach flip. Nervous energy coursed through my veins.

———

Ross sauntered into my office with the confidence of a man who thought he ruled the world.

"What's up, Nora? We were in the middle of a meeting. These things matter to my staff. If we're going to win again, I can't drop everything when you need to talk with me."

"Ross, I need you to sit down."

He must have understood something was off because his demeanor immediately shifted.

"Ross, we are terminating your contract." Straight to the point. It wasn't like I had had much time to prepare a speech beforehand.

"You've got to be kidding me."

"No, Ross, I'm not. At this time, given what the investigation has found, we will be terminating your contract." The words sounded cold, but I didn't care. I was emotionally exhausted and had no energy to sugarcoat things for a man who had spent much of my tenure belittling me. I was done with the platitudes.

"There's no money in the budget to buy me out. Nora, even you must know that. I assumed that you'd be at least half-decent with numbers."

"We won't be buying out your contract. Your actions have voided it. We have evidence that you blackmailed professors into giving favorable grades to your athletes. We have no room in this department for someone who doesn't respect the sanctity of the institution."

"Sanctity of the institution? Nora, this is bullshit. You have no evidence. Did Joel put you up to this? That man is such a coward. You wait, they're going to hang you out to dry. Joel will hang you out to dry. If you fire me, your career is over. No one will touch you with a ten-foot pole. Not after the mess you've made of Renton. The donors are going to be up in arms. Good luck getting anyone to donate next season. Ticket sales are going to plummet. What are you planning on doing for the rest of the season? You don't know who you're up against, you won't have this power for much longer. When Sal hears about this, he'll make things right. Nora, you—"

"Ross, I am going to ask you to leave my office. Or I will have security escort you out."

"You bitch, you don't know what you're doing. Nora, you're a joke. This whole institution is a joke."

He got up, threw his chair across the room, knocking it into my couch, and stormed out of the office.

As soon as Ross was gone, I asked Helen to set up a meeting with Jake, our communication director. I needed him to get ahead of this. We needed to control the story this time. She nodded but didn't move from her chair. Her expression was glassy.

"Helen?"

"Sorry, Nora, yes, I'll set up the meeting. I just need to sit for a moment." I could see tears welling in the corners of her eyes. "This is all so much. The calls we're getting from fans, the investigation, and now Ross. I'm just so tired. How are you handling this so well?"

I could feel a piece of my heart breaking. I opened my desk drawer and pulled out a box of tissues and a bag of M&M's. She took them both eagerly.

"I don't feel like I've been handling it well. I'm exhausted. And honestly, I was scared when Ross started going off like that. I'd expected it, but that didn't make watching it play out any easier. I can't tell you how often I return to my office, wipe the mascara stains from my eyes, and eat a bag of M&M's. I mean, it's to the point where we should approach them for sponsorship."

"Kleenex or M&M's?" she said with a chuckle.

"Honestly, either. I'm sure that I've doubled both of their sales this month."

Helen smiled, let out a long sigh, and pushed herself up from her chair.

"We're going to be okay, Nora. We're going to be okay."

———

Beau Kennedy met me, Helen, Jake, and the rest of the deputy athletic directors in a conference room close to the football wing of the complex. I wanted us to present a united front. The room was much more cheerful than the room I had just left, where I had met with Ross an hour previously. Kennedy had, of course, heard that Ross's contract had been terminated.

Richard Ross had a reputation for screaming. Apparently, after leaving my office he had run through the rest of the athletic complex claiming that if he was going down, the rest of us would go with him. Security had to remove him. Thankfully the press hadn't been there to witness the fiasco.

Kennedy seemed genuinely shocked when we offered him the interim job. I took it as a good sign. I didn't want to hire someone who felt entitled to the job. This building was full of enough entitled people as it was; I didn't need to promote another one. I left him with the deputy directors to sort out the details, knowing I'd be called back to sign the final contract in a few hours.

The day felt like it had spun away from me. I had thought I'd spend most of the day dealing with the volleyball drama, and instead, I'd been dragged back into Higgins's mess. It was hard not to wonder who was next. I didn't have the emotional energy or the relational capital to retool the entire department.

As soon as the ink dried on Kennedy's contract, Jake got to work drafting a press release. I would need to give a press conference. Once again I was left to clean up a mess that I didn't create. I felt myself growing more resentful of Higgins. I kept thinking about him breaking into my office. I still hadn't told anyone what had happened. I'd sent the work order for new locks, and no one had asked questions. Should I have said something? At my next meeting with the investigation team, I'd mention it. I wanted Sal to lose whatever power he had over the department. I would not spend my entire tenure cleaning up what he had left behind.

37.

ANNE

"You're getting really good at answering the phone in a crisis," Graham said as he walked into the lobby. I felt sweaty, and the office felt stuffy. I had spent my whole lunch answering calls as Helen ran around with Nora. I didn't envy Helen—I wouldn't want to sit through the firing of a head coach—but at least it gave her an opportunity to leave our cramped space.

"I think that I'm permanently stuck to this chair," I said with a laugh. Graham walked around behind my desk and tipped me out of my chair, landing me on the floor.

"There you go, problem solved!"

I couldn't help but laugh.

"Wow, so helpful you are!"

"Okay, Yoda," he teased.

"I've also lost the ability to say anything other than *no comment*. My brain has no function left."

Nora's press conference had taken place just after twelve, but even before she addressed the media, news of Richard's firing had broken.

He wasn't the most subtle, and he had taken to Twitter to voice his complaints, even calling on Sal Higgins to vindicate him. It wasn't the media tactic I would've gone with.

"How are things in compliance?"

"We're honestly so busy trying to prep for all the games this weekend that we haven't had time to process the news. Sure, it'll be a headache to wade through all of his violations, but first we have to make sure we're prepped for this weekend."

This weekend, RU would be hosting soccer, volleyball, and football games. It was a compliance and logistical nightmare. On top of the stress of three sports playing at home, the school had recently replaced the ticket scanners, and the new scanners had caused Graham nothing but problems. He'd been complaining to me about them all week.

"How're the phones? Are people as mad at you as they were when Sal was fired?"

"Honestly, this time it might be worse. You'd think people would have something better to do in the middle of their day than sit around and yell at me, but clearly, these people have a lot of time on their hands."

"Wait, this time around is worse?" He seemed genuinely surprised.

"Yeah, because everyone is now panicking about the rest of the football season. I've had the full range of people calling today, some telling me that we must've known that Ross was dirty when we found out about Higgins, so why didn't we fire him then, and others who are saying we should have just waited for the end of the season, seeing as we're already facing NCAA sanctions."

"Hmm, everyone seems to know what's best."

"It would seem like it."

"Is Helen following Nora around all day?"

"Closer than her shadow. But I think it's good, Nora needs solidarity. When Joel came into the office this morning, I could tell Helen knew it was bad news. She started preparing for the worst before he had even finished talking with Nora."

"Have you had any people calling in asking about Beau being promoted?"

"Of course, these callers have an opinion about everything. Most people are worried because he's so new to the program, I think a lot of people were surprised by the pick. But if the administration needed to choose someone who had the least connection to Ross, I think it makes sense. I can't tell people that, of course."

"Yeah, I agree with you."

"Can I ask you something? Did you know about Ross?"

His eyes quickly darted around the empty office, making sure that we were still alone. "No, I didn't have any evidence on Ross. But that's not to say that I didn't hear things that made me wonder if he was clean or not. I assumed that he was involved one way or another, but I didn't say anything to MP because I didn't have any proof. I wasn't MP's only source, though. But I'd assume that if he already knew about Ross, he would have gone public with his findings. This isn't a story that you sit on."

"What had you heard about Ross?"

"Some of his players don't think to look around at who might overhear their conversations. Players talked about how they were going to miss an exam, but it didn't matter, Ross had sorted it out so they wouldn't need to take it—that sort of thing."

I sat for a minute contemplating his answer. "Oh gosh." I wasn't sure what else to say. I wanted to know who else he thought was involved, but gossiping wouldn't help anyone. I'd had to pivot away from the planned schedule to tend to the never-ending phone queue. I was sure I wasn't the only one in this position. The entire department was once again in upheaval.

I didn't have too much time to think before the blaring of the phone interrupted.

"Thank you for calling the—" Before I could finish my greeting, the yelling began.

"Who do you guys think you are? What makes you honestly think that firing Ross in the middle of a record-breaking season was the best move for an already corrupt department? I'm sure that you were all in cahoots with Sal. All of his people know that he still drops by the department. Quit pretending that he's not still in control."

"I'm sorry, sir, at this point I don't have any comment. Nora Bennet made her statement at our press conference this afternoon. I could happily email you the link to her statement if you'd like." Before I could finish my sentence, he hung up.

His words replayed in my head. He had strayed from the normal rants of upset donors. I leaped up from my desk to chase after Graham, who had excused himself when I answered the phone.

"Graham!" I yelled down the quiet hallway after him. He spun around, looking confused.

"What's wrong?"

I tried to choose my words carefully so that he wouldn't dismiss me as crazy. "Nothing's wrong. But can you meet me after work? I need to run a theory by you, and I can't do it here."

"Um, sure. I have to work late to make sure everything's ready for the volleyball match tomorrow, but I can text you when I'm done?"

"Yes, perfect!" I said hurriedly as I rushed back to my desk, where the phone was ringing once again.

38.

ALEXIS

September 30, 1:30 p.m.

"Ross is gone," Beau said when he called me between class and a meeting with Talia.

"Like on a recruiting trip?" I don't know why that was my first thought. I knew the team had a home game this weekend.

"No, gone like fired. The investigation team found out that he was involved with Higgins, and he was fired." He paused deliberately, as if he was trying to catch his breath and wrap his mind around everything all at once. "They asked me to take over as the interim head coach." His voice concealed excitement. He'd just been promoted into his dream job.

My jaw fell open. "What! Beau! You're kidding, that's such an amazing opportunity. Are you okay?" It felt weird to celebrate someone's victory in the face of someone else's loss—even if that someone was Richard Ross. But Beau had worked hard, and he had followed the rules. He was the safe pick, the smart pick.

"Yeah, I'm okay. I honestly just feel a little overwhelmed. I mean, we have a game in like two days, and it's now all on my shoulders." I could almost hear him thinking through all the things he needed to do to prep, as well as how the outcome of this game would affect the rest of his career.

"I'm here if you need anything."

"Thanks, Alexis." I could hear someone yelling for him in the background. "Hey, I gotta run."

Once off the phone, I felt my heart rate rise. Beau was, at least for now, the head football coach. I could only imagine the additional scrutiny he'd be under. If they were looking into hiring him permanently, they'd have to do extensive background checks.

I was sure that he had a squeaky-clean past, with one exception. I needed to come clean. I needed to make sure that I didn't ruin Beau's career, his life.

I scrolled through the contacts on my phone until I found the name I was looking for. The moment before I dialed, Nathan walked into my office and presumptuously closed the door behind him.

"Professor Bennet, how can I help you?" I tried to keep my voice calm; I didn't want to clue him in to the phone call I was about to make.

"I'm sure you heard about Ross and Kennedy?" His voice was flat, unfriendly, almost threatening.

"Yes, I just heard from Beau. He's my boyfriend, after all." I wasn't about to mention any connection I had with Ross.

"I'm sure Ross isn't happy with you."

"What are you talking about?"

"You told the investigation team to check out Ross." He said this as if it were a fact, no questioning in his tone.

"I didn't. I told Ross that when I met with him a few weeks ago."

Nathan scoffed. "Do you seriously expect me to believe you?"

"Nathan, I promise I wasn't the source."

"Really, how convenient is it then that your boyfriend was the one who was promoted?"

"Do you really think if I was the source, they would've promoted Beau?"

He paused as if to consider this. "I think you're underestimating the forces you're dealing with here, Alexis."

"And why are you coming here to do Ross's bidding? You're basically admitting your involvement."

Before he could answer, we were interrupted by a knock. "Alexis?" Talia poked her head into my office. "Did you still want to meet to go over the spring syllabus?" She caught a glimpse of Nathan and quickly added, "Sorry, am I interrupting something? I can come back!"

I stood up from my desk. "Professor Bennet was just leaving. Do you mind if we meet in here as opposed to the conference room?" I suddenly worried about the prospect of leaving my office unattended.

Talia flashed a warm smile. "Yes, of course!" She scooted past Nathan into my now very crowded office.

"Thanks for stopping by, Professor Bennet," I said pointedly.

Nathan bobbed his head and quickly left the office, but not before shooting me a death stare as he closed the door behind him.

"What was that about?" Talia asked as soon as we heard the click of the door. I thought for a moment. I did trust Talia, but I wasn't sure if I could really open up to her about what was going on. I didn't want her to confirm what I felt, that I was guilty.

"Just some departmental drama," I said with an eye roll.

"I never know how to read him. Like, on the surface he seems so nice, but every conversation I have with him, I don't know, it feels like a facade."

I nodded in agreement.

"Do you think he's implicated in what's going on? I heard they fired the head football coach and promoted your Beau-friend!" she said with a wink and a laugh at her own pun. This was not the first time she had made that joke, and I doubted it would be the last. I was glad at least one of us had high spirits.

"Yes, crazy, right? Who knows if he's involved. I guess we just have to wait and see?"

"I guess. But I mean, he had connections, and so far, there haven't been any professors 'convicted,' but the most recent press release said that professors were involved and they're continuing to investigate. I feel like I'm just waiting for the other shoe to drop. I can only imagine what Mason Pont's next exposé will reveal."

"Did you know Mason is my cousin?" I don't know why I felt the sudden need to admit that to her.

"Wait, really? I don't think I knew that! Are you the reason he took an interest in the school's program?"

"Oh, no, he's been looking for a story like this one since we were kids." With that, I steered the conversation back to work.

But I couldn't shake the feeling that maybe she was onto something. Maybe I was part of the reason Mason took an interest in the story.

39.

ANNE

September 30, 8:45 p.m.

Noel had friends over for a study session, so I figured it would be easier to meet Graham at his apartment. He lived off the main College Hill, in a more grown-up-feeling apartment building. The cars parked in the lot reflected the adult paychecks of the residents. Sitting outside the building in my old Impala, I suddenly felt young and naive. I pushed that thought from my mind. I had gone there with a purpose.

He answered almost immediately when I knocked on the door. He looked more tired than he had when I had seen him earlier in the day. I held up a bottle of wine as a thanks for meeting me after an already really long day.

"How did volleyball setup go?" I asked as he poured us each a glass of wine.

"It was a disaster. We picked the worst time to switch to these new scanners. I don't know who approved that. I spent half of my afternoon running around like the guy from those old 'can you hear me now' cell phone commercials, except I was searching for the scanner's signal to come online."

"Oh gosh . . . that sucks." I couldn't help but laugh at the mental image.

"We just need to find some sort of solution before tomorrow night." He took a sip of his wine. "Okay, so tell me about this new theory of yours. Otherwise I'm going to spend the next hour talking about scanners, and no one wants that."

"Okay, promise you won't think I'm crazy?" I asked, holding out my pinkie to emphasize my seriousness.

"What's this?" He laughed, pointing to my outstretched finger.

"It's a pinkie swear!"

With another laugh, he hooked his pinkie finger around mine. I couldn't help but blush at the sound of his laugh. I loved when he laughed at my jokes, even though I was serious regarding the pinkie swear.

"Great, okay, so I think that Sal's still involved in the department."

"Sal, as in Sal Higgins, instigator of all drama who was fired in August?" He didn't sound convinced.

"That's the one. But hear me out, today one of our donors, who is actually pretty high-level, I looked him up, told me to 'quit pretending that he's not still in control.'"

"You don't think he was just blabbing, trying to get you to admit something?"

"No, I think he accidentally admitted something. Think about it, Sal still manipulating the department would make so much sense. Even from within the department, it feels as if he's the one still controlling the narrative. People seemingly refuse to say his name. Ross seemed to think that Sal was going to avenge him. My friend in tickets said that they had a guy who claimed that Sal had promised him tickets the day before a game. That feels like too much to just write off as nothing. I mean, he's your uncle, do you have any theories on where he has been? I think he's still here, lying low, controlling people with invisible puppet strings."

"Okay, other than weird comments people have made, do you have anything else to prove it?"

I realized that it was going to be harder to convince him of this theory than I thought. I had been thinking about it all day, and the more I thought about it, the more obvious it had become. But I had failed to think about how for Graham, this was personal. This was not just his old boss. Sal was his uncle. He was much closer to the wreckage than I was.

"Well, after the first home game, Nora was super paranoid about office security, and had all of the locks changed and brought in a security team to check how secure the office was. Now Helen and I have to change the passwords on our computers every seven days. This makes me think that Sal tried to break into the office or had someone else do it. I don't know if he would be that bold. But I think Nora caught him. Also, on my first day, Noel came by to bring me coffee, and one of her professors was with her, which would be weird for anyone but Noel, she befriends everyone. But Noel told me later that the professor is dating Beau Kennedy. And I saw her, I think her name is Alexis, in the tunnels one night talking to someone. I couldn't tell who she was talking to, but the man sounded mad and threatening. I was so embarrassed that I interrupted them that I practically sprinted away, but it was eerie, I didn't want to be caught in the middle of something. From what I know, those tunnels are only for staff, and most people don't even know about them. It feels so fishy to me."

Graham thought it over for a minute. "I mean, I guess it's not totally out of the range of possibility. But why would he still want to interfere?"

"Money," I said plainly. "Unpaid debts to donors, or maybe he's still making money from all of this?"

"Maybe." I could tell he wasn't convinced.

"What else do you think he could be doing right now?"

"I don't know, I guess I figured that he was fishing or in Vegas gambling or something."

"I mean, maybe, but I just have this weird feeling in my gut about it."

"I'll see if I can find out at least where he is. If he's still involved somehow, this is going to be a really long year . . ." I could tell by the look on his tired face that he wanted all of this behind him. This wasn't just his job; this was his family. This was personal.

40.

LAUREN

October 1, 1:04 a.m.

On the nightstand next to me, my phone shook violently. The sudden noise pulled me out of my dreamy daze. I rolled over and saw the time on the nightstand clock. One in the morning. Maternal panic quickly replaced the confusion about why I was suddenly awake: Why was my phone ringing? Who was hurt? I snatched it quickly from its resting place. The call came from an unknown number. It easily could be a hospital. Or a police station. I quickly answered.

"Hello?" I heard my groggy voice say.

"Lauren." My heart sank and sped up simultaneously.

"Sal."

Where are you? Why are you calling me in the middle of the night? Are you seriously calling me in the middle of the night? I restrained myself from asking the questions that flooded my tired brain.

"You texted me a few weeks ago, asking if we could talk?" The way he said it made it seem as if he was surprised to have heard from me, as if he wasn't the one who had gone silent, and as if I were not his wife.

His voice also implied that to him, it was a perfectly normal time of day to be calling.

"Yes, Sal, I was hoping that you could maybe clear some things up for me. I'm not sure if you know, but you left behind quite a mess," I said sarcastically. I had texted him weeks ago, and he responded with a delayed middle-of-the-night phone call?

"Seriously, Lauren? I thought that you'd be thanking me. You always like to fix my problems for me. I figured that if I removed myself, it would give you more space to work your magic. I'm almost surprised that I haven't gotten a call offering me a new job in the next sleepy mountain town. I was doing you a favor." I quickly realized that he was drunk. He only spoke to me like this when he'd been drinking.

"Sal, you cannot be serious. I haven't heard from you in over a month, and now you're calling me in the middle of the night?"

"You're right. I should've just stopped by, or do you only let Joel drop by the house at night? Letting himself in now, is he? How long have you guys been sleeping together? Did you rush to his house the day I left to tell him the good news?"

"Sal, I'm not sleeping with Joel, are you kidding me?" Anger replaced my sleepiness.

"Cut the crap, Lauren. You don't need to lie to me anymore. I know all about you two."

"You should check your source because there's absolutely nothing going on between Joel and me."

"I'm not an idiot."

"I don't think you're an idiot. Misinformed, but not an idiot. Sal, where are you?"

"Why, so you can run and tell your new reporter buddy? I know you met with him, too. You're really making the rounds. Let me guess, you were the one who told him to look into me in the first place. Did you tip him off? Were you trying to get rid of me, Lauren, so you and Joel could finally be together? How did you find out?"

"Sal, what are you talking about?"

"You looked so surprised that morning when I told you I'd been fired. It was a really believable performance. I don't know why I didn't put it all together. You're the real mastermind in the family, after all."

"Sal, I honestly have no idea what you're talking about."

"Stop playing dumb, Lauren. It's really not a good look on you. Like you didn't have something to do with Ross being fired, either?"

I hadn't heard anything about Richard being fired. I had stopped checking the news; it had all become too exhausting. No one had told me. I would google what had happened once I was off the phone with Sal.

"Sal, I didn't know that Richard was fired. Why, and how, could I have orchestrated that when I had no idea about it in the first place?"

"Keep telling yourself that if it helps you sleep at night. You know you're just as guilty as I am for destroying our family." With that, he hung up.

I lay in bed and watched as the tears stained my pillowcase. I reached again for my phone and realized I had no one to call. I was alone. The walls of my room felt like they were caving in around me. I wished he had never called. I wished I had never texted him. I wished I had never listened to Joel. I wished I had someone to share my pain, my isolation, my confusion. The emptiness of my house laughed at me.

I needed some friends. Friends who weren't involved in this mess. I needed friends who didn't think of me as a basket case.

My mind was spinning, and I had no one to talk to.

I was alone. But the truth was, I'd been alone even before Sal left. I had been alone for years.

41.

ALEXIS

October 1, 12:35 p.m.

Before he'd taken an interest in Renton University sports, I only saw MP a few times a year. Far too little for either of our liking. We would always see each other on Thanksgiving and Christmas, and then, on good years, we got together for a few other scattered moments. Our schedules had never overlapped in a way that made it possible to see each other more often. It was nice to know that I would see my cousin at least six times this fall alone. I felt thankful for the football season. I missed living near my family.

This week MP was covering all of Renton's busy sports schedule—volleyball, soccer, and football—so he was in town for several days, not just flying in for Saturday's football matchup. Someone from the athletic department had asked if the network could send someone to write a special report on the volleyball team. Since he was already planning on being in Renton for the football game, they figured MP could just extend his trip by a day. Just like that, he was a volleyball reporter.

I assumed this last-minute ask was the work of the communication team, trying to rectify the fact that the media had been focusing all of its attention on football, basketball, and Nora. Beau told me the other coaches had complained about the lack of attention. Now that Beau had more power, he had a steady stream of emails filled with complaints from other employees in the department. Each seemed optimistic that he would help them with their latest gripe.

I waited for MP in the lobby of the English building. His flight had landed an hour ago, and he was picking me up in his rental car.

Early fall is my favorite time of the year in Renton. Sunny, warm enough to wear shorts, but cool enough for a sweatshirt, days long enough to enjoy a postwork run, leaves beginning to change. But it had been raining all day. I had grown up with big storms—some of my favorite memories involved watching a storm roll in across the corn-field at my grandma's house—but in Renton, a storm was rare. Instead, on rainy days we just got a constant drizzle, overcast all day. The rain brought with it a sense of gloom. The lazy hazy days of summer were behind us.

I saw a car pull up outside the building, and through the fog I could make out the profile of my cousin. I threw my hood over my head and made a mad dash to the parking lot. I had to pull on the door handle several times before he realized he had yet to unlock the car.

"Did you want to leave me out in the rain?" I joked, taking off my jacket so I could shake the excess water off before I closed the door behind me.

"Sorry, I'm not used to the locks on this car."

"You travel so much now, I figured you would be more used to a rental than your own car." I stopped myself from saying more. Though I wanted to see my cousin, the main reason I wanted to have lunch with him was to ask him why he had started reporting on RU in the first place. The conversation I had with Talia was still ringing in my ears. I needed to figure out a way to casually work it into the conversation. I didn't think it would sound casual if it was the first thing I brought up. "How was your flight?" I asked instead.

"Quick. The flight is only like two hours if the wind is right. I could just drive, but it would take me like ten hours. And I bet the mountains are getting a storm with all of this rain. The airport was busy today. There'll be a lot of people in town this weekend, trying to soak up as many sporting events as possible."

"It doesn't take much for the Renton airport to seem busy. It's like the size of my house."

"True, if there are three people in that terminal, it feels like a crowd."

"Was there a lot of buzz about Ross?"

"Yeah, the guy next to me on the flight tried to talk to me about it the whole way. I didn't tell him I'm a reporter. I think that would have made it worse. He might assume I had some insider information. From what I can tell, people are panicking. Firing him midweek during a winning streak was really gutsy. And right before a home game as well."

"Maybe they were afraid if he wasn't fired as soon as possible, some nosy reporter would expose him." I couldn't help my sarcasm. It was too easy.

"Ha, ha. I'm just doing my job." He pulled the car into an empty spot in front of my favorite Renton restaurant. We both silently got out of the car and headed inside. We arrived just at the end of their lunch rush. I noticed more alumni-age people than normal. The student-to-adult ratio had flipped. MP was right about more people being in town early for the game.

We quickly ordered, then sat in comfortable silence.

"MP, can I ask you something?"

He briefly looked puzzled before he replied, "What's up?"

"Why did you start this investigation?"

"What do you mean?"

"I mean, what got you interested in Renton athletics in the first place? Before this season, you hadn't really focused on one school, and I was just wondering what got you interested in reporting on Renton. I mean, obviously you got an incredible story out of the whole thing." I could feel myself rambling and forced myself to stop talking. I remembered our night at the hotel bar when I had tried to ask him about his interest in the story and Lauren Higgins had interrupted us. I hoped he might be more willing to answer now.

He thought for a minute. I was just about to rephrase my question when he answered. "It was a fluke. I wanted to do a piece on the student-athlete compensation. I was going to look at programs across the country. I'd been talking to one of my friends who used to play for Higgins when he was a coach, and I mentioned the story I was working on. I also said that I had a cousin who's an English professor at Renton. The guy was newer to the network, and I was just trying to connect with him. I hadn't been looking for a story. Almost as a warning, he mentioned how when Higgins was a coach, he always made sure to be friendly with professors. He didn't outright say that it was because he was trying to get preferential treatment for his athletes, but it was implied. I went back to my office and did a quick Google search and saw that he left his coaching job quickly and quietly to take the AD job in Renton. The whole thing sounded fishy. This kid I went to school with is his nephew but also works for the athletic department, so I decided to follow up with him. Everything kind of came together from there. It was just a fluke, I was following a weird hunch that something wasn't right. I didn't plan this, or really know what it would lead to."

I digested what he said. "Would you have continued investigating if you found out I was involved? Like, if I was one of the shady professors in question?"

He looked troubled. "No." He took a long sip of his Coke, gathering his thoughts. "Alexis, what's going on?"

"I'm just curious about what led you here. I try to inspire young writers for my job, remember," I fibbed.

He saw right through it. "Alexis, we know each other too well to lie. What's actually going on?"

I scanned around the restaurant, confirming that I didn't recognize any of the faces. "I might be in trouble. Richard Ross, I knew him, or rather I had met him a few times, and he had a lot of players in my classes. Especially English 101. Almost every athlete takes that class, it's supposed to be an easy A. I never had any problems with his athletes. He would stop in about once a semester, to make sure all of his players were passing, eligible to play. That's pretty common for a coach to do. If a player fails a class, they're ineligible. I think the transition is hard especially for freshmen, I mean it's their first time out of the house, and they're handed all this freedom, and they're athletes at a high-profile school. I think the pressure and excitement make it hard to remember that part of being a student-athlete is to be a student."

"Well, I don't think that this is a problem that Renton has a monopoly on." He chuckled to himself.

"Yeah, I can only imagine," I said, suddenly feeling awkward, the weight of my confession pressing down on me. "So yeah, as I said, I'd never had a problem with Ross, or any coach for that matter. But then, last fall, right when I started dating Beau, I had Austin O'Malley in my class."

"The wide receiver?" If MP could tell where this very predictable story was going, he didn't show it.

"Yeah. Anyways, he wasn't a good student. He just wasn't motivated. Two months into the semester, he had the lowest grade of anyone in the class. That was when Ross came to talk to me. Well, talk is really the kind way of putting it, he actually came to my office and threatened that if I didn't change Austin's grade, he would make sure my tenure at the school was suddenly cut short." I felt the weight of the shame overtake me. "He said he knew I was dating Beau and should cooperate, or he would twist the story and make it look like I used my connection with Beau to get favors from the athletic department, like free tickets that I could resell. Ross said that if I said anything, he would go to Nathan and make it look like I had approached Ross about changing Austin's grade. He said no one would believe I was innocent, that Beau was innocent, because we were romantically linked. He just kept launching threats of what he would do to me, to my career, to my relationship. MP, I was scared."

His expression remained steady. "What did you do?"

"I emphasized our departmental policy, I said that if Austin wanted a higher grade, he would need to come and talk to me himself. Maybe we could work out some extra credit. I had done that for my other students as well, not just athletes. Ross was clearly not happy with me, and from then on he started making regular appearances in my office, checking on Austin's grades. It progressed from there. He started asking if I could meet him in random places. He worried that it would look suspicious if he kept meeting me in my office. So, we would meet in these underground tunnels that connected the basketball arena to the main building. I know now that meeting him outside of the English department looks suspicious, but at the time, I was just doing all that I could to make sure that Austin succeeded in my class. I thought that maybe Ross was also talking with him about his grades. Anyway, I never budged on my position. Then Austin started turning in his assignments, not only on time, but they were really good."

"Alexis, it really doesn't sound like you did anything wrong. You told him no. Multiple times."

"But I continued to meet with him. And, as I said, Austin's assignments started coming back really good. Like probably too good. I think he was cheating somehow. Ross probably got someone else to write the papers for him. I should have said something about it, but I never did."

MP leaned back in his chair, the front two legs coming off the floor, just like he always did when he was a kid. The legs of the chair came crashing to the floor as he plopped his elbows dramatically against the table. I could tell that he was trying not to crack himself up.

"Now can I be honest with you?" he asked.

I twiddled my thumbs nervously together. "Of course."

"Great. I knew all of that. Alexis, you should have known you could've come to me sooner. I had a source tell me early on they saw Ross spending a lot of time in your office last fall. It was one of the first things I looked into. I was being honest earlier. I wouldn't have continued with the story if I knew it would destroy your life. I would've been mad at you, I mean if I found out that you were doing something unethical, I would've been mad, but I would have talked to you. And then, I most likely would have tipped someone off to the story, claiming that I had a conflict of interest. But I couldn't live with myself if I knew that I'd ruined your career to advance mine."

I could feel my eyes welling with tears. "Thank you, MP. I know that even if I tell the truth, I still look guilty. Especially since I didn't say something sooner. Ross is gone, I'm still a person of interest in the investigation, and Austin showed up on my porch the day Higgins was fired, so he obviously thinks that he could get in trouble for whatever went down with him and Ross. Whatever happened was clearly an NCAA violation, and Austin knew it. Plus, Ross cornered me a few weeks ago, trying to get any information out of me that he could. And I'm dating the interim coach. This whole thing is a mess." Tears rolled down my cheeks. "I don't know what to do."

"Alexis, you're cooperating with the investigation, and you and Beau went public with your relationship. Sure, you didn't report Ross, but you also didn't give in to his demands. The way I see it, you did nothing wrong. You had a senior staffer pressuring you in your workplace. If anything, the fact that you didn't give him whatever he wanted shows your commitment to ethics."

"But, MP, I'm almost positive that Austin was cheating. I don't know how, but there is no way his work could have improved so dramatically."

"I think the best thing you can do at this point is hope that the person helping him comes forward. You're just a teacher who wants your students to do the work and turn in their assignments. If you didn't have evidence he was cheating, why would you have thrown him under the bus? You wanted—and still want—to see the best in all your students."

Even as he spoke, I knew that he was too optimistic about everything. I saw the way Ross looked at me. I was sure that he would come for blood.

42.

LAUREN

October 1, 5:52 p.m.

I had to dust the cobwebs off my curling iron before I could use it, that was how long it had been since I had styled my hair. For the first time in months, I was having a girls' night out. I decided that I would pull out all the stops. I was so tired of moping around my house, attempting to be a gardener. I was tired of the voice in my head complaining about being alone. I was going to make the life that I wanted to live, and part of that meant having a night out with my friends.

Planning the night had proven to be complicated. I had barely slept after I got off the phone with Sal in the early hours of the morning, and I was exhausted. It wouldn't be easy to find people who were free so last minute.

It didn't help that most of my friends were somehow connected to the athletic department and hadn't spoken to me much since Sal's firing. Sure, some of the wives had sent me friendly texts to make sure I was okay, but it was clear that they were only looking out for their own families. They wanted to make sure that what happened to me wouldn't happen to them next. The sporadic check-in messages had stopped weeks ago, and I had to face the harsh reality that they weren't real friends in the first place. We had become friends only out of proximity.

I ended up reaching out to two of my neighbors. One, Talia, was a professor at the university. She was young and fun. She reminded me of who I wanted to be when I was in my thirties. The other, my lawyer friend, Joan, had lived in Renton her whole life, yet somehow had no affiliation with the university. Her husband owned a backpacking store in a nearby town, and they spent most of their spare time hiking, instead of sitting in the stands of football games. It was an odd mix of people, but I had high hopes for the last-minute evening.

Talia and I met Joan at her car at six, and we were off.

Renton didn't have many restaurants. The few good ones would be packed on account of the football game. So instead, we headed to an Italian restaurant one town over. I realized that it was the first time in weeks I had spent significant time around people other than my son and nephew. It felt like I was swimming upside down. I knew what I was supposed to do, how I was supposed to react, but it felt like an out-of-body experience. I forced myself to breathe. I looked forward to crawling into bed when the night was over.

I wanted to be there, I reminded myself.

The conversation came easily. The best thing about this random pairing of friends was that we had a diverse range of things to talk about. Our lives only overlapped because we were neighbors. That left so many conversational doors waiting to be opened. After a few minutes at the table, I could feel myself starting to relax.

But then, I saw him, sitting alone at the bar. Or at least I saw someone who looked like Sal. I forced myself to look again. It wasn't him. Of course it wasn't. How could he have known I was coming here? More importantly, why would he care? But since his phone call early this morning, I felt fearful of Sal, of his unpredictability. Who knew what he was capable of?

"Are you ladies in town for the game this weekend?" our waiter asked nicely as he brought us our drinks. Due to the influx of people that would descend upon Renton for home football games, it was almost impossible to get a reservation in town, leaving anyone who procrastinated figuring out their dinner plans to venture to the towns close by.

"Oh no," Joan said warmly. "We're just having a girls' night out."

"Good, I'm glad you guys didn't come into town just for the weekend, the whole athletic department is such a mess, that would've been a waste of your time and money!" Oblivious, our waiter walked away.

"Oh gosh, Lauren, I'm sorry," Joan said awkwardly once he left.

"Oh, no, it's totally fine. This is not my ship to right anyhow," I said with a smile. When Sal and I ate out, it wasn't unusual for people to interrupt our meal to give their opinion on what he was or was not doing right. When he was a head coach, it had been even worse. I had learned to tune out these comments. They were rarely directed at me. If someone did acknowledge my presence, it was normally with some sort of sexist comment about how I needed to be good to my husband so that he could do his job. Or something patronizing about how my husband was a very important coach, did I know that? It wasn't worth listening to. "I'm just glad he didn't know who I was," I added with what I hoped was a lighthearted smile.

"Have you been stopped a lot since everything happened?" Talia asked with concern.

"No, I don't think I'm recognizable without Sal." I didn't mean to sound pathetic, but as soon as the words came out of my mouth, I realized how they sounded. Without Sal, I was invisible.

"How *are* you doing, Lauren?" Joan leaned in. She was a few years older than me. I could tell that she was trying to display empathy. It was sweet.

"I'm okay. I mean, this whole thing has obviously been such a nightmare." I thought about the phone call from Sal. "But, really, I'm okay."

"Have you started working with the divorce attorney?" Joan asked.

She'd given me a colleague's card a few weeks ago, but I had yet to make an appointment.

When she gave me the card, I tried not to read too much into it. I had called her after my first meeting with the investigation team. Even if I hadn't, in a town this small, everyone knew what Sal had done. The whole country knew what Sal had done. This situation reached beyond just neighborhood gossip.

"I guess I should. But I just don't know. It's so hard, I haven't even really had time to talk to Sal, and it's been a lot for me to process at once."

"He's moved out though, hasn't he? I haven't seen his car around a ton," Talia said in true small-town nosy neighbor fashion.

"He hasn't moved his stuff out, and I haven't seen him since the day he was fired."

Across the table, Talia and Joan shot each other concerned looks.

"What?" I asked.

"It's just that we've seen Sal, um, a few times since then. I ran into him last week in your driveway. He was just leaving as I was heading out for my walk." Joan's face flushed as red as a tomato.

"Last week?" My mind was spinning, trying to process the idea of Sal at our house.

"Yes, I figured that you two had an arrangement for him to come and get things while you were out. I've only ever seen him when your car is gone."

That meant that Sal had been in our house—my house—without my knowing. Even though we had been married for years, this felt weirdly violating. He had kept me in the dark about so much, and now here he was, continuing to sneak around. I didn't know if I should be more angry or afraid.

"Lauren? Are you okay?" Joan asked, placing a hand on my arm. I realized I hadn't responded. I couldn't find any words.

"Yeah, um, I'm fine. I guess I didn't realize that he was coming by the house. But it's his house as well. I'll just call him to talk through the logistics." I tried to act nonchalant, as if he and I talked on the phone regularly, but in reality, just saying the words out loud made my stomach turn. I thought about the Sal look-alike I had seen at the bar. I glanced in that direction again. He was there. He had been there the whole time. I hadn't been hallucinating. He was everywhere. He was following me. Smiling.

"Are you sure you're okay?" The words faded in and out. "Do you think we should call someone?" I heard the words but couldn't register where they came from or who they were directed toward.

"Air? Fresh air?" another voice asked.

"Lauren? Come walk?" I felt someone pull my arm around their shoulder and move me away from my seat. And then everything went black.

———

"Aunt Lauren? Are you okay?" I heard Graham's voice through my fog. He sounded concerned. He needed me. Something had happened. I needed to be there for him. My eyes snapped open. He hovered over me, pressing a cold cloth to my forehead. We were outside in the restaurant parking lot. I was too shaken up to feel embarrassed about passing out in public. I slowly sat up, trying to shake off the events of the night.

"Graham? I'm so sorry." I couldn't think of anything else to say. I had caused a scene, pulled him out of his normal life. And on a weekend when he was working.

"Please don't worry about it, it's totally fine. Joan called me, I'm one of your emergency contacts. Are you okay?" he asked me again. I felt relieved that Joan knew who Graham was, that she knew to call him. I realized I needed to remove Sal as my emergency contact.

"Yes." I sat up fully and wiped gravel off my hand. "I'm fine, I didn't sleep well, probably dehydrated." I looked around for Joan and Talia and spotted them both standing nearby, looking very concerned.

"I'll be fine," I said in their direction. "You guys go back and finish dinner."

"I'll drive you home," Graham said, helping me up slowly.

"Are you sure?" Joan and Talia said in unison.

"Yes, of course, I'm just dehydrated. I don't want to spoil your evening." They both looked reluctant. "I'm serious. I'm totally okay."

"Okay," Talia said with a smile and leaned in awkwardly to give me a hug.

"I'll call you tomorrow." Joan repeated Talia's awkward hug, and just like that, they were gone.

Graham and I walked slowly together to his car. He opened my door, guiding me into the seat, as if I were incapable of getting in the car on my own.

"I'm not dying, you know?" I tried to tease.

"I know, I know."

We drove in silence for a few minutes. I wasn't sure what to say. I suddenly felt embarrassed. It was just so much at once, and the thought of Sal following me to the restaurant felt scary.

"I'm so sorry that you got called away from work. I know that this weekend is a really crazy one for you."

"Oh my gosh, are you serious? When Joan called me, I was so spooked. She made it sound like you were dead on the concrete. I had to come." He paused. "Plus, the match was just starting when I left. I have a really good coworker who volunteered to cover for me until I get back. They will be fine."

"Well, I'm happy to know that if I'm ever dead on the concrete somewhere, you'll be there to collect the body. I need someone in my corner."

"So, what happened?" he asked abruptly, avoiding my feeble attempt at a joke.

I sighed.

"I found out that your uncle has been in the house." I didn't really know how to phrase it. When I said it out loud, it didn't seem like it was a big deal. I couldn't explain why it had hit me so dramatically.

Thankfully, Graham's face made my reaction feel justified.

"Wait, what?" His jaw looked like it might be permanently attached to the floor of the car.

"Talia or Joan, I honestly can't remember which, mentioned that she saw his car in front of the house the other day, as in he has been coming by. She said that she figured that he and I had an arrangement that he could come by when I wasn't home. I've barely heard from him since he left. I got a threatening call from him in the middle of the night and he accused me of tipping off the school about Richard, which I had no idea about, and he alluded to knowing that Joel had stopped by." I could feel the tears streaming down my cheeks. I thought about the Sal doppelgänger I saw at the restaurant, but I worried if I mentioned that, Graham would think I was crazy. Before I could register it, the words escaped my mouth. "I thought I saw him at the restaurant tonight. I just have this feeling that he's watching me."

Graham kept his eyes on the road ahead of him. I saw his fingers tighten around the steering wheel, his lips pursed tightly together.

"Do you want me to spend the night tonight?" From his response, I knew that he didn't think I was crazy. In fact, his response confirmed my fears.

"Do you think he's a risk?"

"I'm honestly not sure what to think, but I wouldn't be surprised by anything at this point, including him following you to dinner tonight."

With that, it was settled. Tonight, I would have an ally. Tonight, I would not be alone. I felt gratitude and pride for my nephew, even though I knew that he'd alert Hunter to this new development, and Hunter would insist on coming home. *I should be ready for his arrival.*

43.

Nora

October 1, 7:55 p.m.

There's something about the unity that occurs at a sporting event that makes everything worth it. It's the part I love most about my job. Sure, there would be a fan or two who would make a snide remark to me, but for the most part, especially if we were winning, everyone was just happy to be there.

The volleyball team won their first match. Granted, they played the lowest-ranked team in our conference, but a win was a win. We had our highest attendance of the season, as so many people were in town for the football and soccer games over the weekend. Our marketing and ticketing teams had worked all week to get students to the game by giving out free T-shirts. They had also created an incentive for football season ticket holders to attend the volleyball match.

It all felt worth it.

I found a seat next to Nathan and Margo. Margo pulled herself into my lap and rested her head against me to watch the game.

It all felt worth it.

"Mommy, that will be me," she declared proudly as she pointed to a player. She was in a volleyball phase. I reminded myself that it might not be a phase. She could be a volleyball player. Who was really to say?

"Want to meet the players after the game?" Nathan asked Margo. I shot him a strained look. That hadn't been part of the deal. I had hoped to sneak away quickly after the match. I thought of all the emails that still awaited a response. Having an impromptu meet and greet would make that impossible. But I also didn't want to be the mother who kept her daughter from meeting her role models. Nathan knew about the strained relationship I had with the volleyball coach. I doubted that asking him to let my daughter meet his players would help mend our differences or strengthen our tenuous relationship.

"Really, Mommy?" Her huge eyes stared up at me, full of hope.

"I'll see what I can do," I said with an overly wide smile. "Seriously, Nathan?" I mouthed over her head.

He shrugged as if he didn't understand why it was an issue, as if he hadn't done anything wrong. Maybe in his mind, he hadn't. He was just trying to be a good father, after all.

Margo eventually removed herself from my lap to watch the game sandwiched in between Nathan and me. Her joyful cheers warmed my tired heart. I loved being a mom. I loved being *her* mom.

I checked my phone, scanning through my email. I probably had forty-five minutes until the match ended. That would give me enough time to run to my office, answer a few emails, and make it back in time to introduce Margo to the team.

"Do you mind if I run to my office quickly?" I asked Nathan. "I need to get a few things done before tomorrow. I promise I'll be back before the end of the match."

"Nora, we set aside this time to be together, to have some family time."

"Nathan," I said sternly, "I have to go take care of a few things. I'll be gone for thirty minutes." Before he could argue, I grabbed my stuff and headed out of the gym. When I looked back before walking down the long hallway to my office, I saw Nathan staring at his phone. "If he was so concerned about spending time together as a family, he could start by paying attention to his daughter," I said to myself in a huff.

The back halls to my office were empty. I could hear the crowd cheering behind me. I loved the way the joyful noise echoed down the vacant hallway. It felt like I was surrounded by fans.

I noticed a door to a conference room had been left ajar. After I had found Sal in my office, I instructed the staff to make sure that all rooms were locked when they weren't in use. I dug through my bag to find my keys to lock the door. As I reached in to pull the door shut, I saw two very shocked faces looking at me from the corner of the room. I had apparently just walked in on a heated conversation between Sal and his nephew, Graham. I went inside and closed the door behind me.

"Nora—" both men started at the same time.

I held up my hand in protest. Both mouths instantly shut.

"What are you doing here?" I directed my question as equally to Graham as I did to Sal. Graham was supposed to be working, and I doubted whatever he was doing with Sal was the type of work the university paid him to do.

Both men looked at the floor. I wanted to scream. I wanted to throw something. I wanted to have a job where it was acceptable for me to show emotion. Instead, I stood stoically, refusing to give in. Refusing to be the one to snap. The three of us stood in a lopsided triangle, no one wanting to be the first to break the silence.

Finally, Graham spoke up. "This was not a planned family reunion, I promise. I ran into Sal by accident. I had to go out, I had a family emergency, and I saw him as I was coming back to the court. I wanted to try to talk to him, family member to family member. It was wrong. I should have gone straight to my supervisor." His answer made me respect him. He was just a kid. If he was telling the truth, he was trying to do the right thing.

I figured he was telling the truth because I saw Sal shoot him a chilling glare. Clearly, he thought that their encounter should have been kept within the family.

"Sal," I said, forcing my voice to be strong, in control, "what are you doing in my athletic complex?"

He scoffed. "Your athletic complex? Someone really needs to get off their high horse. I was the one who let you into this building in the first place. You're standing in a building that I built. Your athletic complex? This will never be yours. No matter what you do, who you fire, nothing will ever change the fact that you're only here because of me. This will always be mine."

Graham slowly took a step away from his uncle, moving carefully toward me, as if he was trying to show allegiance to me.

"Do you really think firing Ross will save this sinking ship you're captaining?" he asked, his voice growing more menacing with every word.

"Honestly, Sal, that's none of your business. You have no right to know why I made the decisions I made. You're no longer a part of the department. You have no right to be here. This isn't the first time that I've asked you to leave, but it will be the last. You need to stay out of this building. No attending games, no hanging out at tailgates. I don't want to hear even a rumor that you're anywhere near the university, let alone the athletic department."

"Honestly, dear, who helped you onto that high horse of yours? You're just giving yourself a higher distance to fall from."

I wanted to laugh at his ridiculous metaphor. No matter what stupid thing he said, I wouldn't bend. I wouldn't let him get into my head, not any more than he already was. "Sal, you have thirty seconds to explain to me why you are in this building, and then I'm calling security. I'll also be filing a restraining order first thing, banning you from any athletic-related activities. You have no right or reason to be here."

He gave a leering smile. "You want to know why I'm here? I'm here on some unfinished business. If you really knew what was good for you, you'd let me do my job."

"You don't have a job, Higgins." I pulled out my walkie-talkie and radioed security.

Sal let out a cackle of laughter. "You made a mistake firing Ross, Bennet. You don't know how many people want your head on a platter."

"No, you made a mistake." Graham stepped toward his uncle. "And there's a room full of fans just down the hallway who would like you to pay for it. You're lucky that they don't know you're here. That would be like throwing you to the wolves."

Before Sal could respond, the security guard on duty arrived, walking purposefully through the door.

"I'm responding to a call about a disturbance?" he asked before recognizing Sal cowering in the corner.

"Manny!" Sal said to the officer, as if remembering his name would negate the fact that he was trespassing.

"Higgins, I'm afraid you're not allowed to be here."

"Come on, Manny, after everything we've been through? Remember last year, the Christmas gifts for your kids?"

"I thanked you then. But that doesn't change the fact that you're not allowed to be here." With one quick motion, he grabbed Sal by the elbow and started maneuvering him toward the door. As he was dragged past me, it was impossible not to smell the alcohol on his breath.

44.

The Times

October 2, Sports Page

SAL HIGGINS DETAINED FOR DRUNK AND DISORDERLY CONDUCT

MASON PONT

Last night around 8:00 p.m., Sal Higgins was found at the Renton University athletic complex. When asked to leave by campus security, he refused. He was ultimately detained after refusing to submit to a breathalyzer test. He was released this morning. No one from the athletic department was available for comment.

A fan who attended last night's women's volleyball game reported they heard yelling coming from a conference room and suspects that Higgins had snuck into the building, although his motives for doing so are uncertain. The fan's identity has remained anonymous for their safety.

This story comes on the tail of the firing of Renton's head football coach, Richard Ross, earlier this week.

The Griffons volleyball team won the match three sets to two against fellow unranked conference member Clifton State. Clifton and Renton will square off again tomorrow at 5:00 p.m. Tickets are available through the Griffon ticket office.

45.

ANNE

October 2, 8:10 a.m.

I was sipping my to-go coffee listening to my favorite pump-up playlist when I noticed a familiar figure leaning against the bus stop.

"Taking the bus today?" I teased as I made my way toward Graham.

"I was hoping I'd catch you on your walk to work. I have to tell you what happened last night." He looked tired and concerned. I imagined that he looked forward to the long day ahead of us as much as I did.

"If I'd known you were waiting for me, I would've brought you a coffee."

"I've already had two cups today. I couldn't sleep last night."

"What happened?"

"Ever since you told me your theory about Sal still being involved"—I couldn't help but notice that he didn't call him *Uncle Sal*—"I've been looking into it, trying to figure things out. Last night, well, it was honestly crazy. First, I got a phone call that my aunt had fainted at a restaurant, so I had to leave to take her home. And then as soon as I got back to the complex, I heard someone in a room that was supposed to be locked. So, I went to check on it, and there trying to log on to a laptop was Sal."

I stopped walking and stared at him, mouth open. "What?"

He paused and pulled out his phone, showing me the article by MP detailing the incident. I could only imagine how many irate calls I'd have to field today.

"I don't know if it was better or worse that I was the one who found him. I was trying to figure out what he was doing, why he was there, but he wouldn't say anything. And, as MP reported, he was rather drunk, so even what little he did say didn't make sense. He kept saying names, people who I'm assuming are donors that he owes some sort of favor to. We weren't alone for very long before Nora found us."

"Wait, what?" My mouth seemed incapable of saying anything else.

"I know, I guess she'd been heading to her office for something. But as soon as she arrived, he got mad, like so mad. And at one point she implied that it wasn't the first time that she had told him to leave the athletic complex, which means you were right, he had been snooping around before."

My mind was spinning. I knew that my hunch was rooted in something deeper than just the normal paranoia that I carry around. It felt different, slimy. But that didn't make it easier for Graham. This wasn't just his old boss. This was his family. This wasn't the moment for an "I told you so." He was too close.

"Have you talked to him since?" I asked.

"No, and I hadn't spoken to him in weeks. At first, I was so mad at how he was handling the situation, and then—I don't know."

"So what do you think happened?"

He stopped and looked around. There were a few students on their way to class, but otherwise the street was empty. I was grateful to have a reason to stop and catch my breath; the hill felt extra steep today. "I think he knew I was the one who originally tipped off MP."

"How would he have figured that out? Nothing MP has reported would've clued him in."

"He sent me a text a few nights ago. I'd gone over to my aunt's house, and Joel Bonne was there. I didn't know Joel would be there. Joel has known my aunt for years, but I don't think she knew he was going to show up. But that night when I got home, Sal sent me a text about the importance of not betraying family and reminded me that it was thanks to him that I had gotten my job in the first place. I didn't respond, of course. It was the first time he had reached out to me since he was fired."

"You still interviewed for your job, though, right?"

"Yeah, I still went through the process like anyone else, but he was right, having the AD as one of your references makes you a pretty good candidate. And now I'm forever connected to a man the entire nation knows to be a fraud. I work in compliance; this doesn't look good. Or worse, what if Sal had tried to leverage the fact that he had a family member working in the building? I didn't do anything unethical, but he never asked. I can't help but wonder if the ask was coming. Like if he was biding his time, waiting for me to get comfortable and then connected, then ask me to do his bidding. I don't know. I've been over-thinking every interaction." His voice sounded strained. I had never thought about the fact that he might believe he owed his short-lived career to his uncle.

"You've done nothing wrong. You know that you're good at your job, right? I hear your name mentioned all the time. Sure, you might have used your connections to get the job, but you have more than earned your place." I tried to sound encouraging. I envied his privilege, that he had a connection to help him get the job. It would have been stupid, in my opinion, not to use that connection.

He gave me a weak smile and started walking again.

"Well, I think that seeing me with Joel in his own home was enough to make him think that I might be a traitor."

"You aren't a traitor, you did the right thing."

"Well, a traitor to my family."

"Do you think your aunt believes you're a traitor?" I asked.

He thought about it for a moment.

"I'm honestly not sure. I don't think she has any idea that I was the one who tipped off MP, but I should've gone to her first, before I went to anyone in the media. I thought that she had at least some idea that something shady was happening. I had no idea that she was blind to the whole thing. I would've gone to her first. I didn't mean for her life to be turned upside down." He paused to catch his breath. "When I ran into Sal last night, he was drunk, but he kept firing insults at me, giving words to my deepest fears. One of the things he told me was that I had betrayed my family. He said that I had made my aunt's life a living hell."

I could feel my blood pressure rising. What a manipulative thing to say. "He was the one who made her life a living hell. It's not your fault that he's shady, it's not your fault that he didn't tell his wife what he was up to. You were protecting your family. You reported it before things got worse." I paused to catch my breath. "Do you have any idea what he would want to access on the computer?"

"Contact information? That's my top theory. The computers also have donation records. He might be checking in on people, making sure they stayed true to their word? I'm honestly not sure."

"Can I ask you something?"

He nodded.

"How did you find out about your uncle's, umm"—I wasn't sure how to phrase it delicately—"scandals?"

I had wanted to ask him about it for weeks, since he told me that he had led MP to the story, but I hadn't found the right moment. I especially didn't want to come off as accusatory. But I had to wonder how it was that Sal's wife and the whole department were in the dark, but Graham had somehow known something was amiss?

"He got sloppy. I'm still not sure if it was intentional or not. There's part of me that thinks that he wanted me to find out, because he wanted me on his team, like this was the gateway to getting me to work with him. I'm sure that never in his wildest dreams would he have thought I'd report him. Like I said, he clearly placed a high value on not betraying one's family. I didn't tell him that MP had contacted me about a story, but at that point, MP wanted to write about student-athlete compensation. It wasn't that wild of a story. I mean, it's kind of a worn-out story, honestly, but MP thought he could approach it from a few new angles, like if he followed a school for a season, but with limited people knowing. He'd just started reaching out to professors when I found out."

"Wow, what a lucky break for MP . . ."

"Seriously. His original premise probably wouldn't have really made news. I mean, there's like a story a month about paying student-athletes. It wasn't something that would have landed him on *SportsCenter*.

"But anyway, I found out about everything when we were on vacation, and Sal had forgotten the charger for his university laptop, so he asked if he could use my computer. He has a newer laptop and my charger wouldn't work. You can only access the university servers from a university-issued computer. I didn't think anything of it. When I went back to my computer, I went to pull up my email and noticed he hadn't logged out. I mean, he'd been using his university email to communicate with people. Like, the number one rule of hiding a crime is to have a burner email account or at least one that can't be accessed by your employer. He had left open an email about repaying some debt, I can't remember exactly what it said, but it was enough that I knew something was off. I called MP, and he said that he'd start looking into it. He reoriented his questions and started getting some crazy responses from people. That's when we realized how deep this thing ran."

He stopped to catch his breath. We were almost to the office.

"Once we knew what we were looking for—or I guess it was MP who did all of the research, I just tipped him off to who I thought would be good key people to use as sources—it was like dominoes. Everything fell slowly and then all at once."

"Okay, so what can I do to help? I mean, is there anything we can even do?"

"I guess if anyone makes another comment like that donor did the other day, anything that is suspicious, could you write it down? We can make a list of anything that could be a potential clue as to what he's after?" For the first time since I had known him, Graham sounded insecure, unsure of what we should do next.

"Yes, of course."

He reached out and opened the door, nodding at me as he turned to walk down the hallway that led to his side of the building.

"We're going to figure this out," he said as he walked away. I wasn't sure if he said this more for my sake or his.

46.

ALEXIS

October 2, 2:00 p.m.

"Do you know how hard it is to get caught on a drunk and disorderly?" one of my students whisper-shouted to the girl sitting next to him. "I mean seriously, the dude must have been druuuuunk." He elongated the word as if he were under the influence. This conversation, like many of the student conversations I overheard, made me cringe. On any other day, a comment like this would have caused me to just roll my eyes. But I had spent my entire day listening to students talk about their drunk exploits that had not warranted a drunk and disorderly. It was as if Higgins getting caught added to their theory that they were invincible, somehow above the law.

The joy of being in your early twenties.

It had been hard to get any of my students to pay attention today. The news of Higgins's detention had captivated them.

"I'm sorry to interrupt this very important conversation, but I would like to start my class now," I said, glaring at the student.

He responded by sliding down in his chair and nodding at me.

When Ross had been fired, it had caused a minor distraction. Students talked about it in passing, but with the exception of a few, I never got the impression that they cared about anything other than the social aspect of sports. The detention of Higgins, on the other hand, was personal, relatable. They had all spent time drunk on the streets of Renton.

I found the whole spectacle very annoying. It was a fluke that MP had gotten the latest story at all. He and I were walking to meet Beau in his office during a break in the volleyball match when we heard yelling coming from a conference room. We knew instantly that it was Higgins. He has a very distinctive voice.

It had been easy to tell Sal was drunk. He slurred his words with self-righteous importance. We stood there watching as security showed up and escorted him out of the building. Nora and another exhausted-looking athletic department employee followed close behind. Moments later, Renton PD showed up and pushed Sal into the back of a police cruiser.

There was a small part of me that felt like this was vindication. Not worth the headache and pain of the last year, but a small step toward righting the scales. It's not often that you get to watch your enemy get apprehended by the police.

———

After my class, I found myself walking toward Talia's office. Her class had finished earlier than mine, but there was a good chance she'd still be in her office. I was desperately hoping that she'd join me for an early happy hour.

Her office door was slightly cracked, so I pushed it open, letting myself in. To my surprise, MP sat across the desk from Talia, whose face flushed bright red when she saw me. I looked to MP and back to Talia, feeling like I was going to give myself whiplash.

"Hey . . . sorry, I should've knocked."

"Yeah, no, it's totally okay!" Talia said overenthusiastically.

"I was just heading out anyways. I'll see you at the game tonight?" MP asked me as he gathered his stuff.

"Sure, see you tonight." I don't know why it bothered me to see him there, but whatever was going on between my best friend and my cousin, for some reason I assumed I should've been in the loop.

He quickly finished gathering his things and nodded at Talia before heading out the door.

"Sorry about that," Talia said, straightening things out on her desk, nervously tucking her hair behind her ears.

"I didn't realize you two knew each other?" This felt like the most innocent and nonaccusatory way to ask why my cousin was in her office. I'd told her that MP was my cousin a few weeks after his first article had run. The chatter around the department had died down, and admitting the connection had felt like proving my innocence. If my family member wrote the story, then I must be clean.

She searched her desk nervously until finally, her eyes met mine. "Could you shut the door?"

I took a step aside and shut the door, slowly settling into a chair across from Talia, the one my cousin had just occupied.

"I've been working with MP." She said the words so quickly that they almost came out as one. "He contacted me almost a year ago—he was cold-calling professors that were in athlete-heavy departments. He wanted to interview me for a piece he was working on. At the time it was about student-athletes and preferential treatment, nothing really that hasn't already been reported on by thousands of sports reporters. I shared with him that a few semesters ago, I walked into a conference room that I thought was empty. I needed a change of scenery. But I walked in on Nathan and Sal talking with an athlete about his tutoring situation. I didn't hear much, but I heard enough to know that the athlete was paired with a tutor who would essentially do all the coursework for him, making sure he got a passing grade and continued eligibility. I mentioned this to MP in our first interview. I forgot I'd said anything until he called me a few weeks later, saying the story's angle had changed, and he wanted to know if I'd take part in the piece that exposed Sal. I didn't know the whole scope of the project until it was public. I didn't tell anyone that I was one of the sources. I didn't want to lose my job or my friends. But I don't think it matters now. I think Sal found out somehow that I was one of the sources."

"Oh my gosh, Talia." Instantly I realized what was at risk for my friend. "Talia, are you safe? Are you okay?"

"That's why I was talking with MP. Alexis, I'm not sure what I'm supposed to do. I didn't realize what I was getting myself into when I told him I would be a source. I mean, I work in the English department for goodness' sake. I care about ethics and journalism. But I didn't know who I was dealing with when I first started talking to MP. None of us did. When all this started, I didn't know that he was your cousin. I'm not sure if I could have told you either way, but I would have handled myself differently if I'd known. I should have known." Her face looked pained with remorse.

"It's okay. I just feel like the world's worst friend because I had no idea that any of this was going on."

She smiled. Her eyes had glazed over with tears.

"I didn't tell anyone. I couldn't tell anyone. Especially not someone who's in the department. I didn't want to put anyone else in danger. I didn't want to put myself in danger. But at the end of the day, all that effort didn't matter."

"What do you mean?"

I watched her look nervously around the office as if she was considering whether the room was bugged.

"Sal's been threatening me," she said finally. "At first, I thought it was a joke, or like some weird spam. It started with emails, saying that I needed to stop talking about what I had witnessed. But after Ross was fired, he showed up while I was out to dinner. I had actually gone to dinner with his wife and our other neighbor. Lauren had to leave right after our drinks arrived—it was a weird medical thing—Graham, her nephew, had to come pick her up. When I went to the bathroom, Sal cornered me. He told me I didn't know who I was dealing with, and if I didn't shut my mouth, I would find myself unemployed next semester. Then he stormed out. I think he might've been following Lauren? Then he went to the athletic complex. He must have been on a rampage last night, trying to tie up loose ends." She shook as she spoke. I handed her a tissue.

"Do you think Lauren leaving the restaurant was actually a fluke?"

Talia nodded. "The more I think about it, the more I think she got spooked. She's barely left the house since Sal got fired, and when Joan, our neighbor who was also at dinner, mentioned that Sal had been at their house, it was clear she had no idea he'd been there."

"Wait, what?"

"Joan had seen his car in their driveway. She thought he was there to pick up the rest of his stuff or something, but Lauren had no idea. It might be to her advantage that she's holed up at her house. If Sal only goes to the house when she's gone, he doesn't have many opportunities."

"Okay, circling back to MP, did you actually have other tips for him? I mean, other than seeing Nathan and Sal in the conference room and seeing him at the restaurant?" I worried that she knew I had been approached by Ross, that I was one of the professors that she tipped MP off to.

"I didn't talk about you," she said, as if reading my mind. "I did hear about Ross asking you to fudge Austin's grade, but I knew that you didn't actually do it."

"Wait, how did you find out? And how did you know I didn't do anything unethical?"

"People talk, Alexis." She said this as if it didn't even need to be said. "Someone knew someone who was tutoring Austin. I don't know how you were in the dark about the whole thing. Maybe it was better that way. But people started talking about Ross and the 'tutors' he would hire to help his athletes. In reality, being a tutor meant writing their papers. There was no actual tutoring. As far as I know, no one ever actually met with the athlete they were tutoring. The whole thing was a mess. Early in the spring semester, this was after I heard him talking with Sal, I had my normal meeting with Professor Bennet. The whole meeting felt really off. He started asking me about wanting to advance my career." She paused to look around the office again.

"He asked me if I was interested in earning some extra money. He heard I had just bought a house and asked if I ever thought about tutoring. I know that the NCAA has really strict rules about tutoring athletes, and at that point I didn't even think he was implying that I tutor athletes, I thought he just meant students in the English department. And then I realized, it was all part of a bigger scheme. It wasn't just the one athlete in the conference room. I ended up signing my book deal around the same time, which gave me a good reason to back out. But then MP got in touch, and I told him everything I had witnessed, including my recent conversation with Nathan."

This was beginning to feel like the interconnected plot of a soap opera. I couldn't help but wonder when, if ever, something would come out about Nathan. Was MP waiting to drop that bomb, or was Nora doing something to ensure that it didn't get released?

"Nathan has always given me a weird vibe." I wasn't ready to mention that Nathan had cornered me about meeting with Ross. I wanted to hear the end of her story first.

"Seriously. So, I got myself entangled in this mess, and now Sal knows. I think he assumes that I was the one who tipped off the investigation team to get Ross fired, but I honestly don't think I was. I mean, I don't know who else is a source, but I mentioned Ross in my first interview with MP, months ago. I never talked with Ross. I never had one of his athletes in my class. I've spent most of my time talking about Nathan."

"Were you friends with Sal? I mean, you were his neighbor, right?"

"Like, 'smile at him on the sidewalk' level, but I never really talked to him. But Lauren and I would chat, and we get drinks every couple of months. Like I said, we just went out last night, but I got the feeling that she was scraping the bottom of her friendship barrel, the whole thing was really last minute. I think she's lonely. Most of her friends were from the athletic department. But I mean regardless, he knew who I was. And now he knows what I did."

I thought about that for a moment. "Do you think Sal's trying to preemptively stop you from getting Nathan fired?"

"Maybe."

"What did MP say?"

"Well, he assured me that he didn't leak who his sources were. Like, I don't even know who else he's talked to. He's trying to keep this all as private as possible. I think he realized from the start what's at stake."

"Would you feel better if you stayed at my house for a while?"

"I would feel better if Sal was gone for good."

I was sure that she wasn't the only one in town who had that feeling. Before I saw him last night, I didn't think he was still in Renton. Beau made it seem like no one had heard from or seen him since August. But maybe Beau's naivete to Sal's whereabouts was what made him the ideal candidate for the head coaching job.

47.

LAUREN

October 4, 11:23 a.m.

"The new guy did well," Hunter announced over our makeshift brunch.

Graham had called Hunter immediately after my fainting incident at the restaurant. Hunter used it as an excuse to make the trip home, and he conveniently arrived just in time to watch the football game.

"I heard. The parties on campus seemed to go on all night." I realized that this comment made me sound old.

"Yeah, I forgot how loud this town gets on game nights." He sipped his coffee. "So, anyway, Kennedy wasn't half bad. I was really surprised; I think that Bennet made the right call. He's new, too, so I bet he wasn't involved in the drama. I mean, we were projected to win even before Ross was fired, but it helps that Kennedy held them to three points. Hopefully, that'll shut up concerns about our defense."

I'd had the game on in the background yesterday afternoon. I migrated between reading on the back deck, soaking up the last rays of the sun, and prepping dinner. I had so many conflicting feelings about my fandom. I reminded myself that before I was a coach's wife, I was a fan. But being a fan, if Sal was somehow still intermixed in all of this, felt unethical and like a betrayal of sorts.

"Mom, are you okay?" Hunter's voice pulled me back to the present.

"Yeah, I'm fine, I was just lost in thought."

"No, I mean like overall, are you okay? Graham told me that you thought Dad might be poking around the house without you knowing. If he is, that's creepy."

This was such an odd conversation to have with my son. I knew that he was old enough to hear the truth. He was no longer a kid. I didn't need to hide the harsh realities of life from him. But that didn't change the fact that I didn't want to put him in the middle of this conflict. I didn't want to use him to get information on his father. But it felt like a gray area. I was genuinely concerned for my safety.

"It'll be okay. I don't think your father would actually do something to physically hurt me. I'm more worried about what could still be hiding in the house that he wants access to. I don't want to be found with anything incriminating."

"Okay, so should we search the house?"

I had been intending to look through the house, but I had honestly been afraid to do it alone. I was afraid of what I would find. It felt like a violation of Sal's privacy, even though if he had hidden something in the house, it could cause me to look guilty.

We decided to start at opposite ends of the house and meet in the middle. Hunter started in the garage, and I went upstairs. It was hard to search for something when I had no idea what I was looking for. Would our time be better spent if we searched the hard drives of our computers? Or had he hidden some sort of flash drive under the floorboards? Every possibility felt too dramatic.

As I searched, I found myself wondering if I had enabled him. I always went out of my way to make sure that our family was safe, taken care of. I had been the one to call Joel for a favor after Sal's DUI. I never left Sal to his own devices. So many what-ifs ran through my head. Each one matched with its own type of regret. There was no escaping the reality that I should have known that something was wrong.

I felt robbed of my chance to be the one to walk away for once.

I decided to start in our room because it was the place I knew best. I also doubted that he would've been bold enough to hide something in a room I frequented every day. I didn't find anything, and a wave of relief washed over me.

I padded my way down the hallway to the linen closet, a door I was almost positive that Sal had never opened—the man hadn't folded a towel or done laundry the entire time we were together. I found nothing there, either. I went to the hall bathroom next. Since Hunter had moved out, it had gone almost untouched; in fact, for months I had been meaning to call a plumber to fix the broken toilet.

I wiggled the handle of the toilet. It still wasn't flushing. I'd call the plumber in the morning. Just to be thorough in my search, I lifted the lid off the tank. In shock I dropped it and it crashed to the floor, barely missing my foot. The tank was filled with cash, carefully arranged in neat rows. I could hear Hunter rushing up the stairs. He'd obviously heard the crash.

"Are you okay?" he asked, and then his eyes went to the tank. "Is that . . . ?"

I nodded. "Money."

The toilet lid lay broken on the floor; tiny shards of porcelain had flown everywhere. I didn't even think to warn Hunter to watch for sharp pieces as he made his way into the room. All I could think about was the dirty money that Sal had hidden in my house. How long had it been there? How had I not known? What else could he be hiding?

"Wow, um, okay." Hunter's eyes darted around the room. "A few months ago, Dad told me that this bathroom was out of commission. I guess this was why . . . wait, what is that?"

My eyes followed to where he pointed. A chunk of the lid had smashed against the wall and pushed back a piece of plaster around the bathtub. It had clearly been altered. A corner of what looked like a piece of paper was now exposed.

Hunter navigated his way through the shards and fully pushed back the panel.

"What is that?" I asked. I felt paralyzed. I couldn't believe that what I was seeing was real.

He pulled out a stack of files, each one detailing some high-profile donor or person connected to the department. It looked to be a giant pile of blackmail.

"This is evidence," I said once I realized what we had found. It was real. It had all been hidden in my house. I wondered if this was everything. If Sal had been in the house, there was a good chance he had already removed some things. But looking at how the files had been securely hidden behind the plaster, it would have been impossible for him to remove them without me noticing a giant hole in my wall. Maybe the files were just his backup. It would be ironic if Sal finally had taken my advice and begun making a backup plan.

As I flipped through the documents, it became clear that this was how he manipulated people; he had everyone around him on a string. I found a file for Nora that was relatively blank. It listed her age and experience before taking the job at Renton. It also mentioned that her husband, Nathan, and young daughter, Margo, could be used as possible leverage. Included in the file was a picture of her daughter, taken a few years earlier.

Nathan's file was directly under Nora's and held multiple pages, more than triple the number in Nora's. It detailed conversations the two men had had, student-athletes who had taken Nathan's classes, and transcripts for those students. There was a sexual assault complaint filed by a student, which Sal had managed to make disappear. There was evidence that Sal had used this to blackmail Nathan, ensuring that the English department would always be in Sal's back pocket. I couldn't help but wonder if Nathan and Sal were still in contact, if somehow he was using what he had on Nathan to get him to influence Nora. I didn't know what their marriage was like. What if Sal was prompting Nathan to ask Nora specific questions on his behalf? It seemed ridiculous but plausible. Everything seemed plausible now.

The whole situation felt diabolical. I couldn't believe the web he had woven. He had created fail-safe after fail-safe.

I continued flipping through the stack. Some of the faces and names I recognized, while others were foreign to me. It looked like he had gathered as much information on as many people as possible just in case he found himself needing it. I found a file for me, for Hunter, and for Graham. He had a file for our neighbor, Talia, who he seemed to believe was one of Mason Pont's sources. There was a thin file for Pont; it was clear that Sal had been aware of his existence but hadn't thought him to be a threat.

In the file on Joel, he detailed my family's connection with him. He had assumed that the only reason he got the Renton interview was because I had been sleeping with Joel. The documentation seemed fueled by jealousy. I got the impression Sal had been trying to take down Joel for a long time. Their relationship was clearly closer than Sal had led me to believe. From the file, it was obvious that Sal and Joel had regular contact. Sal kept detailed records of it all.

The whole thing made my stomach turn.

"Mom?" We had both been so quiet flipping through the pages, I had almost forgotten Hunter was still in the room. "What do we do now?"

"I have to tell Nora." I tried to sound as authoritative as possible.

"Do you think we should turn everything over to the police first?"

I thought about it for a moment. For years I had been stuck playing my husband's game. Nora had been an unwilling player as well. She deserved to know what he had on her. What he had on everyone.

I couldn't turn this over to the police and just hope they handled it correctly. I couldn't blindside Nora like Sal had blindsided me. I wanted

Nora to see everything for herself. If we turned the files over to the police, there was no guarantee they'd let her read through everything Sal had documented.

I found myself rooting for Nora. I didn't want the documents to get into the wrong hands and the information they contained about her family to be used against her.

And Nora deserved to know everything. After being in the dark for so long, she deserved to have some control over the outcome. Giving her the information would allow her a chance to make a decision. I would have done my due diligence. What we had found in the bathroom had the power to be the beginning of the end to all of this.

48.

NORA

October 7, 6:04 p.m.

After a long day, Nathan went to pick up our take-out dinner. If I was honest, it wasn't the ideal night for a family dinner. But we were doing it for Margo. Since August, we hadn't eaten dinner together at our table. One of us always seemed to be working late or running late. And after days of my leaving the office later than intended, Nathan had made it clear that he thought I needed to focus more on our family and less on my work.

I was barely keeping my head above water, but this was more important. And even without Nathan's frustrations about my work-life balance, I worried I was neglecting Margo—she was still not sleeping through the night. It felt like I was spinning seven plates piled high with food, desperately trying to keep any from falling to the floor.

The day called for pizza.

Margo had come home from school in tears because one of the kids in her class had teased her. I had another interview with the investigation team. They made it clear that though they were nearing the end of the process, they still needed to tie up some substantial loose ends. I had no idea what that meant for the future of the athletic department. Volleyball was still a mess. And, despite the football team's win over the weekend, I was still getting significant pushback around the firing of Ross.

I was twenty-five minutes into a halfhearted workout when I heard Nathan open the front door. I let out a breath of frustration. I felt like I never had enough time or energy to do anything fully. I would try to work out again tomorrow. Or not. I couldn't do it all.

I heard Margo running down from her room to greet her father, and a few moments later, Nathan appeared in the doorway of the kitchen with Margo clinging like a koala to his leg.

"I bought wine!" he said triumphantly. He handed me the bottle. I recognized it as one I had mentioned liking a few years ago. I uncorked it and poured two glasses as he started setting the table.

"I love this wine," I said, taking a sip.

"I know, I remembered."

The way he said it felt almost romantic, like we were in our early days of dating, instead of sitting at the table with our daughter. As if he was trying to impress me.

Margo went into detail about her traumatic day at school. We listened with compassion. She then launched into describing the class pet, a cockatoo named Bernie, before asking if she could be excused to go play.

Margo's absence was felt. I no longer had a bubbly six-year-old chattering away to carry the conversation. I awkwardly started gathering up the plates, hoping Nathan would take it as a cue that I had no energy to talk more.

"So, how was work today?" Nathan asked as he followed me with more dishes.

"It's been busy. Every time I think I have this job under control, something else comes up. But it'll all work itself out. I'm just ready to move out of survival mode. How was your day?" I realized that I had become so all-consumed by my own life that I barely had asked Nathan about his semester.

"It was okay. I had my upper-level classes today, which I prefer. The students in those classes seem to actually want to be there, which really helps. Hey, I meant to ask you, the night that we went to the volleyball game, that was the same night that they found Higgins drunk hanging around the athletic complex, right?"

Life had been so busy we hadn't even debriefed on that.

"Yes, it was."

"That's crazy. Do you know why he was there in the first place?" I could tell that Nathan was trying to ask casually, but it was clear that he had some sort of agenda.

"You know, I'm not really sure. Maybe he just wanted to walk down memory lane and see his old workplace."

"You don't think he was trying to access anything in particular? I mean, you had just fired Ross, who clearly was still in communication with him."

I couldn't help but note that he mentioned that Ross had still been in communication with Higgins. This was not something that had been made public.

"Nathan, I can't really talk to you about this. I'm in the middle of dealing with a department-wide scandal, it's really not something that I can talk candidly about. I'm sorry. It takes up almost my entire workday, and it's the last thing I want to think about when I'm home."

As I spoke, I watched his expression change. He had clearly been trying to act nonchalant, but when he realized that he wasn't going to get any information from me, his eyes burned with rage.

"Nora, I don't think you understand what you're dealing with. I'm trying to help you."

I tried to hide my shock. I had never heard Nathan use that tone with me. I tried to keep my voice as calm as possible. I didn't want Margo to hear us fighting. "You're right, Nathan, we don't know what we're dealing with, which is why the university and I decided to take the NCAA's investigation so seriously. It's also why I'm not at liberty to talk about it with people outside the circle."

"Outside the circle? I'm the father of your child, we're married, does that mean nothing to you? I'm the closest thing to inside the circle that you have." His voice was steadily getting more aggressive.

"Nathan, that doesn't mean that I can disclose information to you that isn't available to the general public. I'm not allowed to discuss this. It puts everyone at risk. I am not going to put our family at risk."

"Nora"—he lowered his voice to a threatening whisper—"you need to tell me what you know. Who's going to be fired next? I need to know if Higgins got the papers. Or were you able to get your hands on them? I'm trying to keep our family safe."

I tried to make sense of his question. I was still reeling from his sudden change in demeanor. I had no idea what papers Higgins was trying to get ahold of. I thought of the night I caught him in the building and the day I found him in my office. Both times he had been trying to access something on a computer. I had no idea what he was trying to find. It was clear that Nathan knew.

"Nathan, I can't tell you anything regarding the investigation that's not available to the public. I don't know anything about what Sal's up to now, or what papers you're referring to. I'm keeping my family safe. I did nothing wrong. Our family is fine. That's all that matters."

He let out a cynical laugh.

"You think I'm really that stupid? You think that you can feign naivete and I'll actually believe you? You know what I'm talking about. I wouldn't be surprised if you and Helen worked together to make sure that Pont got the right information. You've always been so power hungry. You never could stand the idea of someone else running the athletic department. And you know that Helen is best friends with Talia in the English department. Was that another strategic plant? You were so mad that my career was taking off that you sent her to spy on me?

Are you happy now? While taking down Higgins you had to destroy my life as well? Or what about promoting Beau, who is conveniently dating someone who Ross was trying to blackmail? That was a perfect coincidence, wasn't it, Nora? Stop acting stupid. You're more cunning than the world gives you credit for. But not me, I know what you were up to. I see right through you, I always have. Now I need to know where those papers are, if Higgins is lying about not having them. You have to think about our family. Think about what this would do to Margo."

My head was spinning. I had no idea what papers he was talking about. But they were obviously important enough that Nathan was worried about the repercussions of them getting out. Nathan's reaction clearly signaled that he was somehow guilty.

"Nathan, I need you to leave."

He threw a wineglass against the wall, shattering it and sending beads of red wine across the kitchen.

"You're not as innocent as you pretend to be, Nora. I can't wait to see how they destroy you. You might try to take me down, but don't forget, I know you. If I'm going down, I'll drag you with me."

"Nathan, I'm not going to ask you again, you need to leave my house." I heard my voice wobbling. I didn't care where he went. I needed him gone.

I watched through my tear-filled eyes as he grabbed his keys off the counter and stormed out of the house, slamming the door behind him. I hated that he made me emotional, that he had made me lose my edge. Suddenly, Margo's face appeared in the doorway of the kitchen looking stunned.

"Mommy, are you okay? Where did Daddy go?"

I learned my arms against the kitchen counter, bracing myself, forcing myself to breathe slowly. I was not going to hyperventilate.

"Honey, can you grab my phone?"

With shaking hands, I dialed the only person I could think of who might know how to help, Lauren Higgins.

49.

ANNE

October 7, 8:00 p.m.

I loved October evenings. They felt like a hopeful end to my long days. Noel and I had started walking together in the evenings. Her class schedule was more rigorous than she had originally thought, and I was exhausted after spending all day answering phones, so we decided that we would commit to spending time outside for at least half an hour every day. It helped that Renton was the best version of itself in October. The trees were turning to the most beautiful shades of orange and red, and the sunset crested in a perfect silhouette behind the mountains in the not-too-far-off distance.

I really loved this small town. Part of me wondered if I should stay after I graduated.

Noel had started the process of applying for grad schools. She wanted to get her MFA and then go on to be a professor. The first round of deadlines was fast approaching.

"So, you don't think grad school is for you?" she asked me as we walked slowly along the university's river path.

"I don't know. I think honestly, I just need a break from school for a while. I think that's been the best part of the internship, I've realized how much I really like the routine of a normal job."

"I don't get that. If I could stay in school for the rest of my life, I think I would," she said in a dreamlike voice. I believed her. She was the only person I knew who really never complained about their classes and went to a professor's office hours to actually connect and network with the professor.

"What is that?" Noel said, suddenly sounding scared. She pointed to a group of lights in the distance.

"I don't think there are supposed to be cars on the trail, do you think it's just a really intense bike light?"

"Maybe?"

We both started walking quicker, toward the source of the light.

As we got closer, we could make out voices—angry voices, slightly muffled by the evening wind.

"You're kidding me, did you actually think that would work?" one of them shouted. They clearly didn't care that anyone could hear them. Not that there were many people on the trail.

"I'm telling you, it's only a matter of time. You needed to be more careful," a deeper voice retorted. "What are you going to do now that the evidence is gone? I'm not going to let you ruin my life. And how are we supposed to know it's actually gone, that you're not lying to protect yourself?"

"Would you quit talking so loudly?" a third voice warned in a whisper-shout.

Noel and I cautiously continued on the path. She had her hand on the pepper spray she kept on her key ring. I pulled out my phone, ready to dial for help if needed.

"Should we keep going?" I whispered to her. This part of the trail was almost always deserted, which was why Noel and I liked walking this way, toward the mountains away from campus. The change of scenery was good for our souls, and we liked the peace and quiet it brought. But it now felt secluded and eerie.

"I'm sure it's fine," Noel said confidently. "The sun has barely set, and most likely they're just drunk. Plus, if we get a little closer, we'll be able to see them, you know, in case we actually do have to call the cops."

We rounded the corner, and their figures came into view. The three men stood in the small parking lot that allowed access to the trail.

I stopped involuntarily.

"Noel, I know them."

She had also stopped walking, recognition showing on her face, too. "Me, too . . . well, at least one—that's my professor." She pointed to Nora's husband. I had seen him in the office so many times that I knew his face well.

Without speaking, we took shelter beneath one of the massive oaks, shadowed from view but close enough that we could still hear the conversation.

"He's also my boss's husband. He comes into the office all the time. And that's Sal Higgins, and that's Richard Ross." We listened as the men continued to debate.

A pair of headlights cut through the twilight. We watched as the car drove down the steep, narrow road before it passed out of our view. We heard the tires crunching on the gravel of the parking lot.

"Someone else is coming," Noel whispered, leaning forward. Her voice was a mix of fear and excitement.

The car door opened and slammed. We heard shoes making contact with the uneven ground. The men went silent. They must have been waiting for this person to arrive.

"I can't tell who it is," I said, venturing away from the cover of the oak, my eyes straining in the twilight. Noel stood close behind me. As long as our phones didn't light up, we wouldn't be spotted.

I heard Noel gasp. "It's Joel Bonne, the university's president."

"Gentlemen," Joel said as he approached the group. The other men nodded in greeting. "Well, where are we at?"

Nathan was the first to speak up. "Nora doesn't have them. Or at least if she does, she isn't going to tell me. I wouldn't be surprised if he's hiding them from us." Nathan gestured to Sal.

"Do you think she's just playing into your hand?" Joel asked, ignoring Nathan's accusation.

"I doubt it," Ross said, a little too loudly. "You saw how quickly she fired me. I'm sure that she would have loved to add another person to her body count. Even if that man is her husband. She's relishing her power."

"This is really getting out of hand. I told you to have this cleaned up by now," Joel said, looking at Sal.

"I'm doing everything I can."

"Really? Then why don't I have the files yet?"

"Lauren's home all the time. I can't go over as often as I'd like. I don't want the neighbors to get suspicious and tell her. I hid them behind plaster; I can't just leave a giant hole in the wall. It's not like someone else will find them. They're well hidden," Sal said.

"I cannot let this drag on for much longer. I want this all behind us. I want you two out of this town." His voice turned threatening as he directed it toward Ross and Higgins. "You've made enough of an embarrassment of my university as it stands. I can't have this hanging over my head for the rest of the semester, for the rest of my tenure."

"Nora seems to be taking the investigation very seriously," Nathan interjected.

"Of course she is, that's why she has his job." Joel looked directly at Sal. "You guys better clean this up before she finds out you were involved, too. If she finds out, Nathan, I will have to fire you. At least one professor has already come forward accusing you."

"Good luck covering up another one of his scandals," Ross said under his breath.

"Who was it?" Nathan demanded, the anger in his voice almost tangible.

"You know I'm not going to tell you that."

"I bet it was Alexis Baily. She's dating Beau Kennedy," Ross said with poorly disguised disgust.

"And she told you that she wouldn't help your student cheat," Sal said dryly.

"The identity of the informant is beside the point. I'm warning you, Nathan, if Nora comes to me and tells me that you're involved, I will have to let you go. It wouldn't look fair to make her fire Ross and then the university doesn't fire you. I won't let anything happen that would cause her to point the investigation toward me."

Ross made some sort of protesting noise and started to interject, but Sal spoke up before he got the chance.

"I'll get the rest of the files. I'll get this taken care of as quickly as possible."

"Good," Joel said, turning on his heel, walking back toward his car. "Don't give me a reason to regret this."

The other three lingered for a few awkward moments before they got into their own cars and dispersed.

"Oh my gosh!" Noel said as soon as they drove off.

"I know!" I couldn't come up with a more intelligent response.

"What do we do?"

"I think we should call Graham. He might know what files they're talking about. It sounds like they're still at Higgins's house, and Graham mentioned that Lauren was living alone now. Also, I knew Nathan was a sleaze. Every time he visited Nora at her office, he always showed up unannounced, and he never even seemed to care if she was busy. As if his presence should trump whatever it was she was working on."

"I have to say, I'm honestly a little crushed. I was going to ask Professor Bennet to be one of my references for my MFA application."

"Does it make you feel better or worse that our very esteemed president is trying to make excuses for him to stay on staff?"

"Definitely not better."

"Okay, I'm going to call Graham."

———

Thirty minutes later, the three of us found ourselves on Lauren Higgins's doorstep.

"Are you sure we're not intruding?" I asked as the door swung open and the tired but smiling face of Lauren Higgins greeted us. I instantly recognized her as the woman I'd seen crying in the bathroom. I couldn't help but wonder if she remembered me as well.

Lauren welcomed us into her house with a hospitable smile. I guessed that she was raised in the South, the drive to be a gracious hostess ingrained into her fiber.

"Do you guys want a cup of tea, wine, coffee? Hunter and I were just finishing dessert if you wanted something sweet?"

We all politely declined. Nonetheless, there was a pitcher of water with five glasses already on the living room coffee table. A young man, whom I assumed to be her son, Hunter, sat on a couch. He looked almost identical to his mother. Hunter, Graham, and Lauren all had the same shade of rusty-brown hair, the same olive skin, and high cheekbones.

"So, I heard you've seen my dad recently?" Hunter said with a slight laugh.

"Um, yes, we did," Noel spoke, her voice sounding out of place. "I'm sorry," she added in a rush.

"Nothing to be sorry about."

"Why don't we sit?" Lauren said, gesturing to the couches.

Graham flopped down comfortably next to his cousin. It was like Noel and I were outsiders in the middle of another family's drama. I suddenly felt the gravity of the situation. This was not a game. This was not just some fun Nancy Drew investigation. This affected real people's lives. These people counted on us to be reliable witnesses.

"What happened tonight?" Lauren asked. She sounded tired. I could only imagine how exhausting it must be for her.

"Anne, do you guys want to explain?" Graham gestured to Noel and me. We both sat on the couch nervously twirling our thumbs. I had hoped that he would take the lead and explain what had happened.

"Um, sure," I shakily replied. "Well, Noel and I normally walk along the river in the evening, and we were on our normal walk when we heard some angry voices farther along the path." I went on to explain what we had seen, Noel helping me remember the specifics.

The room fell silent for a few moments as Lauren and Hunter digested our story.

"You said that Nathan Bennet was there?" Lauren asked.

"Yes," Noel and I said in unison.

"Interesting." Lauren seemed to ponder this. "His wife, Nora, called me this evening asking for advice on what to do about Nathan. It was funny, I was actually just about to call her, but she got to me first. I'm assuming that Nathan had planned to go straight from dinner with Nora to meet up with this motley crew. I'm sure they were expecting him to bring intel from Nora. She seemed really shaken up on the phone." Lauren paused to fill her mug with tea. "I had wondered if she would ever call. I wasn't sure if she would. We were always friendly, I like Nora a lot. But we never talked much outside of events. My reputation as a fixer must precede me."

"Clearly you were great at fixing Dad's life," Hunter added sarcastically. "If he was meeting with Joel, that basically means Dad was handed into the arms of the beast."

I expected Lauren to look hurt by this comment, but her expression remained steady.

"He was beyond fixing, your father. No matter where we ended up, he was going to make some sort of trouble. I knew that for a long time. I needed him to get a job that had less press. I didn't want his mistakes to ruin your life." She looked at her son. "But clearly, I underestimated how easily he could make a mess. Blame your father and his stubbornness, not my inability to fix this problem."

"So, I think the biggest question I have after hearing this"— Graham inserted himself, interrupting the family bickering—"is where are the papers Sal is looking for? He mentioned they're somewhere here, behind plaster."

"They're in my safe."

"What?" Graham, Noel, and I exclaimed at the same time. Had Lauren known everything all along and was just playing the part of the innocent wife?

Lauren said nothing, sitting there sipping her tea, clearly waiting for one of us to speak.

Hunter broke the silence. "Oh my gosh, you're so dramatic." He rolled his eyes at his mother. "You were not this calm, cool, and collected when we found the files."

"What's going on?" Graham asked, interrupting again.

"I found out that Sal had been coming into the house while I was gone. One of my neighbors told me they'd seen Sal here while I was out—remember, Graham, I found out at the restaurant that night."

Graham nodded solemnly.

"Well, I was talking to Hunter about it, and he suggested that we search the house for anything that he might be coming back to get."

"And?" Graham probed eagerly. We were all on the edges of our seats.

"And we found it," Hunter said matter-of-factly.

"Are you going to tell us what you found?" Graham asked impatiently.

Lauren got up from her seat, crossed the room, and grabbed a locked box that sat on an old bar table in the corner. The moment felt dramatic, as if we had been sitting next to the ticking time bomb for months. But then again, I could only imagine how Lauren felt, finding files in her house.

"These were all hidden in the wall of the upstairs bathroom," Lauren said as she fiddled with the lock on the box, opening it. "Once Hunter and I found them, I put them in this safe so that Sal wouldn't have access to them anymore. We searched the rest of the house and didn't find anything else; I'm assuming this is everything. Who knows if there are more files that he already removed from the house."

We all moved to the box. Inside sat a huge stack of files labeled with the names of various people connected to the athletic department.

"Is this for blackmailing?" Graham asked.

Hunter nodded. "That's the most likely explanation. He was smart enough to keep these files somewhere other than his work computer. Unlike his careless use of the university email." I assumed that Graham had confided in Hunter what he had seen on Sal's email.

"This has to be what Joel was after," Noel reasoned.

"He literally has a file on everyone," Graham said as he thumbed through the pile. I could hear the fear in his voice.

"Yeah, and they check out. He must have had some great spies," Hunter said with the same fearful tone.

"What are you going to do with all of this?" Graham asked his aunt.

"I'm going to give the papers to Nora. She deserves to know the truth. Then she can do with them whatever she sees fit."

The room fell silent as we digested the information. I couldn't help but notice everything that went unsaid in her answer.

"I'm going to see Nora tomorrow," Lauren said.

"She has a free morning. I don't think she has a meeting until ten thirty," I piped in. When Lauren gave me a confused look, I quickly added, "I'm her intern."

"Wow, what a year to do that job," Hunter said with a laugh.

"We should probably be going," Graham said as he gathered his things.

"Thank you for coming over. We're going to figure this out," Lauren said. It was impossible not to believe her, not to trust that she would make everything okay.

50.

Lauren

October 8, 9:00 a.m.

I prayed it would be my last visit to the athletic complex. Anne held an opening for me in Nora's morning schedule. I didn't want anything official on her calendar. I worried that Sal could somehow still access that information. If he was trying to break into the university computers last week, who knew what he had access to.

I called my liaison with the investigation team and told them I needed to push our meeting back. I didn't want to hand the files over without Nora seeing them first.

Talking to her last night, she sounded desperate. It was the first conversation I had with her where her every word didn't seem calculated. She was normally straightforward—never as eloquent as Sal, but always composed. Last night she had been anything but. Last night, she sounded like a woman who was scared for the safety of her family. I understood that feeling completely.

I wore an old Renton University baseball cap to blend in inside the building.

I had a weird sense of déjà vu walking down the hallway to the athletic director's office. I had so many memories in the building, good and bad. It was hard to push them away.

I remembered the day the building opened, when I stood proudly next to Sal, beaming at his great accomplishment. I might not have agreed with the heinous waste of money to build this eyesore, but I knew what it meant to Sal. To his legacy.

As I made my way to Nora's office, I felt like I was grieving. The last few days, it had been easy to distract myself from my feelings. No matter what ugly truths I found out about Sal, they would never fully erase all that we had gone through together. It would be impossible for me to throw away the image of the man I had fallen in love with. The man who had taught our son to play baseball. Who held my hand as I cried saying goodbye to another city, another university I had fallen in love with. I had loved him through all of that; I had seen him put in the hours, work hard to be the best at his job.

No person is all bad. Being back in the building, in this hallway, made it impossible for me to forget Sal's good works. He had made a difference in the lives of many of his student-athletes. He encouraged his coaches to scout recruits from overlooked schools. He wanted his teams to win. He wanted to build the best program he could. At least parts of his legacy were good.

"Hi, Lauren!" Anne said warmly as soon as I opened the door to the small waiting area.

"Hi, Anne. Helen." I nodded to Helen, who didn't look surprised to see me. Anne must have told her that I was coming in.

"I mentioned to Nora that you might be stopping by. She had to jump on a quick phone call, but she should be done in like two minutes."

"Thank you." I was glad Sal had hired Anne. She seemed competent and professional, and acted like she actually enjoyed doing her job.

I sat awkwardly on the small couch that was relegated to visitors. I had never had to wait in this room before. I wasn't sure what the protocol was.

"How are you, Helen?"

She flashed me her warm smile. "It's been quite a year. But all will be well."

I couldn't help but wonder what Helen thought of me. She didn't seem like the type of woman who would let something like this happen under her nose. She remembered everything and everyone. It'd be impossible to sneak something past her, or so I had thought.

Given that she still had her job, she must have been in the dark about Sal's doings. I wondered if she, like me, questioned all the signs she missed.

"Hey, Lauren, you can head back." Anne's voice interrupted my thought spiral.

"Thanks," I said, then walked down the familiar hallway to Nora's office.

The room was the same. The same size. The walls the same color. Even most of the furniture was the same. Except nothing was the same. The room felt different. It felt lighter than it did when Sal had occupied the space. Nora had pulled the blinds fully open, letting in the late-fall morning sun. An oil diffuser sat in the corner, filling the room with the relaxing smell of lavender.

"Hi, Nora." For some reason, my voice sounded sheepish. I felt like I should take responsibility for the mess that my husband had caused. If I had known, could I have changed things? Would I have changed things? Or would I have been a coward, tried to cover up yet another of Sal's scandals? Quickly moved. Left behind the mess for someone else to sort out?

"Hey, Lauren, thank you so much for coming in today." She looked tired; I wondered if she'd gotten any sleep.

"How're you holding up?" I figured my best strategy would be to lead with empathy. She sounded so tired last night, so defeated.

She looked uncomfortable, as if she was constantly on edge, worried about letting her guard down. Slowly, she sank into her chair and let her forehead fall into her hands.

"Honestly, I'm still so exhausted. As soon as I think I'm about to put all of this behind me, something else comes up. I just don't know how to handle the day-to-day responsibilities of this job while constantly waiting for the other shoe to drop. Sorry, I don't mean to unload on you. Like I mentioned on the phone last night, I couldn't think of anyone else who might understand what this feels like."

I sat in the chair opposite her. I wanted to reach out and put my hand on her arm, but I worried the comforting gesture would scare her off. "You're handling this better than I would be, better than I am," I admitted. "I honestly feel like I can barely manage just the day-to-day tasks of life; I can't imagine having to face the same stress every moment at work as well."

Her eyes started to well with tears. "Thank you, Lauren."

I reached into my purse and handed her a tissue.

"I don't want to add something else to your plate, but I'm hoping at least what I'm about to share with you will be the beginning of the end."

"Don't worry about it. At least whatever news you have will come from a friendly face."

I realized then that it might be better if I had Anne explain what she overheard, give some background to my visit. I asked Nora if Anne could join us.

Nora paged Anne, and she tentatively entered the office and sat in the chair next to mine. It was clear from the way that she spoke that she had rehearsed her story; she seemed much more put together today than she had last night. It was clear how much she looked up to Nora.

"Wow," Nora said as Anne finished explaining. "Wow," she repeated. "So, Joel and Nathan? Wow." I watched as she tried to control her emotions. I could tell she'd been trained well. You couldn't be a woman in sports and show your feelings. Even when those feelings involved your husband. She had already cracked more than I'm sure she wanted by tearing up earlier.

"So, like Anne mentioned, Joel was looking for some files. I found them in my house earlier this week." I passed her the thick stack. It felt like I was letting go of precious cargo. As much as I wanted to hold on to them and keep them as insurance for myself, I owed it to Nora to give them to her. I had gone back and forth about it all night. I reminded myself that I told Hunter and Graham that I was going to tell Nora. I couldn't go back on my word.

But still, I wasn't really sure I would go through with it until I saw the threatening outline of the athletic complex in the skyline as I drove to campus.

It needed to end. Letting her have all the information would be a massive step toward the investigation closing, even though I knew that by surrendering the documents I'd be surrendering my own control. I had photocopied the files, just in case I needed backup copies.

I didn't tell her about the money. Hunter was the only other person who knew about that. I wasn't ready to lay all my cards on the table.

I sat in silence as Nora began to quickly flip through the stack. I knew whom she was looking for. Nathan. She wanted to protect her family. I watched as she removed the file and examined it. For a split second, I thought she was going to tear it in half, but instead, she scanned the page, over and over again, as if rereading it would change what was written.

"Sexually assaulting a student." I could tell that she hadn't known. "I can't believe that Sal would hide this from me, from the university. This is a serious allegation. All so that he could ensure he maintained control over the English department? I can't believe this. I don't even know who I'm supposed to talk to at this point. Obviously I'm not going to report this to Joel. I can't believe Joel was in on this. What a shit show." Nora's face fell.

"Nora, I'm so sorry." I felt guilty. I felt like I should've done something to prevent this. I also knew how she felt. When I found out about Sal, when the world found out about Sal, all I wanted was for someone to sit across from me and acknowledge the all-consuming pain. I didn't want to be a topic of gossip. I wanted people to see me as a person.

"Thank you for telling me before you went public with this, Lauren. I really appreciate it."

"Trying to not repeat the mistakes of my husband. But if you ever need anything, you have my number, please use it."

As I walked away, I found myself hoping that she would call.

51.

ALEXIS

October 16, 8:45 a.m.

The stack of midterm essays sitting on my desk seemed impossibly high. At the beginning of the semester, I had promised myself that I wouldn't have any last-minute grading sessions. That promise had obviously been broken. I was in a rush to grade as many essays as I could before the weekend.

For the first time, I was going to travel with the football team. Well, not *with* the team, but I was going to meet the team in Clifton. The NCAA didn't cover the travel costs for spouses or partners. Given how much a coach makes compared to a professor, this felt a little ridiculous. But Beau and I were committed to doing everything by the rules. So Talia would come with me, and we planned to make it into a girls' weekend. We were even staying in a different hotel than Beau, to make sure we sent a clear "we're not breaking the rules" message to the world.

"Thank God, you're here!" Talia said, bursting into my office.

"Yes, desperately trying to catch up on my midterm grades," I said, pointing to the pile of papers on my desk. "How's your grading coming along? You're not planning on trying to grade on the plane, are you?" This had been her failed strategy on our last girls' trip.

"Yeah, whatever, I'll get it done. But, Alexis, bigger news than grading papers—Nathan was fired."

I dropped my pen on the floor. I watched it roll toward the door. Shock rippled through me.

"Wait, seriously? When?"

"I know, I know, it's crazy. I didn't actually think it would happen. But they found some damning evidence. He has to be out by noon, he's packing his office now."

"Oh my gosh. How did you find out?"

"My contact from the investigation team told me. He called me to tell me that the investigation is over. He thanked me for my courage in sharing my story. And then almost immediately after, MP texted me. I honestly don't know if I should be relieved that they believed me and fired him, or paranoid that he's going to come for me and ruin my life."

"I can't believe they actually fired him. Nora can't be too happy about that."

Talia poured herself a cup of coffee from the pot I had brewing, and flopped into a chair.

"Do you think it's really over?" It was clear that she was trying to keep the relief at bay.

"I honestly don't know. Man, he was always such a sleaze. But I'm surprised he actually got fired."

"I was starting to wonder. I mean, I bet he thought his position was secure. Wasn't he the one who confronted you about talking to Ross? So he was clearly not too worried about trying to hide his involvement."

"Do you think that he thought that Nora would protect him?"

"Maybe, but that doesn't seem like a truly fail-safe plan, especially since Nora was the one who fired Ross, and in every press conference she made it super clear that she was committed to purging her department of anyone else involved. I mean, I know she doesn't have jurisdiction over the English department, but still, she's a major player in university politics."

"Who do you think will take over as the head of the English department?"

We talked about the future of our department until we heard yelling coming from the hallway.

"Is that a student?" Talia asked as we got up to investigate.

One of the voices was clearly Nathan's. It had gotten everyone's attention. Faces peered out of office doors all along the normally quiet corridor.

"Can you tell who else is yelling?" I whisper-shouted to Talia.

"I can't. And I'm not about to leave your office to find out."

"Seriously . . . do you think we should call the police? Campus security?"

A voice from the office next door responded, "I called campus security; they should be on their way now."

In the meantime, we listened in curious horror.

"I think it might be Ross and Sal," I whispered to Talia.

"Do you really think they'd be that stupid to show up here?"

"They might be at a point where they really don't have anything else to lose."

Moments later, campus security stormed down the hallway and quickly dragged four men out of the small office—Nathan Bennet, Sal Higgins, Richard Ross, and Joel Bonne.

"Dr. Bonne?" The entire hallway peanut gallery said his name almost in unison, shocked to see their esteemed university president with a group of men who had just been fired for blackmail and fraud.

"Well, that was unexpected," Talia said as soon as the parade of ashamed men had passed.

"Seriously. Why would they all show up here?"

"Maybe to claim some last-minute incriminating evidence?"

"Well, three out of the four have already been fired, and the fourth basically admitted guilt by being seen associating with them," I said, still not believing what I was overhearing.

"Unless," I wagered, "maybe he didn't know that the others would be here this morning. Maybe Dr. Bonne thought that he'd have Nathan's office to himself, so he could gather whatever evidence he needs to save himself from going down with the other three."

"That would actually make a lot of sense. I wonder if Nathan assumed that Bonne would try to get information from his office and preemptively called for backup?"

"Maybe, or maybe they were all here searching for the same thing. Every man for himself? I mean at this point, sure, their careers are over at Renton, but they could still start over somewhere else. Maybe not the same jobs, but any job would be better than a lifetime of unemployment. I wonder if Nathan had something in his office that would be a guaranteed career-ender?" Talia questioned.

"Gosh, who knows. What a mess."

I checked my watch. I never hated my nine thirty class more than I did at that moment.

"I have a class now. But will you let me know if anything else happens?"

"Deal," she said with a nod. "I doubt anyone will get much grading done this morning."

52.

Nora

October 16, 2:30 p.m.

I hoped it would be my last time sitting across from this man. When I had pictured this moment, I thought I'd meet it with an unshakable feeling of relief. That wasn't the case. Sure, I felt some relief, but it was hard to actually believe what he was telling me, that we could soon put the investigation behind us. As much as I wanted my last moments with the investigation team to be all business, it wasn't. It had become personal.

For the first time since the investigation began, I wasn't sitting alone on my side of the table. I sat next to members from the board of trustees who had been informed of the situation. I'd had mixed experiences working with the board over the years. But regardless of our past, it was clear that today we were allies—and it was clear we were the good guys.

The investigation team laid out its findings, confirming much of what I already knew. I had spent most of my spare time in the past few days going over the files Lauren had given me. After reading the pages multiple times, I honestly couldn't believe that Sal had gotten away with the scheme for so long.

It was clear that Sal believed himself to be the ringleader—that was why he had been the primary gatherer of information. But while he might have viewed it as a mark of his leadership, to me it indicated something different—that he was afraid. He had to have information on everyone around him, even those he claimed to trust, to guarantee that if he went down, he could drag everyone else with him. It was more than just a means to get what he wanted. It was an insurance policy.

No one wants to believe they're playing second fiddle in someone else's show. Nathan, Ross, and Sal each believed they were in charge, but in reality, all signs pointed to Joel Bonne being the real mastermind.

Joel's integrity had been questioned when he hired Sal. But Joel had made a substantial effort to downplay the fact that Sal had been fired from his previous position after getting a DUI. Joel had reframed things, claiming that because he was family friends with Lauren Higgins, he and Sal had been in talks privately for years about the possibility of Renton University hiring Sal if an opportunity arose.

It was clear now that Sal's shady history had played perfectly into Joel's plans for the university's athletic program. He needed someone unafraid to bend rules to advance the program. Sal's track record made him the perfect candidate.

Then there was Ross's involvement. As the program began to improve after hiring Higgins, the school started to attract higher-ranked recruits, recruits who were more interested in their athletic performance than their academic performance. This posed a problem because the NCAA takes GPA and grade rules very seriously.

Sal gave Ross an ultimatum—Ross would either figure out a way to turn his students' grades around or he'd be fired. Sal opened the door for Ross to join him in the complicated scheme, including guaranteeing some additional financial gains if Ross cooperated. The only missing piece was finding a department willing to bend some academic rules.

That's when Sal remembered that the woman he had just hired as his assistant athletic director was married to a professor. At that time, the only job Nathan had been able to find was at a university a few hours away. He had been desperate for a job closer to home and was willing to do anything. He had made this clear to Sal the first and only time our families got together outside of work. With Sal's influence, Nathan landed a job in Renton's English department, and as luck would have it, the head of the department decided to take early retirement.

And just like that, the final piece of the puzzle fell into place.

But Nathan turned out to be more of a liability than anticipated. In his second year as the head of the department, he was accused of sexually assaulting a student who also happened to be an athlete. Joel made sure it was resolved quietly, but he couldn't risk another slipup, especially since Nathan was married to the assistant athletic director. Sal wanted to prevent anything that would cause an investigation into his athletic department. My relationship with Nathan just gave Sal another potential angle to blackmail our family. He had assumed that I would never do anything to compromise my family. He had assumed that Nathan had told me about the assault.

Looking at the evidence, I felt a wave of sadness wash over me. When the team finished presenting its findings, I sat in stunned silence. So many people had deceived me for so long. Things would never be the same. My husband had torn apart our family. He pretended to be the sort of father, the sort of husband, that a woman could only dream of.

Oh my gosh, Margo. How was I going to explain all of this to Margo? How do you tell a child that one of the people they look up to the most in the world is actually a fraud? I wouldn't do anything to compromise her. And that meant cutting Nathan out of our lives.

"Given the results of our investigation, we would advise that, in addition to the measures that have already been taken, Dr. Joel Bonne should be removed from his position as president of the university," the lead investigator announced.

Around me, the trustees nodded. What other choice did they have? Conclusive evidence pointed to Joel as the master manipulator, the ringleader.

"We also have multiple sources reporting that this morning all four men in question were in Mr. Bennet's office, trying to remove additional documents Mr. Bennet had been storing, and the group caused quite a scene. We're assuming that each of the four thought that they could remove the evidence from his office before it was cleaned out."

"Do you know what they were looking for?" one of the trustees asked.

"We think Mr. Bennet had started his own set of blackmail files, following Mr. Higgins's example. We have a few members of our team currently searching the hard drive of his computer and checking the office for any sort of hidden evidence," a member of the investigation team answered.

"Thank you for your cooperation during this difficult time. Please know that we're at your disposal, and we'll let you know if we find any additional evidence from Nathan Bennet. We doubt that anything we find will be substantial enough to reverse our current recommendations."

And just like that, the investigation was over.

Epilogue

"Coach Kennedy, knowing that Renton University has voluntarily forfeited from the postseason while awaiting the NCAA sanctions for Level 1 violations, how did that affect the way you coached the second half of the season, especially given the immediate suspension of your team's star player and a potential first-round draft pick, Austin O'Malley?"

The English professor in Alexis cringed when she heard the question. It was unnecessarily wordy. More importantly, his question ignored the fact that Beau had just led the team in a conference championship win. This would have been impressive in any situation, but she couldn't help but be extra proud given the fact that he had taken over midway through the season. Instead of focusing on what he had accomplished, most journalists only cared about getting any additional gossip about the scandalized program.

They'd be disappointed to learn that since the firing of Joel Bonne and Nathan Bennet, the drama had all but dried up. It was clear that regardless of the sanctions imposed on the school, Nora was going to appoint Beau as the head coach for the next season.

Alexis looked down at the ring that was newly on her finger. Thanks to Nathan, she knew exactly what not to do as a professor and spouse of someone who worked for the athletic department.

From her spot in the wings, close enough to show her support, but not too close to draw attention, Alexis waited for the press to fade away. She could hear the squeals of delight coming from Margo. The field teemed with people celebrating. Despite the security team's efforts to keep fans from rushing the field, elated Griffons were still on the field celebrating almost half an hour after the game ended. Margo held hands with Anne and Graham. All three had euphoric joy on their faces.

Alexis was sure that MP was somewhere close by, trying to figure out his angle for whatever new story he was working on. Or, more likely, he was searching the field for Talia.

The feeling was surreal. It felt like they were celebrating their survival. They had made it through. This confetti-filled field was their party. The world had watched them. The world had spent the past four months analyzing their every move, looking for any hint of evidence that would prove guilt. But they weren't guilty, and they had made it. They had survived.

Alexis turned to watch Nora giving an interview. She would likely spend her entire career proving to the world that she had truly earned the job. If it bothered her, she didn't let it show. The people who knew her—Lauren, Helen, Anne—knew that she hadn't set out to speak on behalf of all women in sports. She had set out to do her job. And this year she proved that she was very good at it.

A few states away, Lauren sat in front of the TV and couldn't help but overflow with pride. She caught a glimpse of Anne and Graham, who had officially started dating as soon as the investigation was closed. She noticed Helen, directing people to steer clear of Nora, who was giving an interview. Hunter had gone to the game as well, but she doubted he would have joined the crowd on the field. He tried to avoid doing anything that would draw attention to himself, to his last name. Lauren suspected that the scandal would plague him for the rest of his life.

She had the freedom to change her name, to go back to who she was before Sal. Though no name change could ever undo the past. The fallout of the trouble her now ex-husband had caused would follow her for the foreseeable future. Lauren had cooperated with the NCAA and surrendered all the information she had on him. Sal had been given a lifelong ban. He could never be employed by an NCAA institution again. The findings of the investigation team were being surrendered to the state, which was considering pressing charges.

When she had told her mother about the scandal, her mother was more upset by Joel's involvement than Sal's. Her mother had always worshipped Joel and assumed that he could do no wrong. She clearly wasn't the only one he had fooled.

But Sal and Joel were no longer her problem. The consequences of their actions were no longer her burden to bear. She cleared all of Sal's stuff out of their house. All four of the men had moved away from Renton, each to somehow start his life over. She honestly didn't care where Sal ended up or what he was doing. She had stopped trying to manage the lives of others.

She couldn't help but smile, knowing that no matter what the future held, she would be okay. She had a toilet tank full of cash. It had been hard to figure out what to do with the money, given its origin. She set aside a significant portion to donate to the City of Renton's girls' sports league. She planned to put the rest toward the MBA she had always dreamed of pursuing. She wanted to prove to herself that she wasn't too old to follow her dreams. She was already the hero for finding the files Sal kept on everyone. The investigation team had assumed that the money had disappeared with Sal.

Nora was desperately trying to wrap up the interview. She saw her daughter out of the corner of her eye and wanted nothing more than to celebrate with Margo, the person she loved the most in the world.

"Yeah, um, could you tell me how you think your victory impacts the future of women?" the reporter in the generic navy suit asked. He clearly thought that he was asking some groundbreaking questions.

"Wow, you're throwing softballs tonight," Nora answered dryly. "I think this victory signifies to women that we have a seat at the table. This isn't the guys' club it used to be. In fact, I think that what happened at our university shows what can happen if this is a guys' club."

"Well," the reporter started defensively, "you can't really believe that that's true for all men, can you? I think that comes off a little sexist."

"You could say the same thing about your question to me about women." Nora looked dramatically at her wristwatch. "That's all I have time for today." She turned on her heel and ran to embrace her daughter.

The cameras continued to click.

The world was watching her, and she was learning to accept it.

ACKNOWLEDGMENTS

I started writing this book at a time when I desperately missed the sense of community that comes from sports. Writing this book not only filled the football-size hole in my heart, but it allowed me the chance to reflect on my first real job, which was with my university's athletic ticket office. I am forever grateful to my family at the Washington State University ATO: Hannah (who hired me!), Becca, Keeley, Aaron, Jamie, Paul, Matt, Collin, and Corinne. I am so grateful for the years I worked at WSU. Go, Cougs!

Thank you to Lauren Bittrich for believing in this book. I am so grateful to work with you. Your care and insights have made this book shine and helped it find the perfect home. I am also infinitely grateful for my team at Lake Union. Thank you to Lauren Plude and Jodi Warshaw for being the perfect editors for this book.

I remember watching my first football game alongside my dad when I was six. I asked him who he was rooting for and, in an act of six-year-old defiance, decided to cheer for the other team. I had little concept of the rivalries that would ensue. Dad, thank you for fostering all my obsessions, sports included. I love you.

My extended family has played a huge role in shaping me into who I am today. To my aunts, uncles, and cousins, I love you all. Even if we will never agree on what team to root for, there is no one else with whom I'd rather spend a Saturday yelling at the TV. But, just for the record: Go, Cougs! Go, Steelers! Go, Mariners! (Or Pirates, or Nats, I never really could decide on a baseball team.) And a special thank-you to my aunt Pix, uncle John, and Jack for opening your home to me while I was working on this book. The next order of wine is on me! Three-dog night forever!

To my sister, Grace. I love you so much. You are my harshest critic and fiercest companion. You make my life, wardrobe, and writing so much better. I'm so glad that we live in the same time zone again!

Thank you to all my friends who have cheered me on along the way. Especially thank you to Ashley for being there for every victory and heartache; I love you so, so much. Gwen, thank you for being my faithful first reader. Amy, you have taught me so much about love and compassion, which has been reflected in the way I wrote these characters. Beth, thank you for being my favorite pom-pom girl (and vodka collins buddy). Casey, thank you for being my oldest and wisest friend. Molly, Ellen, and Marie, you have walked with me through so much of this crazy adventure, and I could never have done it without you—thank you for being there with me through it all. Mary, thank you for encouraging me to keep going (from our running days to now). Brooke, I will always remember drinking wine out of coffee cups together the night I found out I got a book deal—thank you for keeping me sane. Josh, the RV scene was inspired by tailgating with your family—go, Cougs—and your socks are in the mail. Bill and Terri, you have been so encouraging to me throughout this process. I love you both so much.

To the "We Have Plans" group chat—Elizabeth, Lauren, Kelsie, and Molly—you made NOVA feel like home. I cannot put into words how grateful I am to have found you.

I owe an incredible debt to my writing friends Liz and Jordan. Liz, thank you for always being an encouraging voice in this crazy adventure—I'm so glad we are in this together. I am so grateful for the thousands of hours of voice notes we have sent back and forth. Jordan, thank you for always taking time out of every Refuge meeting to talk about writing and books. You both have encouraged me to keep going, and the feedback and impact you've had on my writing are sprinkled throughout this book.

The Renton Griffons were named after my dog, Luna, who is a Griffon Nivernais I adopted while living in France. You might assume that having a multilingual dog means she is better behaved, but in fact it just means that she ignores me in two languages. Allez les Griffons!

Et, pour tous mes amis en France, je vous aime. Merci de m'avoir soutenu quand je me réveillais à deux heures du matin pour regarder le football américain. Allez, allez! Grâce à vous, je soutiendrai toujours les Bleus.

And always, I write in memory of my mother, who taught me the joy of storytelling.

ABOUT THE AUTHOR

Photo © 2022 Ashley Fleck

Olivia Swindler was raised in Spokane, Washington, and lived and worked in France for over five years. The author of *Cynthia Starts a Band*, she believes that through fiction we can grow and learn from one another, and hopes to create and foster hard, real-life conversations with her novels. Olivia is also a graphic designer and a reader of many, many books. She currently resides in Virginia with her dog, Luna. For more information, visit www.oliviaswindler.com.